Micah Persell

# HARD work

*Sin City Gigolos, Book 1*

Crimson Romance
New York London Toronto Sydney New Delhi

CRIMSON
ROMANCE

Crimson Romance
An Imprint of Simon & Schuster, Inc.
1230 Avenue of the Americas
New York, NY 10020



First Crimson Romance ebook edition NOVEMBER 2017



Manufactured in the United States of America

ISBN 978-1-5072-0805-2
ISBN 978-1-5072-0702-4 (ebook)

*For Nielle—*
*Who selflessly offered to research this book with me.*
*Such the giving heart.*

# Chapter One

"Oh, God."

*That's right, baby.*

"Oh, *God!*"

The woman beneath him arched her back and dug her nails into his abdomen before raking them down to where they joined. She pressed her manicured fingers over her clit and bit into her lip. Kip picked up the pace of his thrusts, the telltale fluttering of her orgasm against his cock signaling that he could finally—*finally*—come.

He grinned down at her—his payday was just minutes away—and allowed the knot of restraint at the base of his spine to loosen as he tipped over the edge with her.

He swallowed down the small moan that rose in his throat as he spilled into the condom, maintaining control even as he allowed himself to slip it a bit.

Her dazed eyes opened, and her gaze scoured his torso as his stomach clenched and unclenched—something he did intentionally, because they always liked to see it—before the last of his own orgasm faded.

*Job well done.*

She sighed. "Fuck, Kip."

He chuckled as he leaned down and brushed a kiss against her damp neck. "Good?"

"The best."

*Job* very *well done.* He glanced over at the clock beside the bed, and even he raised an eyebrow. Two hours. Two hours of delayed gratification for a woman who had claimed she had trouble orgasming at the start of it. Two hours of taking her right to the edge and backing her off over and over and over again.

*Damn, I'm good.* This was going to mean a tip. A big one.

She sighed again, and Kip frowned slightly as he tried to remember her name. As he grasped the condom and pulled out of her, he mentally shrugged. It didn't matter anyway. Her eyelids were already drooping, and in moments she would be asleep. "I'm going to take a shower, doll."

She murmured something and nodded. Hopefully, she wouldn't fall too deeply asleep. If he had to wake her up to get payment, it could get awkward. Then again, there wasn't much in his line of work that wasn't awkward, so *c'est la vie.*

In the bathroom, he tossed the condom and turned the shower on all the way to hot. As he waited for it to warm up, he caught a glimpse of himself in the mirror, his gaze automatically falling to the red, angry stripes she'd given him on his stomach.

He sighed. Those needed to be gone by the next client. Despite obviously knowing he was a gigolo, none of the ladies liked the reminder that he slept with other women, and it usually affected his payout when they caught sight of a love bite or scratch someone else put there. He relied half on networking at casinos and bars, half on word of mouth to maintain and add to his client list. No traceable agencies for him. So, he had to keep the ladies—he didn't believe in types and serviced all kinds—happy. His livelihood depended on it.

He stepped under the water and started lathering up with the hotel's provided soap, ready to get out of here and on with his night, which was now free, having thoroughly pleasured his last client of the day. Once he'd washed the woman's scent from his body, he toweled off and walked back to where his clothes lay in a pile beside the bedside table where—hallelujah—Sated Beauty had left his money before slipping into a slumber deep enough that her tiny snores filled the hotel room.

He took a moment to thumb through the crisp, green bills, and … holy shit. Who cared if the scratches were gone by the next client? She'd tipped him more than he could have ever expected.

Kip did some quick math in his head. Nineteen thousand dollars. Nearly there. Thanks to this woman's generosity, he now had half the amount he needed to start his own business and get out of one in which he had to shower several times a day and hide hickeys on the reg.

*This calls for a celebration.* But somewhere off the Strip, where he wouldn't feel like he had to be *on* and could enjoy a cocktail in peace.

He pulled on his clothes and slipped his payment into his wallet before shoving it in his back pocket. His favorite place was open for several more hours yet, and if he remembered correctly, Steve was behind the bar tonight. He mixed the best Blue Hawaiians.

Kip cast one last grateful grin at the woman sleeping spread-eagled in the middle of the bed, then slipped out of the hotel room and into the night.

# Chapter Two

Victoria clicked send on the e-mail and then leaned back in her chair with a slight smile. Another job well done. Her client was going to love the idea she'd just sent, and that meant that she was going to be her boss's new favorite.

Or, continuous favorite. Six of one; half dozen of the other.

The only thing that mattered was she'd just closed the gap between her and the newly vacant corner office, even if it was only by a few proverbial inches. Just one more big success, and she was surely in.

Her computer chimed. "Already?" she muttered. She clicked her inbox, and when it refreshed, there was a new e-mail, but it wasn't from the client she'd just contacted.

It was a Google alert, and when she saw the subject line, she forgot how to breathe.

She clicked on the e-mail so hard, the mouse emitted a creak beneath her fingers. Her gaze moved over the words too quickly for her brain to understand, and she had to start over again. Several times.

When she finally grasped the news release she was reading, she leaned back in her chair, stunned.

The Ricchezza was switching advertising agencies. A fairly new casino on the strip, The Ricchezza, which meant *wealth* in Italian, had launched onto the scene, becoming a must-stop casino within hours of opening its doors for the first time.

And now it was up for grabs.

*It's finally happened.* Since beginning her career in advertising several years ago, Victoria had kept a wishful eye on the big casinos located just a few blocks away from the offices of Precision Media Services. Surely, one of them would want fresh ideas at some point.

Hardly daring to take her eyes from the screen, Victoria groped in the laptop bag beside her chair and unzipped the secret pocket on the inside. She dug through the myriad pencils and pens until her fingertips encountered the well-known and oft-visited flash drive.

Her thumb brushed over the peeling tape label she didn't have to read—the one that said "Hopes and Dreams" in black Sharpie—as she plugged it into the computer tower. She tapped her foot against the plastic carpet guard beneath her desk chair as her computer worked to open the files, and when it did, she clicked open the ready-made proposal. The perfect one. The one she'd made only a few months ago on one of her regular "What-if Weekends" with The Ricchezza specifically in mind.

As she quickly scanned it, the firm set of her lips relaxed; as she typed a few final edits, the relaxation turned to a full-fledged smile.

It was brilliant. Just as she remembered.

She composed the body of the e-mail, attached the file, and clicked send.

She flicked a glance at the bottom, right-hand corner of her screen; she'd managed to send off a damn fine proposal within ten minutes of The Ricchezza releasing the news. Not even "The Master" over at Precision's biggest competitor could top that.

There wouldn't be enough fussy French-pressed coffee in the world for Masterson when she received word tomorrow that Victoria had scooped The Ricchezza account right from beneath her nose. A bubble of giddiness roiled in Victoria's belly.

This was it. That corner office was as good as hers.

She looked at the clock again. Plenty of time to celebrate before she went to bed for the minimal five hours of sleep she needed to function.

She shut down her computer, waiting until the screen was completely black and her files secure before turning off the lights and walking through the office that had been abandoned for a good four hours already on this Friday evening.

"'Night, Earl." She waved over her shoulder as she passed the watchman.

"'Night, Ms. Hastings."

She felt his careful gaze follow her across the parking lot to her Mercedes, and when she backed out of her spot and drove past him, he kept his eye on her until he couldn't any more, always watching out for her safety, though she didn't know what he would do if someone ever threatened her. He was older than God and walked with a pronounced limp thanks to his regular gout flare-ups. If there were trouble, she would have to protect him.

As she stopped at a red light, the Bluetooth in the car started ringing, and a rare bloom of happiness lit in her chest.

She pushed a button. "Hey, Cassidy."

"Please tell me you're not still at the office."

"I'm not. Swear to God."

A heavy sigh. "You just left it, didn't you?"

Victoria shrugged with one shoulder, though Cassidy couldn't see it. "Hey, I've got some good news."

"She said in a shameless ploy to redirect the conversation."

*Guilty*. "So, The Ricchezza is in the market for new advertising blood."

There was a pause on the other end. "Okay, I'll allow this new topic, but we will revisit the travesty of spending your Friday night at the office as soon as it's done."

Not if she could help it. "I already sent a bid."

"That's right, you did. You're an ass-kicker. And?"

"It's good." She drummed her fingers on the steering wheel as she pulled into the lounge's parking lot. "Really good."

"Well, yeah. I meant *and* as in, what did they say?"

"I just sent it. I won't hear back until probably Monday." *Oh, God, that's a long way away.*

"Nah, you'll hear from them any second. Just keep your phone on." There was a cacophonous spat of gunfire on the line. "Damn it," Cassidy muttered.

"You die?"

"Yes. Fucking again."

Cassidy's ability to carry on and be present in a conversation while button jamming as she wrote and tested video games never failed to leave Victoria in a state of awe.

"Programming error?" Victoria asked. "Or player—?"

"Nice try, Tori. We were discussing the sad state of your life. You're not getting out of it this time."

"The sad state of—" Victoria shook her head. "I think I'm offended."

"Good. When's the last time you got laid?"

"*What?*" She pulled into a parking spot and applied the brakes a little too vehemently. The car lurched to a halt. "I'm not talking about this with you."

"Because I'm willing to bet money it was before my brother died."

Victoria swallowed hard. "Cassidy …"

"I'm right." The sudden gentleness in Cassidy's usually brash tone was jarring. "Aren't I?"

She wasn't right. Victoria rubbed the vacant spot on her left ring finger, even though the indentation there had long disappeared. It had been much, much longer than the two years after Jeremy's death since Victoria had been laid, owing to the fact they'd slept in separate rooms for that last year before his suicide, an invisible wall erecting itself between them despite their best efforts to battle his mental illness together. She wasn't going to tell Cassidy that, however. "Cassidy, I don't need sex."

She definitely needed sex.

"You forget I've seen the rate at which you burn through AA batteries."

"Okay, we're done here."

"Tori, go get some already. Burn off the stress—"

Victoria pushed the end button, dismayed to find her fingers shaking as she did so.

Immediately, her phone chimed. It was a text from Cassidy.

Do it! Do it! Do it!

And, nice, she'd been sure to include two emojis: a pointer finger followed by an okay sign.

Victoria's lips thinned. *File under things you should never hear from your sister-in-law.* She texted back:

Seriously?

Cassidy: LU

Victoria sighed, and her thumbs moved once more over the keyboard.

Love you, too. But I think I now need therapy.

Cassidy: Then my work is done.

Victoria slipped her phone into her purse and locked the car behind her. *Get some.* It was so far out of the question, it was laughable. Sex meant a relationship; she'd never get caught in the trap of one of those again.

She walked into the bar, industriously named "The Bar," and headed to a stool by rote, too distracted by both her conversation with Cassidy and the huge, impending realization of her biggest dream to pay much attention to her surroundings. As she ordered a whisky—straight, over the rocks—she slipped her phone from her purse and checked her inbox.

*Empty.*

She put the phone facedown on the bar but kept it right at her fingertips. She'd be checking her inbox nearly every other breath until she heard back from Davis, the owner of The Ricchezza.

"Whisky for the lady."

A crystal tumbler appeared in her line of sight, placed on a square, black napkin. She raised her head and gave her best efforts toward a thank you smile. Apparently that failed, because the bartender just raised an eyebrow and asked, "Starting a tab or—?"

She sighed. "Sure. Why not? I'm celebrating." *Hopefully.* She checked her phone again. *Damn.* Still empty.

"If you say so."

She looked back at him to find his gaze taking in everything from her business attire to the laptop case sitting on the stool next to her—the one she optimistically referred to as her purse—with a smirk on his face, and she bristled.

*First Cassidy, now this guy.* Everyone was suddenly a critic.

She tossed back the whisky in one bracing gulp. "I'll have another." The badass effect was ruined by the strained quality of her voice as the liquor burned its way to her gut.

"Yes, ma'am." He turned his back, but not before she caught the hint of a patronizing smile on his lips.

*Ass.* She distracted herself as she awaited her second drink by checking her e-mail again. Nothing, naturally, but this time, the sting was dulled slightly by a pleasant fuzziness in her chest.

*Quality whisky.* She'd have to take time and actually taste it the second time around.

The bartender dropped off her second glass, and Victoria wrapped her fingers around it, squeezing tightly to keep them from wandering to her phone again. She raised the glass to her lips and drew in a deep breath, the dark scent of the spirits filling her lungs. Really quality whisky. The bartender probably thought he could pull one over on the little lady and give her something expensive without her noticing until the check came, but she couldn't bring herself to mind. This was one damn fine drink.

She took a sip and let the alcohol hover over her tongue before swallowing, and as she did so, she let her gaze wander around the bar for the first time since entering. It was shockingly abandoned for a Friday night, which only meant she was far enough from the Strip to have found a neighborhood bar the tourists had yet to overrun. Florescent lights at least a decade out of date and advertising various beers peppered the wall, but the booths were crack free and the dark wood tabletops gleamed.

Her gaze landed on one patron seated beneath the neon Bud Light sign. She swallowed the whisky in a gulp that nearly stole her breath.

*Lord have mercy.*

Victoria quickly checked to see if the other people in the bar were aware of the flawless specimen of manhood in their midst. No one was paying him any attention. Aghast, she looked at him again.

He was Michelangelo's goddamned David. His head was tipped back as he watched the TV above the bar, and his wavy brown hair cascaded past his shirt collar. His elegant Roman nose led her gaze down to a chiseled jaw and a neck she could happily nibble, which disappeared into the open collar of his shirt and branched out to broad shoulders a girl could really hang on to in the event of a rough ride.

Her pulse raced, and she ducked her gaze, hiding behind another sip of her whisky as she drank him in.

While she'd fought so hard not to think about it when on the phone with Cassidy, her body suddenly and vehemently reminded her that it'd been exactly three and a half years since she'd had a man between her thighs. And, her body helpfully suggested, here was a prime candidate to fill that missing spot in her life.

Her cheeks heated, and she snapped her gaze away. She squirmed in her seat as the spot between her legs began insistently beating along with her pulse.

*Damn.* This was the worst it'd been since Jeremy's death. Usually, she could distract herself with work or—*yes, Cassidy*—something battery operated, but she hadn't ached this bad for sex since she could remember.

She found her gaze sliding back over to the dream man, and this time she didn't fight it, certain she'd discover he hadn't really been that good-looking anyway and this would be over just like that.

*Gah*! He was even more handsome than she had initially given him credit for. He shoved some fingers through his hair, and his hands caught her attention. They were perfect. Just like the rest of him. So big, with gorgeous, blunt fingers. She'd always been a sucker for hands.

She took a nervous sip of her whisky, and her gaze fell to his drink. She relaxed a bit. Finally, something unattractive about him. Whatever he was drinking, it was blue. Smurf blue. It even had an umbrella in it.

Which is why she had no idea what she was doing as she raised her hand to get the bartender's attention. He walked over, flicking a glance at her still-full drink. Victoria nodded toward Dream Man. "Another round of whatever he's drinking. On me."

The bartender grinned. "Hmm, we *are* celebrating, aren't we?"

She barely resisted the urge to scowl at him. Luckily, she was so confused by what she'd just done, the bartender was gone before she could give in to the impulse.

*What did I just do?*

She shouldn't have done that. What was she thinking? She knew how anything like this went. How it eventually ended.

*Jeremy.*

No! She shoved the thought aside. This man, whoever he was, was not Jeremy. And a drink was not a relationship. As the asshole bartender mixed up another blue drink, Victoria began to calm down. Maybe this was exactly what she needed. She was right: a drink wasn't a relationship. Most people had sex without a relationship, too.

*Maybe I could have a one-night stand.* She'd never had one before, and, if she had to guess, she wasn't a one-night stand type of girl. But anything was better than celibacy, right?

She swallowed hard as she watched the bartender carry the drink to Dream Man. She winced when she saw his current drink was all the way full. She couldn't even flirt right. The bartender sat the new drink down in front of him and then nodded her direction.

Victoria straightened in her seat and tried to take a nonchalant sip of her whisky, but she damn near choked as Dream Man's full attention landed on her.

The man was even more incredibly gorgeous from the front than the side. Where did his handsomeness end? Surely there was a finite limit to such things.

Dream Man's eyes—she could see now they were a vivid blue—met hers, but his gaze didn't stay locked with hers for long. It fell to her lips, and he began to grin wickedly as he then looked at her neck. And breasts.

Victoria's breathing grew shallow. *Oh, God.* She felt as though he were touching her. Those big hands cupping the breasts he stared at as he brought the blue travesty of a cocktail to his lips and took a long draw on the straw.

She pressed her knees together and set her drink down with a *clink*. Dream Man abandoned his own full cocktail, picked up the one she'd ordered for him, and pushed to his feet.

*So tall.* Even seated across the bar, Victoria had to tip her head back to take in his full height. And damn if those broad shoulders didn't taper down to the sweetest narrow hips.

He started walking her way, and the angels began singing as his thighs moved beneath the fabric of his pants.

He was walking her way.

She'd done it. She'd flirted, and it'd worked. What in God's name was she going to do now? She took a gulp of her whisky, her gaze never leaving his while she fisted her other hand in her lap to control the tremble in her fingers.

He stopped right beside her. She stared up at him, her lips still around the rim of her glass. She blinked.

Had she thought his eyes merely blue? There was an appalling lack of descriptors in the English language for the shade of his deep, icy gaze that somehow warmed her from her pebbled nipples to the tips of her curled toes.

"Hello."

She lowered the glass but had to clear her throat before she could speak. "Hello."

His lips curled, and her gaze followed the small tip at their corners like her ovaries depended on it. "Thanks for the drink."

"Yep." *Oh, God.* Yep?

His smile widened, showcasing a dimple in his left cheek. "May I join you?"

She nodded toward the vacant stool next to her, unable to manage even the inane, one-syllable responses she'd spewed thus far as she caught scent of his cologne. *Delicious.* Dark and spicy, just like the whisky she'd held in her mouth moments before. He'd taste much better; she knew it.

She was suddenly desperate to not fuck this—whatever *this* was—up. "I'm Victoria."

He sat down on the stool but kept his body facing hers, putting them in such close proximity that their knees brushed. Heat licked her body, and she swayed his direction.

His gaze moved over her body again before pausing on her lips and then meeting hers. "A pleasure, Victoria," he said in a deep voice that, given the right circumstances, could send her straight into orgasm.

*Oh, fuck.* One thing was for certain. She was going to do wicked, wicked things to this man tonight.

# Chapter Three

*So much for taking the rest of the night off.* But if he had to go on the job again …

This Victoria was a stunning woman, with her blond hair up in a prim and proper bun that couldn't detract from the sensuality of her porcelain skin and those enormous brown eyes. *Doe eyes* a more romantic man might call them.

Which was why Kip shied away from that description as soon as it popped into his head.

Victoria was also jumpy as hell. As he intentionally pressed his knee into the soft muscle of her inner thigh, her drink jostled in her hand, nearly splashing them both.

That's when he noticed she was drinking whisky. He raised a brow as he scooted her cocktail napkin closer to her hand so she could set her drink down.

He didn't subscribe to the belief that one's drink choice was a reflection of the person—his own affinity for Blue Hawaiians was proof enough of a cocktail's inability to diagnose personality—but straight whisky …

Damn if he wasn't already impressed.

When she kept her fingertips near her drink, Kip set his own down and placed his hand a mere breath away from hers, the possibility of touch at any moment a latent promise.

And she definitely noticed. Her pulse was a rapid flutter beneath her jaw and, at its current speed, would feel like butterfly wings against his lips.

He noticed how her pupils expanded when she gazed up at him over the rim of her glass. And the way she couldn't keep her eyes off his body. And the way she consistently shifted in her seat as though she were swollen and achy between her legs.

She wanted him.

She could have him, of course. Anyone could for the right price.

"So, Victoria." He grinned at her and focused on her lips, a move that made her straighten in her seat. "What brings you to The Bar—business or pleasure?"

She blinked several times, and just as Kip was planning to repeat himself, she said, "For me, business is pleasure." She seemed to immediately regret the statement, as she blushed the prettiest shade of pink he'd ever seen. His gaze traveled down her neck and then to her chest as he watched that blush disappear beneath the vee of her shirt. How far down did it go?

Despite the fact that he had thoroughly worn himself out a couple of hours ago with his last client, his dick twitched. "Hmm." He nudged his fingers forward until the tip of his middle finger brushed the tip of hers. "Business is pleasure for me as well."

That blush deepened, but then she surprised him when her eyes narrowed and she tipped her head back and laughed. Not a delicate, tinkling laugh like some women; oh, no, not for *Victoria*. Her laugh was deep and husky—as potent as her drink.

He drew his brows together. This was … not the usual reaction he got when he seduced a woman.

"You've got to be doing that on purpose," she said when she looked at him again.

Kip tilted his head. "Doing what?"

She gestured to all of him with a flit of her fingers. "This."

The fact that he had been doing everything he'd done from the moment he left his seat until now on purpose did not keep him from feeling offended. And not a little embarrassed—something he never felt around women. "I'm always purposeful around a beautiful woman."

He could tell she was still amused, but she sobered and looked at the bar, rolling her shoulders.

Because he'd trained himself to pick up on a woman's every mood, he recognized that she was uncomfortable being complimented, which probably meant that it had been a good long while since someone had told this woman she was beautiful. And she was more than beautiful. Stunning. Unique. No, he definitely didn't believe in "types," but she seemed to check every single one of his boxes. Something panged behind his sternum, and he reached for his drink, disconcerted.

As he took a sip, Victoria said, "Well, you don't have to be quite so purposeful around me." Her gaze skittered away from his, and she drew an invisible circle on the bar. "I find I like authenticity best."

*Noted.* Astonishingly, he wanted her to like him, which was a new situation for him, and one he didn't find particularly comfortable—not to mention, it wasn't necessary for his line of work. Maybe it was because she'd called him on his act. Maybe it was her delicate blend of vulnerability mixed with hints of a woman who would chew you up and spit you out if you crossed her.

Whatever it was, if he was going to get her as a client, he was going to have to be present and try. No autopilot for Victoria who liked authenticity—God help him. And yet, he had to fight his knee-jerk response to say something smarmy, like *You'll find me authentic*. He swallowed. "All right."

"So"—she licked her lips, and those gorgeous eyes met his—"What kind of business do you do that's so pleasurable?"

Kip pressed his lips together. Authenticity, in this case, was going to get him nowhere. Time to employ a trick he'd learned worked on every woman in existence: turn the topic back to her. And a little touch never hurt either. He pressed his knee into her inner thigh again, and, like magic, her legs parted a bit, nearly distracting *him*. "What's your pleasurable business?"

She tilted her head, and her gaze grew increasingly piercing until Kip had to squelch the urge to shift in his seat. Her delicate throat worked beneath a swallow. "On second thought, there's probably no need to get personal."

Kip blinked twice in rapid succession. *What?* His brain worked overtime. She wanted authentic but impersonal. How in the world was he supposed to do that?

*What a challenge!*

He nearly groaned. He shouldn't like this. He shouldn't like this at all. In fact, he should thank her for the drink, get up, and go home. Right now. He should do that right—

Her fingers brushed against his, jerking him from his thoughts.

She straightened. "Do you want to get out of here?"

Kip inhaled quickly through his nose. "Get out of here?" he repeated, as though he'd forgotten the meaning behind those words.

"Get a hotel room. For the night."

Her fingers were hot against his, but they trembled a bit, and that's when he knew he hadn't misheard or misinterpreted her.

Holy hell. Whatever he'd done had worked. An unaccustomed tightness that felt like excitement filled his gut. Victoria, who had been nervous seconds ago and who was now propositioning him, was full of surprises. He couldn't wait to see what more he'd unearth with her beneath him. Would she be a vixen? Passionate? Or one of those tender lovers—the ones that made him nervous? Only one way to find out. He shifted his fingers slightly until they were intertwined with hers. Best to just get this part out of the way, and yet, he found himself hesitating. The word *sure* was perched on his lips, though he hadn't slept with any woman without being paid for it in four years.

That simple *sure* terrified him. He leaned forward, and, with his lips only a few inches from hers, said, "My rate for a night is a thousand dollars." He stroked the inside of her wrist with his thumb. "But I'd be happy to give you an hour for much less than my usual rate."

*You'd what?* He gritted his teeth. What the hell had he just said?

Victoria sucked in a breath.

*Say yes*. Please, fuck, let her say yes.

• • •

*My rate …*

Those words echoed on repeat in Victoria's head as she stared into this stranger's unimaginably beautiful eyes. With each repetition, they grew louder until they were a roar.

*Victoria, you've fucked up this time.*

The truth became undeniable. She'd propositioned a prostitute.

Of course, she'd propositioned a prostitute.

She snatched her hand away from his, and he let her go without the slightest resistance. Irrational disappointment crashed down around her.

She lurched to her feet. Not-So-Dream Man's gaze as he looked up at her burned her anew. She snatched her laptop bag and jerked it onto her shoulder. She'd finally decided to take the plunge and ask for a night of sex, and this happened. "I don't have to *pay* for it." *Oh, God,* do *I have to pay for it?* Was she that hopeless?

He sighed, and the sound contained something that made her pause instead of storm out right away like she'd been planning. "You certainly don't," he said. His gaze roamed her body again, and his eyes flashed. He rubbed his pointer finger across his bottom lip. "You certainly don't."

And despite knowing now that his words weren't genuine, her body surged with heat once more. Why would he be regretful … other than possibly losing his going rate for an entire night?

A grand. Naturally, he would be regretful over losing that amount. His regret was no more trustworthy than his compliment.

She groaned and clenched her fingers in the strap of her bag. What a nightmare. She'd really liked this guy, even when he'd been trying too hard. And that body—

Well. When your body was your office, you had to keep it up, didn't you? She tossed some bills on the bar.

"Victoria—"

She couldn't even meet his eyes. Her cheeks flushed, and her body was already lamenting the fact that she was going to go without sex. Again. And tonight, no vibrator would help matters.

"Victoria," he said again.

She closed her eyes for a moment, pinched the bridge of her nose, and then forced herself to look at him.

His hand was extended toward her, and in his palm sat her phone.

Her phone! She snatched it and saw the blinking light that meant she had a new e-mail. She hadn't thought it possible, but this was strong enough to distract her from her current humiliation.

Can't-Believe-She-Thought-He-Was-Dream Man was saying something, but Victoria didn't expend any energy trying to translate it through the dull roar in her head. She waved a hand at him—more a *not now* than a *see you later*—and left The Bar without another word.

She was breathing quickly as she walked toward her car, and when she closed herself inside, her heartbeat accelerated to the point she was lightheaded. This could be it: the moment her life changed.

She unlocked her phone, and a noise slipped past her lips when she saw the e-mail was, in fact, from The Ricchezza domain.

Dear Ms. Hastings,

We thank you for your excellent proposal …

She was unable to keep herself from skimming down to the bottom of the e-mail where she saw not the name of Mr. Davis after *Sincerely*, but the name of his assistant.

She frowned. With her throat suddenly dry, she scrolled back up to where she'd left off and read the e-mail thoroughly.

"Okay," she said to the silent interior of her car. "It's not a no."

*But it's not a yes, either.*

With a sudden calm—the kind she always felt when she went to work—Victoria placed her phone in her laptop bag.

The Ricchezza had gotten another promising proposal. They were going to pursue both options until they could make a more informed decision.

Another promising proposal? She drummed her fingers on the steering wheel. "Masterson." Had to be.

Damn it, Masterson had gotten to them, too. Of course she had. She was the best.

Victoria lifted her chin. "But I'm the best, too."

And this was all she'd ever wanted. Time to go to war.

# Chapter Four

A ringing phone penetrated Victoria's dream. The one in which she was licking up a particular prostitute's thigh as she worked his erection with both hands.

She groaned as she rolled to her side, her body aching with unsated lust, and she slapped blindly on her bedside table until her fingers encountered her cell. She raised the phone to her ear.

"Hello?"

"So, did you do it?"

"Cassidy?" Victoria squinted at her clock. "It's five-thirty. On a Saturday morning."

"Stop dodging. Answer the question."

"I'm not—Dodging?" She rolled to her back and flopped her forearm across her eyes. "I'm asleep. Like you should be."

"That's cute. You think I sleep."

Victoria could hear the distinct sounds of a fistfight in the background. "How do I get in trouble for staying late in the office, but you're allowed to stay up all night doing your job?"

"Because my job is cool."

"Hey."

"I mean, oh, no, what was I thinking. I've seen the error of my ways."

"You're a dick."

"Welp, you definitely didn't get laid, Grumpasaurus Rex."

Victoria rubbed her eyes. "When's the last time you got laid?" Turnabout was fair play.

"Tuesday."

"Wait, what?" She was suddenly very awake. She jerked upright. "Tuesday?"

"Yeah, you know, the day between Monday and Wednesday." Cassidy sighed. "It was no good though."

All of Victoria's protective instincts surged to the forefront. "I can't believe I haven't met the guy. You're in a relationship?"

Cassidy snorted. "Not if I can help it."

"Oh." Victoria frowned, not sure how she felt about that.

"God, I can hear the disapproval in your voice all the way across town, Mother Time."

"No, that's not it." In fact, hadn't she been aching for a no-strings-attached fling herself last night? She propped her elbow on her knee and cradled her forehead in her palm. Her bedraggled hair dangled around her face, and she took a big breath. "I tried to. Last night."

All video game sounds abruptly ceased. "I'm going to need you to repeat that, because I swear, for a second, you sounded like a real woman."

"And I already regret this conversation."

"No, seriously. You tried to hook up last night?"

The disbelief in Cassidy's voice was insulting, but what was worse was that she was right to be disbelieving, because Victoria couldn't even pick a fling properly. "He ended up being a …" Was she truly going to confess this? "Prostitute." She winced.

"A—"

Victoria nibbled her bottom lip as she waited for Cassidy's response.

Laughter, so loud and abrupt that Victoria had to pull the phone away from her ear, spilled out of the line.

Victoria hung up with a vicious jab of her thumb and flopped down in bed. Almost immediately, her phone rang again, but she silenced it and stared up at her ceiling, which was just starting to brighten with the beginning of the day.

After some sleep—interrupted though it had been—she was not so mortally angry at the man who had never even told her his name. The truth was, he had done nothing wrong. For that matter, she had not done anything wrong either. But she had sent over the drink. She had propositioned him. She'd even noticed and commented on how hard he was working with her; she just hadn't realized he'd literally been working.

It had just been a massive misunderstanding.

Her phone chirped. With a sigh, Victoria raised it, already knowing what she'd find.

ILU. I'm sorry. Pick up the fucking phone.

When the phone rang again, Victoria answered it but didn't say anything. Cassidy would first anyway.

"So, why didn't you have sex with him?"

*An excellent question.* "With a prostitute?"

"I believe they prefer the term *gigolo*. And yep, that's who we're talking about."

"Cassidy—" Victoria groaned. "I honestly don't know how to answer that."

"Hey—" The sudden gentleness in Cassidy's tone set Victoria on edge. "I know your last relationship was painful. *Really* painful."

There was something that sounded like fear in her sister-in-law's voice. *Oh, Cassidy.* "Honey, that's not why you're avoiding relationships, is it?" Victoria wouldn't be able to stand it if that was the reason. She wouldn't allow her failed marriage with Jeremy to ruin another life.

"We're not talking about me." Any sign of vulnerability had been vanquished.

"We could be—"

"The thing is," Cassidy said, cutting her off, "a gigolo is kind of perfect. You know, if you're trying to avoid relationships. I wish I would have thought of it instead of sleeping with Chris, who is now making *awkward* take on new definitions."

Victoria was silent for a moment. "Huh," she said finally. Cassidy was right. A gigolo *was* kind of perfect. *And you let the perfect one get away!* "Damn it."

"Excellent. So, here's what we're going to do."

"Do? We're not going to do—"

"I can set everything up for you. I'll text you the details, and all you'll have to do is show up."

"Like my pimp?" Please, God, let this horrific conversation be a dream and not real life.

"Oh, sweet Victoria, no. Like his pimp. Silly girl."

Victoria cleared her throat. "I think we should talk about family boundaries again."

"Trust me, sis. You won't be sorry."

"Now wait a second—"

Dial tone.

"Well, shit." New definitions of awkward indeed. "I can't think about this right now." She groped the space beside her bed until she found her laptop where she'd left it after drafting a response to Davis's assistant last night. She'd known better than to send it after a couple of whiskies and some disappointment.

Work was the perfect solution to everything. So, she'd work. And she'd sweep the floor with Masterson.

But while she typed away, her mind wandered, and her defenses crumbled. What could it hurt, going along with this scheme of Cassidy's? After all, the only opinion that mattered to her anymore was Cassidy's, and she was, obviously, on board with this madness.

When Cassidy's text arrived, Victoria might just read it. *Might.*

# Chapter Five

"Kipling."

"Mother." He dutifully leaned down for a kiss that never reached his cheek—his mother could never bear to smear her lipstick. Her perfume nearly choked him as he caught a particularly unlucky lungful.

When they both stood upright again, she patted a hand near, but not on, her silver hair and took a moment to peruse him. Kip braced himself as her blue eyes took on a sharp glint.

"Is your shirt pink?"

"Intentionally so."

"Hmm." She pursed her lips, and Kip marked the time down as three seconds—only three seconds since he'd arrived, and he'd already managed to earn her disapproval.

*A personal best.*

"Where's Dad?"

She turned from him, already losing interest. "I'm sure I don't know."

Which meant he was probably in the game room watching television for entertainment and not research—a pastime his mother hated and therefore pretended didn't exist.

He started that direction but hadn't made it two steps before his mother said, "Don't get too comfortable. Dinner will be ready any moment."

"There's no danger of me getting comfortable," he muttered beneath his breath.

God, he hated Sundays. But he still showed up every week, because if he started thinking about why he came, he'd have to face some of the feelings he'd been avoiding for years.

He straightened the cuffs on his pink button-down shirt as he rounded the corner and found his father just where he knew he'd be: watching golf from the leather lounge chair that was permanently conformed to his shape.

Kip took the empty lounger next to his father, who grunted by way of greeting. A commercial came on, which was when his mother would have focused, but Kip's dad turned his way. His brown eyes took on a merry glint as he scanned Kip's attire. "Bet your mother loved that shirt."

"For Christ's sake." Kip tugged at his collar. "It's just a shirt."

"Nothing is just anything in this house."

He took a page out of his dad's book and grunted. *No kidding.*

There was a squawk from behind them, and neither of them turned toward the intercom system that had been in the house since his childhood—the house his mother optimistically referred to as *the mansion.*

"Dinner is served," said a tinny, compressed version of his mother's voice.

With a heavy sigh, his dad pushed from his chair and clicked the television off before dropping the remote on the side table. Kip eyed his father's browbeaten expression. *Does my face look anything like that?* There was a definite tugging at his eyebrows. He intentionally tried to straighten them just in case.

"Let's go to supper," his father said in the same tone someone might say *Let's go to the DMV.*

"Right behind you."

They walked through the house silently until they arrived at the formal dining room where his mother was already seated at the head of the table. Father took the other end of the table, and Kip took the place setting in his usual spot halfway between the two.

*And so it begins.*

He tipped his wrist so he could snag a peek at his watch. Two more hours. A person could do anything for two hours, and he often had.

He smiled, thinking of one particular time when a client had been very generous with more than just her money—

"And how was your week, Kipling?" His mother cut into the lobster tail Mary, their cook, had prepared. "That smile you're wearing looks promising."

Kip cleared his throat and reached for his own silverware. "It was a good week," he said carefully. He always said everything carefully. Too much cheer would make his mother suspicious—happiness was always questioned in this house. Too much gloom, and his mother would remind him that he had only himself to blame.

"Anything in particular stand out?"

He chewed thoughtfully and then swallowed. "No."

It was the same conversation they had each Sunday, and so far so good. It was the Sundays during which they deviated from the script that made him cringe.

"Any luck on the job front?"

*Annnnd, we're deviating from the script.* Kip set his knife and fork down, what little appetite he'd had vanishing into the lush carpet beneath his feet.

"Oh, Georgiana, leave the boy alone."

She sipped from her wine before saying, "I believe we have. It hasn't helped."

"I'm still looking." Kip rubbed his finger over a water spot on his fork, one that—had his mother seen it—would have been taken out of someone's hide in the kitchen staff.

"Hmm."

God save him from his mother's *hmms*. He sighed and placed his hands in his lap. His parents didn't know he had a job, and he certainly wasn't going to correct that impression, as the knowledge that he made thousands of dollars a week selling sex would only turn up the heat in the hot seat.

Luckily, they hadn't paid close enough attention to his life—except in this one area of employment—to notice that he was able to support himself nominally well since they'd cut him off without any aid about a year ago when he had refused to follow Georgiana's footsteps and join her firm after college graduation. He knew they expected him to come crawling back any moment, unable to make it on his own. That was not going to happen. In fact, earlier today, Kip had secured a brand-new client for tomorrow evening. His client list was increasing, not decreasing.

"Your charm can only get you so far, Kipling."

*Ah, yes.* Now they were back on script. It wasn't a Sunday Dinner if his mother didn't remind him that all he had going for him was his looks and personability.

It had always been Kip's opinion that those two things counted for a lot in this world, but it wasn't an opinion his mother shared. Little did they know his charm had made him a successful man—well, semi-successful. Okay, no one else would define prostitution as success, but give him a break.

He'd probably stroke out if his mother looked at him during one of these Sunday Dinners and simply accepted him for who he was. Loved him. Put him above her ambition for one second—

And, he shoved those thoughts aside—the very ones he'd be trying to avoid by not thinking about why he showed up at this house every week like clockwork, seeking approval from his family like some sap whipping boy who hadn't learned better by now.

He didn't need approval or acceptance. He'd make it on his own. Hell, was already *halfway* to making it.

Technically, Kip knew, the money he'd already managed to save was enough to open a business. A small one, but one that belonged all to him, and one in which he would have to answer to no one. The problem was, he didn't know what kind of business he wanted to open. Which would be worse: working a little longer while he saved more and figured out his path or starting a business now only to find out his mother was right? That he didn't have anything going for him but his charm?

And because Kip was good at fucking everyone, including himself, he'd managed to raise his money in the one way that would keep him from being able to go legit if word of it ever got out. Georgiana was far too well known in this town. That her son was a gigolo would spread far and wide if anyone found out, and then no one would do business with him and he wouldn't be able to join her firm—the backup plan that still made him shiver.

"He knows all of this, Georgiana."

Kip pressed his lips together as his mother turned her attention fully on her husband. "Does he, Avery?" she said softly.

They both knew that tone. His father broke eye contact and reached for his own glass of wine. Had his father dared to challenge Mother as she presided over Sunday Dinner? When was the last time that had happened?

Dear old dad was a kept man. Georgiana had come from money; Avery had married into it. At one point they'd probably been in love, but that point was far, far behind them. Avery didn't work, and, as far as Georgiana was concerned, that meant he didn't get a say in running the home.

Kip was a feminist—a gigolo kind of had to be; his mother was something else altogether. Equality? Nope. She wanted everyone in the world beneath her boot, and for some reason, his father had volunteered to be at the bottom of the pile.

"I do know," he said softly, hoping to deflect his mother's attention back to himself—something he usually did everything in his power to avoid. His dad owed him. Big.

It worked. Her attention nearly audibly snapped his way, and as she set down her own silverware, he knew he was in for it now. He tucked his chin into his chest and pretended to listen as she launched into a lecture on how he was wasting his life and blah, blah, blah.

He kept his father in his peripheral vision as Avery turned back to his meal, suitably cowed by his wife's dominance. *The fuck I'll ever end up with a woman like that.*

No other woman would ever strong-arm him. Boss him around. Make him live a certain way.

Look at him like he was a waste.

Because if he had to live the rest of his life like he'd lived under Mother's thumb for the first eighteen years, either under her roof or under her dominance at the firm …

*I'd rather turn tricks for the rest of my life.*

# Chapter Six

Victoria paced the room of the Desert Oasis Hotel & Spa, a luxurious hotel well off the Strip, until she could see the imprint of her sensible heels in the pattern of the carpet. "I can't believe I'm doing this." She nibbled on her thumbnail. "I can't believe I'm *doing this!*"

Her stomach flipped as she paced, but she wasn't sure if it was from nerves or anticipation. In just a few minutes, she could finally be having sex again.

"Okay, I'm definitely doing this." The guy—whoever it was Cassidy had hired yesterday—was on his way over here this second. It was too late to back out now, and she wasn't sure she even wanted to.

*Don't lie to yourself. You definitely don't want to.*

She'd taken extra care with her grooming today, shaving places she hadn't shaved since Jeremy had been alive. As she walked, her bare lips rubbed together, creating a silky slide so pleasurable that this guy Cassidy had hired was not going to have to touch her at all to get her ready.

She was already good to go and chomping at the bit.

At least, she thought she was. But when there was a soft but firm knock at the door, Victoria jumped.

She placed a shaky hand over her stomach. *What am I doing?*

This was crazy. She'd been so adamant a couple of nights before with her *I don't have to pay for it.* Here she was, paying for it.

*It's never too late to back out.* With a breath for courage, she walked toward the door. She'd simply tell him this had been a mistake and then head back home, stopping by the gas station on her route for more batteries.

She had dignity. She had—

She opened the door, and her lips parted. "You!"

Maybe-Dream Man stood outside the open door, his hand still raised for a knock, and those gorgeous blue eyes of his widened for a moment before he grinned lopsidedly and leaned a shoulder against the doorframe. "Hello, Victoria."

*He remembered my name.*

Her mouth opened and closed a couple of times, but nothing came out. Her mind, however, worked at a million words a minute. Her body, already primed, surged white hot, and she had to fist her hands at her side to keep from reaching for him and hauling him into the room.

He laughed softly. "Are you going to invite me inside?

Automatically, she moved aside and gestured for him to enter before she could think twice about the action. She inwardly cursed as he walked by her. What happened to calling everything off?

But then she caught sight of his broad shoulders from the back, and her gaze traveled downward across that broad expanse until it narrowed to the tightest ass she'd ever seen or imagined.

She closed the door.

At the quiet *snick*, Definitely-Dream Man turned. His hot gaze gobbled her up, and in response, her nipples tightened. "I confess," he said in a low rumble, "I was more than glad to see you on the other side of that door."

Victoria narrowed her eyes. The truth or an act? This man's profession was making women believe what they wanted to believe. In fact, he probably remembered her name because he'd trained himself to always remember a woman's name.

As though he'd heard her thoughts, he said, "I'm being honest with you. I promise."

She straightened her shoulders, lest she appear vulnerable. She'd have to do better guarding her thoughts. This wasn't a relationship. Would never be one. Emotion had no place here.

He stepped toward her and didn't stop coming until they were so close she could see the fine shadow of a beard on his clean-shaven jaw.

*He must have to shave constantly.* He'd probably shaved right before he came to the hotel, but his jaw would still leave a burn all over her.

"I'm Kip, by the way."

She jolted. He hadn't told her his name that night at The Bar. Was his name something he only gave away to paying customers?

*Stop it. Stop thinking that way right now!*

"Kip," she mumbled. She frowned. "Is that short for something?"

He shrugged. "Just Kip."

*My ass.* But his hedging answer reassured her more than anything else could have. They were both on the same page. No strings. No emotions.

Just pleasure.

She hoped.

She nibbled her bottom lip again, and his gaze narrowed. "Nervous?" he asked.

"You have no idea." Her words were quiet in the room, but she felt so much better once she'd said them.

"Don't be." He raised a hand, but paused with it several inches away from her cheek. He raised a brow in obvious question, and she found herself nodding. His brow relaxed, and he brushed the tips of his fingers across her cheek until he cradled it in his palm. "I will take very good care of you, Victoria."

*Oh, God.*

She hadn't realized she'd spoken out loud until Kip smiled. He lowered his head, and just as she thought he was going to kiss her—panicking that he was moving so quickly—instead, he asked, "What made you change your mind?"

Her befuddled mind scrambled to keep up. "Change my mind?"

"About paying for it."

She couldn't prevent a wince.

"Victoria, there's nothing wrong with this."

"I know that."

He brushed her cheek with his thumb. "Do you?"

*No.* She nodded.

With his other hand, he wrapped his fingers around her wrist, pressing his thumb into her pulse point before stroking there in a circle. "Tell me what you want. What you like."

She swayed toward him. "Everything."

The thumb stroking the inside of her wrist paused. "Everything, huh?"

His lips were quirked at the corners, and she felt her cheeks flush with heat. She stepped backward before she could stop herself.

*Why did you say that?* Shame she hadn't felt in years flooded her chest. Shame she hated and knew was ill placed, but shame she couldn't keep at bay nonetheless.

"Hey, now," Kip said, placing a hand on the curve of her waist. "Victoria—" He tightened his fingers in her soft side and pulled her back to him. "Honey, you're thinking too hard."

The endearment shocked her, but, even more shocking, after he uttered it, she immediately calmed. Damned if she knew why.

"That's better," he murmured. "So—" He moved his hand to the small of her back and now his arm was around her. She could feel the heat of his broad chest hovering a breath away from her breasts, and her nipples strained toward that warmth with all their might. "Victoria likes everything. What a pleasant surprise."

Her breathing quickened.

"Before we get to *everything*," he said, wrapping his other arm around her back. "How about we start with a kiss?"

*A kiss*. While moments ago, she'd been panicking at the thought of one, now, with his arms around her, she was trembling for his lips against hers.

She'd gone without a kiss even longer than the years she'd gone without sex.

The sudden thought clogged in Victoria's throat, and unwelcome memories forced their way through the haze of her lust.

*No. Anything but that.*

She reached up with the hands that had still been at her side and grabbed hold of Kip's shirt right over the shockingly firm planes of his chest. She didn't allow the feel of his body to shock her for long though—couldn't afford to—and she jerked him toward her, stood on her tiptoes, and crushed her mouth to his.

Her eyes were still open, so she was able to see how his widened, his eyebrows shooting toward his hairline.

But he didn't release her. And after a moment, the muscles that had stiffened against her fists relaxed, and he wrapped his arms more securely about her.

Yes. This is what she'd set out to do. And she'd been successful.

She was already breathing hard—much harder than the mere two seconds of kissing merited—and she waited for the pressure of Kip's lips against hers to drive away the onslaught of the unforgiving past.

His eyes closed; his brow relaxed. One of his hands smoothed up between her shoulder blades until his fingers wound into her hair. He skated the tip of his tongue along the seam of her lips.

He was doing everything right, and she could recognize that he was good at it.

*It's not working!*

She moaned, a sound he echoed, but she was already pushing her fists against his chest, barely keeping herself from beating against it as she wished to beat against the tide of the memories.

As soon as he felt the pressure of her hands, he stopped, an immediate halt to all activity as he lowered his arms and stepped back. As her chest billowed, she noticed his cheeks had a slight red tinge to them, and his lips were shiny from her mouth.

"Victoria?"

*Victoria, I'm so sorry. Victoria, please stop. Victoria, I just … can't.*

The distance that cropped up in their marriage, no matter how hard she'd tried to keep it at bay. The resentment that, as his caretaker, she'd felt toward his illness, and even him when, instead of getting better, things just got worse and worse. And then, the immediate guilt that would overrun her, because no matter how hard things got for her, they were infinitely harder for Jeremy. And she should know that! Should shove everything she was feeling aside before it made him do something stupid, like …

She shoved her hand over her lips, spun, and sprinted to the bathroom.

• • •

*Okay.*

Kip blinked at the closed bathroom door several times, hoping either the view would change or he would reach some level of clarity as to why his arms were suddenly and achingly empty of woman.

Of Victoria, whose body had felt unexpectedly good against his. Whose kiss had tasted of the orange juice he'd spied on the table when he'd come in. Whose fists in his shirt had driven him slightly wild, as though he'd never had a woman fist his shirt before instead of it being a regular occurrence.

The erection that had sprung to existence as soon as he'd placed his hand in the lush curve of her waist several minutes ago jerked within his pants, and he hissed in a breath, taken aback by how much it ached.

Nothing here made any damn sense!

He shoved some fingers through his hair as he drew in a deep breath and blew it out harshly.

He'd never had a woman run away from him before. He wasn't sure he was a fan.

With a grimace, he rearranged his cock in his pants so that he could move without pinching the thing to death. Then, he strode across the room and knocked on the closed bathroom door.

"Victoria?"

Silence.

"Are you—are you sick?" She'd had her hand over her mouth as she ran. He eyed the orange juice again, looking for any sign of a mini liquor bottle nearby. Nothing.

There was still no response from the other side of the door, and he felt a flare of uncharacteristic impatience. Then he jolted. Was he truly impatient to get back to the kissing—a part of his job he did solely to arouse his clients and not for any sort of self-gratification?

"The hell's wrong with me?" he muttered. He rapped the door with his knuckles once more. "Victoria!" he said more sharply than he'd intended.

There was finally a noise from the other side, but it was so faint that he barely heard it except for making out the wounded quality of it.

A chill slid up his neck. "Honey?" He reached down and wrapped his fingers around the doorknob, giving it a twist.

*Locked.*

"Victoria, open the door, please."

Another one of those noises dripping with hurt filtered through the door.

*Fuck this.*

He rammed his shoulder into the door, and it gave way with a surprising lack of resistance. Kip stumbled into the dark interior of the bathroom, and his eyes scanned frantically as he groped for the light switch.

The light was shards in his eyes, and he held a hand up against the glare, squinting into the sudden glut of illumination.

He caught sight of her immediately, and his hand dropped. She was huddled between the toilet and the tub, her knees tucked into her chest and her arms wrapped around her shins.

She was rocking back and forth, and that same, horrifying sound that had scared him so badly kept traveling his way at regular intervals.

One thing was very clear: she was hurt.

"Honey!" He rushed over, sliding on his knees as he hit the tile. He brushed a hand over the back of her head. "Look at me."

His heart seemed to be trying to climb up his throat.

"I know. I'm sorry."

The words were garbled, but he heard them nonetheless. His hand stilled on her hair. "Sorry?"

"I just wanted a kiss. I'm sorry."

Kip attempted to swallow past the throbbing that seemed lodged at the base of his throat, but it didn't quite work. "I'm going to lift you. Okay?"

She didn't respond in any way other than a string of unintelligible words and more rocking.

"Shit," he muttered. "*Shit.*"

Something was very wrong with her. He slid one arm beneath her bent knees and pulled her far enough from between the toilet and tub by sliding her on her bottom to be able to wrap his other arm around her shoulders and stagger to his feet with her cradled against his chest.

She tucked her face into the crook of his neck, and her frantic breaths raised gooseflesh along his chest. "I'm so sorry, Jeremy." She hiccupped.

The muscles along Kip's shoulders stiffened. He squeezed her close. "Shh, honey." He carried her through the doorway, turning sideways to keep from bashing her into the doorframe, and walked to the bed.

He kneeled on the mattress and crawled to the center on his knees before settling against the headboard and arranging her in his lap. She curled into him, wrapping an arm around his neck, and when she pressed her face against his throat, he could feel wetness.

Tears.

He tightened his arms and started rocking her back and forth.

*Why are you doing this?* Even as he snuggled her hair with his cheek, he recognized that this was crazy. He should have called hotel management when he couldn't open the door. Hell, at the very least, he should have called the odd woman who'd hired him and told her to come get Victoria.

He absolutely should not be here in the middle of the bed rocking her and trying to calm her tears. This was not what he did. Was outside of his job description.

And a mob of *shoulds* would not be able to pull him away from Victoria at this point.

*Honey*, he'd called her at several opportunities. Another oddity. He often used a pet name with his clients, but it was always *baby*. He never once had called someone *honey*, because it wasn't a pet name, it was an endearment and therefore had no place in his vocabulary.

He tucked her head more securely into the notch between his neck and shoulder. "Why are you sorry, honey?"

"He died. It's all my fault he died."

Kip frowned, but he didn't pause as he rocked her and stroked her hair. He had incredible people instincts. Whereas a confession like this would have sent him running with any other client, it seemed unlikely Victoria would try to choke him to death or, one of his least favorite client memories, whip out a pointy nail file and jab it his direction. "Why do you think that?"

"I … needed sex." She sobbed. "His medication … he didn't want me anymore, no matter what I did."

His heart grew sick. He pressed a kiss into her hair.

"He loved me so much," she murmured. "He took himself off it, and—"

*Oh, shit.*

"It was our anniversary. I f-found him. His gun in his hand." She sobbed again. "There was so much blood. Why couldn't I just control myself? The meds were finally working. If he hadn't felt pressure from me, he would have been fine!"

A sudden rush of tears slid down his neck, pooling in the dip of his collarbone. "Oh, honey."

What a thing for someone to have to live with. What a thing for a woman to have to live with when women's sexuality carried such a stigma as it was.

*To feel as though your need for sex killed the man you loved …*

"Was Jeremy your husband?"

At the word *husband*, she stiffened. "Yes—" She straightened in his arms and blinked up at his face, tears streaming down her cheeks. Her eyes widened. "Kip?"

He felt his eyebrows rise. She'd obviously forgotten where she was and whom she was with. That was some serious trauma. He cautiously raised his hand and brushed his fingertips across her cheek. "Yes."

Her cheeks paled. "Oh, God. What did I say?"

*Probably your deepest secret and fear.* "Nothing to be ashamed of."

She gasped and pushed at him a bit, but, unlike what he would do in a similar situation with someone else, Kip didn't release her. "Hey, now," he said.

"I told you about Jeremy!" She struggled against him.

He attempted to exude extreme calm—hopefully, some of it would be catching. "You did."

Her expression grew stricken, as though her every nightmare had been realized. "Oh, God."

Her tone was far different from the one he was used to hearing those words spoken in.

"Let's just take a breath, hmm?" He stroked her hair again. "You've told people before. It's no big deal. Just pretend I'm one of them."

"I've told nobody before!"

He drew his head back. "Seriously?"

"Yes!" She pulled her knees up again and buried her face in her hands. "Not any of my friends. Not my sister-in-law. Nobody! All they know is that Jeremy killed himself." She shook her head. "Ugh, I just wanted to fuck! And now the one guy who will fuck me is looking at me like that." She waved a hand his general direction, keeping her forehead pressed to her knees.

Properly chastened, Kip cleared his expression, but his mind was rioting. "The one guy." He laughed without humor. "Victoria, be realistic."

Men were lined up for this woman. He knew it.

She raised her head, and her eyes were sharp. "Yeah, that's why I'm paying for it. I have so many people wanting to screw me."

He frowned. She wasn't serious. Was she? This woman was a catch with a capital C. He fucked for a living, and he hadn't been able to stop thinking about her since running into her at The Bar. "Is everyone in this world idiots?"

She looked down at her knees and wiped the tears from her left cheek, which was now stained with one of her blushes.

"Victoria, I'm confident that if you really looked around you at the men who are drooling all over themselves, you'd find that isn't true."

She laughed humorlessly and still wouldn't meet his eyes. "My own husband wouldn't sleep with me."

He reached out and tucked a strand of hair behind her ear. "You know that's a different situation. I know that's a different situation, and I don't even have particulars. He—"

She waved a hand at him and squeezed her eyes shut. "We are not talking about this. I don't even want to remember that I told you."

Kip shut his mouth. "Okay."

She flopped back on the bed and threw her forearm over her eyes. "I can't believe I managed to screw up a screw with a hooker."

His lips twitched. "Technically, we prefer the term—"

"*Gigolo*. I know." She sighed. "I'll pay you for your time."

"Victoria"—he shifted so he faced her fully—"if you're under the impression I'm not going to fuck your brains out still, you're gravely mistaken."

He saw the rapid rise and fall of her ribcage halt abruptly. She slowly removed her arm from her eyes, and her gaze connected with his. "Fuck my brains out?"

He winced. *Really?* "Okay, I recognize in hindsight that wasn't romantic." What was it about this woman that made him completely inept? "I'll make lo—"

"Nope, stop right there." She sat up, and a glint of something he hadn't seen yet in her fired through her eyes. "Fucking my brains out sounds … perfect."

Kip pressed his lips together to keep his jaw from dropping. He tried to manage a nonchalant shrug, but it felt like a spasm more than anything. "Okay."

She smiled softly. Shyly. "Okay."

For the first time in his profession, he was unsure how to proceed. Normally, he'd take charge at this moment—lean over and kiss her until she was breathless and achy. But, he knew things about this woman. Deeply personal things. It was preventing him from viewing her as a client, and that was throwing him off his game. What was he supposed to do no—

Victoria launched herself at him.

With an *oof,* he landed on his back with her sprawled on top of him.

She immediately pushed up, her hands planted in the mattress on either side of his shoulders, and he could see her brightest blush yet stealing across her cheeks. "I'm sor—"

He placed his fingertips over her moving lips, and her words petered out. Then, the tip of her tongue met the tip of his middle finger.

He shuddered, and every drop of blood in his body surged to his cock. "What were you planning to do with me"—he tried to collect his cool and failed—"when you got me in this position?"

She still wasn't meeting his eyes, and her arms were still taut. She shrugged with one shoulder.

He shook his head. "This from the girl who likes *everything.*" He brushed his fingers along her bottom lip, hoping against hope she'd lick him again.

She wiggled on top of him, probably in an attempt to slide off his body, but then she halted. The blush deepened and swept down her chest and as far as Kip could see down her shirt—and he was definitely looking, staring at the valley between her breasts with utmost concentration.

She moved against him again—she'd found his erection. It was sandwiched, not unpleasantly, between their bodies and pressing into her stomach. When she moved a third time, a noise he never made in bed slipped from somewhere deep in his chest.

"Oh, *shit,*" she muttered.

An insistent ache panged in his gut. This was going to fly out of control in 0.0 seconds if he didn't do something. Didn't take control. She was merely lying on top of him, and it was driving him crazy in a way he never thought a woman could. In a way a woman never had.

He gripped her arms. "Victoria—"

Her gaze suddenly met his, and her eyes were already hazy. Her gaze dipped to his lips, and her own parted. "I'm going to kiss you."

*Yes.*

No! Control!

*Roll her over. Get her beneath you—*

Her arms suddenly gave way, and she collapsed to his chest, her breasts two firebrands scorching through his shirt. Her lips found his, and she immediately wound her arms around his neck, playing with the hair that tumbled over his collar. Her tongue dove into his mouth without preamble, and sensations lit inside him like a fireworks display.

The fingers in his hair tightened and gave a little tug, and suddenly, his hands were groping her ass without his permission.

She moaned, then lifted her lips long enough to say, "Harder," before diving back into the kiss.

He obeyed, palming her ass with so much strength, it would have been a slap if he hadn't held himself back at the last second.

*A slap? What the hell are you thinking?*

But then, as she sucked his tongue into her mouth, she jerked at his hair. "*Yes*. Harder, Kip."

This time, he did slap her.

He'd had clients in the past who'd wanted it a little rough. Those he could convince to direct the attention to his own body, he'd stayed with for the hour or two they'd hired him to fill. But the ones who'd insisted he do anything that could end up on a police report if his client had a change of heart? He'd walked out without a backward glance, more than willing to forfeit a few hundred dollars. Police reports stuck around forever, showing up at the worst times, such as when one tried to go legit in a judgmental world.

So when Victoria moaned so loudly it vibrated against his teeth, and when she bucked against him, thrusting against his hard cock crammed into his jeans, he still couldn't believe it when he smacked her ass a third time, this time on the other cheek.

She bit into his bottom lip and muttered unintelligible words at him.

Even through the haze of his lust, he needed to know what she was saying. Needed to make sure he still had her consent.

He pulled back from the kiss, but he squeezed her ass, unable to make himself take his hands from her yet. "What was that, honey?" His voice was nearly unrecognizable, hoarse and throaty.

"Naked." She pressed frantic kisses along the line of his jaw as she reached for the buttons of his shirt. "Please."

His own body flushed so hot, his skin had to be getting just as red as hers was. "Yes." He kept one hand on her bottom, and with the other, he helped her with the buttons of his shirt. As soon as the breeze from the room's air conditioner wafted against his skin, however, he badly needed her skin against his. In a moment, he switched his fingertips from his own buttons to hers.

The satin of her blouse slid against his fingers and against her breasts, quickly warming against his touch, and the swells of her breasts were so distracting that he abandoned her buttons to curve his palm around one firm, voluptuous curve.

Victoria immediately bowed her back, thrusting her breast into his palm, and, in the same movement, thrusting her stomach against his dick. He hissed in a breath, and she was kissing him again, mewling into his mouth with every stroke of her tongue.

His groin tightened, and he groaned, arching into her before the dimmest recesses of his mind screamed loudly enough to get his attention.

*Orgasm inevitable!*

His gigolo side was strong enough to get him to halt thrusting against her stomach as what he now realized was a powerful orgasm began sweeping up his spine in exquisite pleasure.

He broke from the kiss, gulping in great lungfuls of air. "Fuck."

"Yes!" She suddenly straightened, now straddling his hips. She swept the sides of his shirt away and pressed her palms over his pectorals, groaning and tossing her head back as she shifted over the throbbing dick she now captured between her thighs. "Fuck me."

*Not helping.* This situation was about to detonate, in more ways than one. Kip closed his eyes, blocking out the view of Victoria with her gorgeous flushed skin and blond hair tumbling from her careful bun. Blocking the view of her kiss-bruised lips and the way her nipples thrust against the fine fabric of her blouse.

He drew in a slow, aching breath, and with it, gained a slight bit of control back so that when she next slid over his lap, thrusting the head of his erection against what had to be her clit, he was able to keep from spewing inside his pants.

But only just.

She was writhing atop him now, the crescents of her blunt nails digging into his chest. Her breathing was frantic and catching on every exhalation. She sounded as wild as he felt.

"Kip," she gasped. "I'm going to—" She bore down on him, her thighs squeezing his hips, and her head tipped back, revealing the long length of her neck.

His eyes widened. She was as wild as he was feeling. She jerked along his length. Her breath hitched, and then she cried out.

He tightened his fingers on her hips as he helped her keep her rhythm, her hands slipping over his nipples in the sheen of sweat that had broken out over his chest.

"Shit," she cried. "*Shit!*"

Her body stiffened visibly, and then, just as suddenly, she collapsed, falling to his chest once again. Her frantic breaths cascaded over his exposed skin, tightening his nipples and causing him to shiver, though the possibility that the reaction was from the sight of Victoria at the height of her pleasure was highly likely.

A fine tremor racked her slight frame, and Kip smoothed a hand up her back. The other hand cradled the back of her head.

He was so damn horny he was going to explode. *Needed* to explode. And yet, he found himself wanting to simply hold her as she came down from what had been a nearly violent release.

As her breathing calmed, she pressed a kiss to the hollow of his throat. "God, I've been needing that for three years."

Kip jerked. "Three—"

She looked up at him, alarmed, and placed her fingers over his lips. "Forget I said that."

*Like hell.* This woman had gone without a man for three years?

"I can't believe I didn't even get my clothes off."

He flipped them suddenly, pressing his hips between her thighs and forcing them wider to accommodate him. "Your clothes will be off for the next one, honey. I promise."

She blinked up at him. "I get more?"

He smiled down at her, and, with fingers that trembled only slightly less than they had minutes ago, set about undoing her buttons at last. "You get everything."

She breathed a laugh and arched her back. She reached up with both hands and undid the rest of her bun.

Like a dream, all of this rich, blond silk tumbled down around her shoulders and chest, thoroughly distracting him once again from his goal of unbuttoning her blouse. As the waves slipped over her breasts, the scent of her shampoo wafted up, and Kip found himself bending down and stroking the tip of his nose along her throat so he could get a better whiff.

He found her pulse point and indulged in an open-mouth kiss, just like he'd fantasized about the first time he met her. The flutter of her heartbeat strummed against his lips, and he touched the tip of his tongue to her skin.

She moaned and wove her fingers into his hair, pulling him up until she could kiss him once again.

This kiss was a little different. With one orgasm out of the way—one she'd desperately needed, apparently—she wasn't as frantic for him.

Instead, she was wicked.

Slow, languorous sweeps of her tongue against his. Her nails scraping against his scalp. The way she raised her knees on each side of his hips, cradling him between her legs and bringing his body flush to hers.

He had to be crushing her; he had no desire to lift himself from her.

*No finesse with this woman. None.*

She was dangerous. Made him forget his purpose here. He should distance himself, both physically and emotionally.

Instead, he deepened the kiss. Bringing both hands up, he cradled her face, his thumbs stroking across her cheeks, where he knew without looking that a delectable blush spread.

He would get control of himself but not to gain distance. He'd get control so he could make this as good as possible for a woman who deserved it more than anyone he'd ever met.

He poured himself into the kiss, showing her with every weapon in his arsenal how badly he wanted it. Wanted her.

She pulled from the kiss, gasping, and stared up at him with heavy-lidded eyes. Her gaze scanned his features, and he kept stroking her face as she did so, letting her look her fill. "God, you're fine," she breathed.

"And you're fucking gorgeous."

As she breathed a disbelieving laugh, Kip mentally kicked his own ass. He had not said anything right since carrying her out of the bathroom. He was supposed to be a gentleman—women *paid* him to be one—and he couldn't keep from swearing around her, forgetting what he should be doing.

By some miracle, it was working for her. Half of his previous clients would have already walked out in a huff, pissed that he wasn't delivering on the fantasy they'd purchased.

But he didn't like that her small laugh had been disbelieving. Self-deprecating. So he let all the *please let me fuck you* he was feeling rise to the surface. He tenderly brushed a tendril of that beautiful blond hair from her brow, and then he pushed himself up until he was kneeling between her spread thighs.

She'd lain content before him, all her limbs relaxed, but his sudden shift made her slightly nervous if the new glint to her eyes was any indication.

Maintaining eye contact, he shrugged his shirt from his shoulders, knowing as he did so that every muscle in his torso would flicker for her.

He loved it when her gaze heated, and her lips parted around suddenly shallow breaths.

Smoothing his palm down his stomach, he then worked at his belt, and her gaze narrowed, rapt on his groin. The clack of his belt buckle was stark in the quiet room amid their increasingly ragged breathing.

He pulled the belt through the loops, his biceps flexing, and then dropped it off the side of the bed before next undoing the button of his pants and lowering the zipper.

She licked her lips, and he felt it like a lick to his skin. His fumbled as he pushed his pants past his hips. He always wore black briefs when he was seeing a client, but he'd never been as thankful for their particular cut as he was when Victoria made a desperate, short sound in the back of her throat when she saw them.

In a practiced move, he stretched out over her on straightened arms, grinding the erection that was barely contained in his underwear between her legs as he kicked his pants the rest of the way off.

And, just like that, Victoria was done observing. He could see in the flicker of her gaze that she was going to touch.

*Yes.*

She reached up and placed both palms over his chest, and then she leaned up and opened her lips over his collarbone, sucking hard before giving him a sharp nip.

He grunted, his hips jerking forward without his permission.

"Liked that?" she murmured right before she did it again.

*Oh, God.* What he liked had no place in his work, but damned if he didn't like that so hard. "Yes," he groaned.

As she nipped and sucked her way up his neck, her hands traveled down. Her delicate fingers trailed along his abs, and then, with a boldness that was at odds with the vulnerability she'd displayed earlier, she cupped his erection and aching balls with both hands.

She squeezed.

"*Fuck!*" He thrust into her hand with all his strength, driving the sensitive head of his cock against her hold.

Just as quickly, he bit his lip and locked down every muscle in his body, keeping himself from thrusting again.

*This is about her!*

The fingers of one hand stroked up his length while the others cupped his sack. "You feel so good."

He breathed a laugh. "This is not going like it's supposed to." His words were clipped and strained as he tried to hold himself still.

She nibbled the underside of his chin. "How is it supposed to go?"

"*You're* supposed to be losing your cool."

"Trust me." She kissed the corner of his mouth. "I am."

Her hands moved to the band of his briefs, and he knew he was seconds away from feeling her skin against his, at which point, he would be less than useless.

Shaking his head to clear it, he grabbed her wrists with one hand and pulled her arms over her head.

"Hey." She frowned up at him. "I was playing with that."

Another short, breathless laugh. "I know." He leaned back and kneeled between her legs again. "But now, I'm going to play with you."

Her eyes flashed.

He resumed the task he'd set out to do several times already, dismayed to find that he'd only managed to undo one of her buttons—the one right beneath her throat—in all the times he'd tried to get her out of her clothes.

The fabric of her shirt was slick and soft, and with it clinging to her sweat-damp skin, he could see the lacy outline of her bra through it. His erection jerked as he slipped the second and then third buttons free. They were tiny, delicate pearls, and his large fingers had trouble with them when he'd never had trouble with buttons before in his life.

He blamed the shaking that racked his entire body.

On the fourth button, her blouse began to part, revealing the lingerie beneath. And it was definitely lingerie.

Victoria had dressed for him.

Something odd thumped in his chest, exhilarating and paining him at the same time. Now he was desperate to see her, and he moved quickly as he unbuttoned the rest of her blouse, shoving it aside with uncouth vigor.

"God in heaven," he breathed.

He stared so hard, she squirmed beneath his gaze, but even then, he couldn't pull his focus from her body long enough to ensure her she was rocking him down to his core.

She wore a cream-colored lace bustier that pushed her breasts up and wrapped around her svelte curves until Kip thought his brain was going to explode. Delectable patches of pale skin peeked through the lace's pattern.

Propping himself up on one arm, he traced with his fingers one of the corset-like ribs of the bustier from the base right above her belly button up to the curve of her breast. "This is incredible," he murmured.

She squirmed again, and he struggled to get his gaze up from the flesh he was making love to with his eyes. At last, his gaze met hers. "Incredible," he repeated.

As expected, she blushed. But the way she bit her bottom lip and traced her own fingertips along the strap of the bustier let him know she was pleased by his compliment and attention.

*Good.* Finally doing something right.

And then he realized that if she'd taken such care with what was beneath her top, what awaited him beneath her pants was going to be just as life changing.

He grabbed her free hand and pressed a quick kiss into her palm before directing it to her parted blouse. "Take it off, honey."

She obeyed him without question, and he stowed that knowledge—that she was agreeable to being directed—away for future use. While she was occupied with removing her shirt, his fingers stroked down her stomach to the button and fly of her slacks.

Her breathing hitched as the sound of her zipper filled the room, but as she dropped her shirt over the side of the bed, she lifted her hips, giving him wordless permission to take her pants off.

He controlled himself enough to keep from ripping them off in his bid to see all of her, but he was less than suave. He also had no concept of where her pants went once they were off, because his entire world narrowed down to the tiny slip of a G-string that encircled Victoria's hips.

His hands were suddenly fisting in that delicate lace as though he were going to tear it from her body.

His gaze hungrily poured over her exquisite body. "You've got to be kidding me."

She stiffened. "What?"

"Women don't look this good." His gaze shot to her face. His brows drew together. "You can't be real."

She seemed stunned for a second, and then a soft smile spread her lips. "God, you're good for my ego."

"Give me some time. I'll be good for a lot of other things, too." He stared at her bustier once again. "I want to keep that"—he nodded at the lace molded around her breasts—"on for a bit longer, but I want this off." He tugged at her G-string. "Okay?"

She nibbled her bottom lip and nodded, once again lifting her hips. This time, it afforded him the most fortuitous glance he'd had of a woman's body in memory. The lacy underwear was a vee that dipped down below her navel, and with her legs and ass taut from her current position, he could stare his fill at the way the G-string disappeared between her ass cheeks, making him want to slap them all over again now that he knew how firm they were.

The shake alone would give him a heart attack.

He swore beneath his breath as he tugged the lace over her hips. As he pulled it down her thighs, he learned something else new about Victoria.

She was a groomer. Everything—from her mound to her slick lips—was bare.

His hips jerked, his cock longing to thrust along that sweet, wet flesh in a smooth glide. He gritted his teeth and pulled the G-string off entirely, tossing it over his shoulder. "I can't wait to touch you." He hadn't meant to say the words, but they were so true, he couldn't find it in himself to regret them.

"Then touch me," she whispered, planting her heels on either side of him and spreading her knees wide.

She was going to kill him. All her constant contradictions were driving him wild. This woman, with her legs spread so wide he could see the shadow of her opening, was the same woman who had apologized for kissing him minutes ago.

He wouldn't leave her boldness unrewarded. He could feel his cheeks straining to contain a smile as he wrapped a hand around each of her ankles. Her body beneath his fingers was delicate, and he stroked a circle on the inside of her ankles with both thumbs.

A simple touch, but her lips parted, and her eyelids fluttered as though she were fighting to keep them from closing.

Which meant she had started thinking again in the wake of her first orgasm. If she was fighting natural responses, he still had some work to do to make her completely let go. He wanted her to revel in those natural responses. It would only be fair, because he couldn't wait to find out what she did, what noises she made, when she was lost to pleasure.

"Your skin is so soft," he murmured.

He stroked her again, but this time, his thumbs traveled higher, over the curve of her calf muscle. Gooseflesh suddenly leapt from his touch to race over her entire body.

He stopped holding back his smile—just the slightest bit—as he smoothed his palms over her knees and down the slope of her spread thighs. As he did so, he stretched forward, spreading out on his belly between her legs.

He traipsed his fingertips over her hipbones, and a shuddering sigh sounded from her.

Kip glanced up to find her eyes closed. He indulged in a moment of self-congratulations, and he felt his grin broaden.

But then he looked down at her spread sex, and his smile fell away. A sudden, intense yearning to lean down and place his open mouth over the clit that visibly throbbed before his eyes nearly overtook him.

But he couldn't do that. He didn't have her medical records. She didn't have his.

*Fuck.* He frowned. He'd never wanted to go down on a woman so badly in his life—professionally or privately.

He felt cheated.

He ... *felt.*

That got his attention. He licked his dry lips and forced himself to focus once more. Curving one arm around her thigh, he rested an open palm over her belly. The gentle thud of her heartbeat flicked against his palm as, with his other hand, he trailed the curve of her inner thigh to her sweet, tantalizing, bare lips.

"Gorgeous," he whispered, knowing his breath would waft against her aroused sex.

Like he expected, she squirmed.

He pressed down with the hand over her belly, keeping her in place. Staring up at her expectant face, he stroked down her center, from clit to opening, with his thumb.

"Oh, God."

She bucked against the hand holding her down, but he showed no mercy, this time tightening his arm around her thigh to help keep her still.

She was more responsive than he could have dreamed. The way she was breathing right now, the fine tremor that racked her body—Kip had no doubt that he could stroke her less than five times and make her come again.

Victoria had been without a man for far too long. And that lack ended tonight.

His pinky brushed against the edge of her bustier. He needed, for both their sakes, to get her out of the last of her clothes and his dick inside her body in the shortest amount of time possible. Neither of them were going to last much longer.

"Okay, honey." He stroked her one last time, and she moaned. "Sit up for me." *Before I lose all my control.*

She blinked down at him. "W-what?"

Her eyes were glazed. Beneath the cups of her bustier, her nipples were so taut they looked painful.

"Sit up. Let me get this off you."

She nodded, but he wasn't sure she'd understood his directions until the muscles beneath the palm over her stomach bunched. She sat up.

Kip pressed a kiss to her stomach just beneath her belly button, opening his lips and giving her warm skin a slow lick.

Her belly dipped, and she sucked in a breath. He rasped his chin against her soft skin before looking up at her.

Her breasts rose and fell in quick succession over the top of her lingerie. With what he hoped was a wicked smile—God knew if he had *any* game left—Kip reached around her and began unhooking her bustier one tiny hook and eyelet at a time.

Her breaths increased in frequency, and the color along her cheeks heightened. By the time he finished and gently pressed her back to draw the bustier down her arms, his breaths were just as frantic as hers.

As he caught sight of her nipples for the first time, though, breathing at all became a challenge.

Perfection. Her breasts were high but generous—the unicorn among all breasts. Her tight nipples were the color of a delicate pink rosc.

He was afraid he would fall on her and devour her.

With measured slowness, he knelt over her and lowered himself until his stomach stretched over her bare pubic bone. She was so aroused that, when she wiggled, she slicked across his stomach. By that time, Kip was already closing his lips over her left nipple, so his harsh groan was muffled by her taste.

She arched her back and threaded her fingers through his hair. "Kip." She squirmed beneath him, and he had to bite back the desire to tell her to hold still or she wouldn't get her money's worth. "No more seduction. *Please.*"

Like words from a dream. He should protest. Victoria deserved seduction. Needed seduction.

But he was just desperate enough that her lust-filled order sounded brilliant to him. He pressed a kiss to her shoulder, then leaned over the end of the bed, groping for his jeans. Yet another sign that he was out of it. He was always sure to slip a condom under the pillow when he undressed so he could protect his partner and himself smoothly and imperceptibly when the time came.

And here he was fishing through his discarded pants. After an embarrassingly long amount of time, his fingertips finally encountered one of the several foil packets he'd stuffed in his back pocket before heading over here.

Before he could turn back, there was a tugging at his briefs.

His gaze snapped back to Victoria and then down at where both of her hands were fisted in the waistband of his briefs.

She tugged again. "Off now."

God, he hadn't even remembered that he still wore them. "Certainly."

Her brow furrowed, and she bit into her bottom lip. She gently pulled his briefs' waistband out before pulling down, and his cock leapt to be free.

"Oh, God," she whispered.

Kip bit back a harsh moan as her fingertips moved toward the crown of his erection. But when her touch breezed over his sensitive skin, that moan escaped with a vengeance. He fisted the sheets on either side of her hips and gritted his teeth.

God help him if she wanted to explore for long, because he had about five seconds left before something embarrassing happened. He wasn't sure exactly what it would be, but he knew for sure that it would call his professionalism into question. "Victoria," he begged as she wrapped her fingers around him and stroked him down to the root.

Her name on his lips seemed to break her from a trance. She jolted—he felt it all the way down to his aching balls—and then she looked back up into his eyes. "I can't wait for this."

Like a lay with him was freaking Disneyland. "I can't either." He gently nudged her hand aside and breathed a sigh of relief when she obediently relinquished her hold on his cock, as it bought him precious seconds to get himself together.

He shucked his briefs as though they were on fire, and then he was tearing into the foil packet, not at all unlike a starving man digging into his first meal in days.

"Let me."

Kip glanced up. Victoria was staring at the condom in his fingers with her hand held out.

"Yes, ma'am."

Her brow quirked at that, but she bit back a smile as she plucked the condom from his fingers and placed it against the crown of his dick.

Which immediately jerked upon contact, displacing her efforts.

*Get a hold of yourself!*

Smiling grimly, Kip thought about animal shows where something cute got eaten. Nope, not strong enough. A trip to the mall during Christmas time. It was hopeless. Nothing was stronger than the sweet torture of her fingers against him as she repositioned the condom and began rolling it down his length. When they were fully protected, she wrapped her hand around him and squeezed.

The most mortifying sound imaginable rumbled deep in his chest—something between a whimper and a plea. She grinned up at him, a surge of confidence in her eyes, and he nearly groaned again.

This confidence was going to kill him. It promised adventure. Innovation. Memorability. He was doomed.

She tugged him forward by his erection, and with very little finesse, he obeyed in the form of flopping down on top of her.

Just as he was getting ready to scramble up on extended arms and apologize, she moaned and wrapped her arm and—holy shit—*legs* around him, and he slid all the way to the hilt inside her luscious body.

"Fuck." He pressed his forehead against her shoulder. "Oh, *fuck*."

She canted her hips, and he sank even farther into her tight heat. He wanted to beg her to stay still. Give him a moment.

He could never be that weak.

And, so, since the chance that this was going to be appallingly short was a very real possibility, he vowed to make it the best short encounter she would ever have.

They could do longer later.

He propped himself up on one elbow and gave her his best smoldering look. He was semi-successful if the small hitch in her breathing was any indication. Before he could mess up this tiny victory, he leaned down and covered her mouth with his, licking inside with infinite tenderness.

With his other arm, he wrapped up her thigh and pinned it against his side, sliding his hand down her exposed underside until he could clutch her bottom. With sprawled fingers, he squeezed her beautiful ass and then began to move with slow, measured thrusts.

She whimpered into the kiss, and her tongue dueled with his.

His fingers squeezed again, and the pressure of her tight sex around his went straight to his gut, where the dull ache there became an insistent throb.

*Holy fuck, this is good.*

Like, top-ten good. Hell, maybe even top five.

He was being paid for his services, and this was the best experience he could remember having in recent memory.

That sobered him quickly.

His eyes popped open as he kissed her. Luckily, hers remained closed, so she couldn't witness him freaking out as his body tingled all over, all the way down to his usually dormant heart, which was now beating like a freight train against hers.

He forced his muscles to stay relaxed. Forced himself to keep pleasuring her. And all the while, he shoved every errant, warm sentiment toward this *paying client* into a giant, figurative box in his mind, kicking it into a corner.

*Give her what she's paying for. Nothing more.*

Just as his panic was ebbing, her eyes popped open, and her gaze clashed with his. He put his game face on and turned the passion of the kiss up a notch while grinding his pelvis against her swollen clit as he thrust into her once more.

She pulled from the kiss slowly but decisively. "Kip?" Her brows drew together. "Everything okay?"

*Fuck.* She'd felt him change.

He ducked his head and kissed and then licked her neck. "Oh, yeah," he muttered against her skin, deepening the angle of his next thrust.

She sucked in a breath, then moaned, melting into the bed and grinding right back against him as he circled his hips, pressing into the spot he knew would send her into climax.

*Distraction achieved.*

Now he needed to finish this. Before his control slipped. "So gorgeous." He nipped her shoulder and thrust again, this time harder, and the breathy moan of a few seconds ago now turned into an earthy groan. "So perfect."

"Shit." She lifted her hips, thrusting with him now. They were moving together in beautiful synchronicity, their bodies conversing as naturally as if they'd been doing this together for years. "It's so good, Kip."

He screwed his lips together tightly around words he shouldn't—he couldn't—say. *It is so good. It's not usually like this. I could get addicted to this. I don't want you to be a paying customer. I want to do this all night.*

Tomorrow night, too.

Desperate, he palmed her breast with his left hand, tweaking her nipple with a soft pinch that made her arch her back and call his name to the ceiling.

*Slipping more.* "Shit." He was panting. Filling his hand with her breast again, he cupped it to his mouth and sucked her nipple between his teeth.

She was writhing beneath him now. They were no longer moving together in perfect motion, but it was even more earthshattering than before.

With a sudden surge, Kip sprang right to the edge of orgasm. *You can't do this! Stop this right now!* He was going to come before a client. For the first time in his life.

Her sex clamped down on his dick so hard, he couldn't thrust anymore. She arched, threw her head back, and keened.

"Victoria." Her name tripped over his lips in an adrenaline-inducing rush of relief. "God, yes." He shoved into the tight hold she had on him and circled his hips against her clit as stars lit behind his eyes.

He shut them tightly and buried his face in her breasts as his orgasm overtook him. He bit her—much too hard—but it kept his mouth occupied with something other than all the sentiments that wanted to burst out of him as he filled the condom to capacity.

Her thighs trembled against his hips as she squeezed him there and with her arms, hugging him with her entire body.

Both of them relaxed in unison, their orgasms ebbing at the exact same time.

Kip opened his eyes and stared at the perfect nipple in his vision. His breathing was still far too erratic. His heart thundered.

And then he did something incredibly stupid.

He wrapped his arms around her, nestled his cheek against her chest, and closed his eyes again.

As though, for all intents and purposes, he intended to cuddle this woman and bask in an after-sex glow.

Her thighs released their death grip on his hips and ass, and as she lowered her legs, she brushed her foot down the length of his calf in what could only be construed as a tender caress. She next wove her fingers into his hair and hugged him against her.

And, forget top ten or top five—it was the best thing he'd ever felt.

As she began massaging his scalp with her fingertips, Kip forced himself to withdraw. But it took two tries for his body to listen. With a groan that sounded like he was in pain, he clutched the condom and pulled out of her.

Her hands fell to her sides, and something hollow resounded in Kip's gut. "I'll be right back, honey," he murmured, not quite able to meet her eyes.

She mumbled something sleepily and rolled to her side.

Kip padded into the bathroom and tore the condom off, the little corresponding snap a much-needed wake-up call. After tossing it in the trash, he looked at himself in the mirror.

His eyes were haunted.

He scrubbed a hand down his face and swore under his breath. Forget a shower; he needed to get out of here and now. Before he turned right back around, pulled out *another* condom and fucked her again—slowly this time.

He snatched a washcloth from the rack over the toilet and turned the water to scalding in the sink. Wetting the cloth, he gave himself a quick whore's bath and then stalked from the bathroom, his mood descending with every step.

He stopped abruptly, however, when he entered the main room once more.

Victoria was asleep, which was not an unusual way to find his clients. But in the short time he'd been in the bathroom, she'd put a stack of cash on the bedside table, which was also not unusual.

Because he was a gigolo.

The money was highlighted in the bright yellow glow of the lamp as though standing on stage beneath a spotlight.

His clothes were folded neatly at the end of the bed.

His feet heavy, he walked as silently as he could so he wouldn't wake her, because God knew what he would say to her if she did wake.

Something unacceptable, surely, given his current mindfuckery.

He pulled his clothes on as quickly as possible, then walked over to the table.

Holding his breath, he fanned out the bills with the tips of his fingers.

His breath rushed out of him. His glance jetted over to the clock.

*Two hours and fifteen minutes since I arrived.*

She'd paid him much, much more than his hourly rate, which he had told to the woman who'd arranged this appointment. In fact, she'd paid him more than his nightly rate, which—he grimaced now—he himself had told her at The Bar.

Kip pinched the bridge of his nose and sighed silently. Then he rearranged the bills into a nice, neat stack.

He straightened his belt as he turned to look at her one more time before he left.

Her lips, swollen from his kisses, were parted. Her lush lashes curved against her cheeks. Her neck was red from whisker burn.

Of its own volition, his hand moved. Stroked her cheek. Tucked a stray lock of hair behind her ear. Pulled the comforter up and over her shoulder. "Good night, honey," he whispered so softly she wouldn't be able to hear him.

Then he turned and walked to the door.

When he clicked the light switch off, the halo of light surrounding the stack of bills on the table disappeared.

But the bills remained.

# Chapter Seven

Victoria sighed and snuggled into the pillow beneath her cheek. Warmth and satisfaction filled her to bursting, and, rolling to her back, she stretched, arching her body and pushing against the headboard.

The apex of her thighs twinged uncomfortably.

Her eyes fluttered open, and as she stared up at the ceiling, she cocked her head to the side. *Not the ceiling of my bedroom.*

That fully awoke her in the span of two heartbeats.

She blinked several times as last night rushed back.

*I had sex last night.*

A burble rose through her chest and up into her mouth until it exploded from her lips in the form of a giggle.

"I had sex last night!"

With another giggle, she snatched the pillow from the other side of the bed and buried her face in it.

Kip's scent filled her senses. She pulled in a deep breath of it, and, holding it, closed her eyes.

He had been incredible. Worth every penny and then some.

God, how had she lived without sex for so long?

Her smile crashed. She pulled the pillow from her face.

*How am I going to live without it again?*

She hugged the pillow to her chest, and it was so like the brief moment she'd held Kip the same way last night that her bottom lip trembled.

She couldn't. Couldn't do celibacy again.

Before, after Jeremy's death, her grief and an overwhelming sense of guilt had distracted her. With her heart so broken, there had been no way she'd wanted to have sex with anyone ever again. But, as the years had gone by and that grief had ebbed—though not vanished—her needs had become insistent, and now that she'd had the best sex of her life and knew for certain what she was missing …

She sat up and shoved a hand through her knotted hair. "Okay, so you don't have to be celibate again."

She straightened, the simple, spoken words taking root and lifting her mood immediately. Hadn't she just had sex with a prostitute? Hadn't it met her every need while enabling her desire to avoid a relationship?

She would just do it again! Whenever she needed to.

"Sleeping with strangers."

As soon as she said it out loud, her fingers tightened in the pillow. "Sleeping with strangers," she said again. "No big deal."

Her gut knotted and her heart instantly plummeted. She wouldn't be able to do it.

Yes, she didn't want a relationship, but … *strangers*? What if they were bad at it? What if one of these complete strangers tried to hurt her? What if …

*They are nothing like Kip.*

"Oh, dear." She nibbled her bottom lip. The truth was, he had been perfect. Every touch, every word—he had delivered the kind of night a woman rarely was lucky enough to experience.

And he had left right after.

Perfection.

She couldn't take the risk of disappointment—or worse—with someone else. She was far too busy.

*So, hire Kip.*

She tilted her head to the side. Slowly, a smile spread her lips. That was it. The ideal plan.

She would contact Kip, offer him an exclusive employment opportunity, and never have to worry about this part of her life again.

She could focus on more important things without distraction.

*Wait, exclusive employment?*

Her smile dimmed. Yes, why the exclusivity? Her brow furrowed as she tried to get to the root of why, in the deepest recesses of herself, she knew that part of it was non-negotiable.

It couldn't be because she wanted him to herself. That would be unacceptable. An unforgiveable slight against Jeremy. No, it had to be someth—

*Ah!* Safety. Obviously.

Every muscle in Victoria's body unclenched itself. Yes, she would want to be able to forego condoms, and the only way to ensure they could do so safely was if they were sleeping only with each other.

She nodded. This was brilliant. The best idea she'd had outside of work in years.

Grinning, she reached for her phone on the bedside table and froze.

She narrowed her eyes. Surely, what she was seeing was a figment of her imagination, but the narrowed gaze did not change anything.

Kip's money was still on the table.

"What in the—?" She reached for it but drew back before she could touch it. Why on earth would he have left it?

*He forgot.* It was logical and the most probable reason, so … Her frown would not relent.

Well, whatever the reason, she could fix this slight snafu. She'd be seeing him again, thanks to her business offer, and she could give it to him then.

She grabbed her phone, skirting the cash as though it were poisonous, and opened her messaging app. Cassidy was at the top, like always.

"Need Kip's number."

After she clicked *send*, she nibbled her bottom lip. It could be hours until she heard back. Cassidy had a sporadic sleeping schedule at best, and—

Her phone buzzed in her hand, and Victoria nearly dropped it.

"Who the fuck is Kip?"

*Seriously?*

"The gigolo!"

Her phone immediately rang, and Victoria groaned. She did *not* want to talk about this. But Cassidy would dog her until she answered.

"Good morning, Cassidy."

"Details. Now. Especially since you want to contact him again."

"You want details about my illicit night with a male prostitute?"

"Hells yeah, I do."

"I'm your sister!"

"In-law. There's a difference, you know."

"Yeah, a difference that makes this conversation worse not better."

There was a pause. "Why would that make it worse?"

Victoria flopped back on her pillow. "Cassidy, I just want the man's number."

"So, you're saying it was good."

Before she could stop it, the most girlish, giggle-sounding noise escaped Victoria's lips.

"Oh, my God!" Cassidy practically shouted into the phone. "It was!"

Victoria jerked the phone away, winced, and put the phone back toward her ear with an inch's space this time. "Okay, deduce from my side of the conversation what you will, but I'm not giving you details."

"But—"

"No way!"

"You are just a ruiner of all good things."

"Thank you. Now, Kip's number."

"Fine. I'll text it to you. But when I sleep with a prostitute, I'm telling you nothing. No, don't even bother begging."

Astonishing, the rush of relief she felt. "Thanks, Cassidy."

"Yeah, yeah. I love you, too." There was indiscriminate grumbling from the other side of the line, and then the call ended.

Seconds later, her phone buzzed with a text. They were the longest seconds Victoria had suffered in her life. When she saw simply ten digits, her heart flipped over.

Straightening in the bed, Victoria attempted to smooth her hair. *Smoothing my hair down? Really?* She glared down at herself. *Idiot.*

He picked up on the second ring. "Hello, this is Kip."

"Kip!" Victoria cleared her throat and drummed her fingers against the pillow in her lap. "This is—"

"Victoria?" His voice sounded odd as it said her name.

"Er," she licked her lips, "yeah. It's me." *How would he know my voice after one night?* It had to be something he'd trained himself to do for his profession.

An awkward silence filled the line, and Victoria … *this had been a brilliant plan, right?*

"I'm—" There was another brief pause, and when he spoke again, he was as smooth as he had been in her bed last night. "I'm glad to hear from you."

His voice shot straight through her and all the way down to her sex. "That's … good." She squeezed her eyes shut. *Okay, get it together*. She had a business proposition. One she would make sure he was happy to hear about. Start with that. "The money was still on the table this morning."

*Shit!* That wasn't the business proposition at all!

Silence reigned once again. She winced. Maybe she should just hang up the phone? Forget she'd ever—

Luckily, Kip rescued them both. "Oh, was it?"

Victoria raised her eyebrows. "Yes."

He cleared his throat. "I can't believe I forgot it."

*Yeah, me either*. She swallowed. *Just go with it*. "Well, that's an easy fix, don't worry."

"Oh, I trust you." His words were quick and careless.

This time, she paused and generated the awkward silence. "Do you."

He sighed. "Maybe we should hang up and start this conversation again."

Her laugh startled her. *Pull the thought right from my head, why don't you*. "How about we just pretend we did and go from here."

A husky chuckle. "I can accept that plan."

"Okay, well." She shifted in bed. "Since you're in the accepting vein of thought, I actually have a business proposition for you."

"A business proposition." His tone could only be described as careful.

"Well, yes. It's one I think you'll like."

"I'm listening." His voice was back to normal.

"I'd like to hire you."

"For tonight?"

"No." She shook her head and closed her eyes. "I mean, maybe tonight, but ..." *Oh, for fuck's sake, just say it!* "I'd like to acquire your services for a prolonged period of time. Exclusively."

There was a lengthy pause. "Oh."

This was not going at all the way she had thought it would. *Mention the money*. "I'll pay you $20,000 for the rest of the month." There were eighteen days left until the thirty-first. "That's a few thousand more than your nightly rate." And if, after eighteen days, she needed more, she would simply buy more.

His puff of air was audible over the phone.

She relaxed. Now he would jump at the deal. Why hadn't she led with that? Her business was deals, and here she was messing one up.

"Victoria, thank you for the offer."

Her lips parted. She heard a definite *but* in his voice. "Don't answer now!" She'd practically yelled the words at him. She covered her lips with her fingers and pulled a long breath through her nose. *Try again. At normal person volume.* "How about you just think about it, okay?" Her fingers started hurting, and she looked down only to discover they were knotted in the pillow so tightly they were bloodless. "You have to get your money from last night at some point, so whenever you're ready, just let me know. We can talk details at that point if you want."

There was a heavy sigh. "I'll think about it. Of course, I'll think about it."

His obvious reluctance stung. "Well," she said shortly, "thank you for last night."

"Oh, Victoria—"

She hung up.

And immediately regretted it. *Right, because throwing a tantrum on the man will certainly convince him to see things your way.* "Ugh!" She flopped back on the bed and tossed her phone at the chair a few feet away, not even looking to see if it made it or reached a shattering death on the floor.

If her phone were broken, she wouldn't be able to call Kip again and torment him with lucrative offers to sleep with her.

If she were lucky, she'd never hear from him again. Then she could forget this mortifying moment and focus instead on the earth-shattering sex of the night before. An experience that she would now have to seek from strangers. Because Kip had as good as said no, and she couldn't go without anymore.

This day was off to a great start.

With a groan, she rolled from bed and began gathering her belongings. She had a meeting this morning. The most important meeting of her career, and she wanted to get ready for it at home where she was surrounded by her things instead of the scent of her and Kip's sexual escapades and the indentation of their heads in the pillows.

She was having her first face-to-face with Mr. Alan Davis from The Ricchezza in two hours. She needed her head in the game.

She was a whirlwind as she pulled on her clothes and tossed her phone into her purse. But she stilled suddenly as she turned toward the bedside table. She gave the stack of bills the side eye.

Finally, with a huff, she stormed over, grabbed the meticulously straight pile of bills, and slipped it into the cell phone holder of her laptop bag. Tugging the strap over her shoulder, she straightened her spine and walked toward the door.

It was harder than she'd imagined to close it behind her without one final look at the bed. But she did it, and as soon as the door nestled into its frame, Victoria snapped free from her stupor as though released from bonds.

An hour and a half later, she was walking into the office, perfectly coifed and ready to review her marketing plan before presenting it in detail to Mr. Davis.

Victoria's personal secretary, Daniel, rushed over as soon as he saw her. She could tell by the panic in his eyes that something was up. He fell into step beside her and ducked his head to speak to her without anyone overhearing. "Ms. Hastings, Mr. Davis is already here."

Her steps faltered, but she kept on through sheer force of will. *What?* She straightened her laptop bag. "Early. I like that." *Shit!*

"He and his lawyers are waiting in the conference room." Daniel paused at her office door while she rushed over to her desk with as much poise as possible. "Mr. Kincaid is in there with him now."

Victoria gripped the back of her leather chair and closed her eyes. She hadn't told Mr. Kincaid about the potential deal with The Ricchezza yet, because—

Well, selfishly, she wanted to tell her boss about the deal when she'd secured it. And then accept his congratulations and the corresponding promotion on the spot. Now he was going to want a say in things. Would want to be a part of the process.

*Double shit.*

"Excellent." She turned to Daniel. "Can you contact our delivery service and let them know we'll need the coffee and pastries immediately?"

He jerked a nod. "Yes, ma'am."

"Thank you." She straightened her jacket and breezed by Daniel, who was already rushing back to his desk and reaching for the phone.

No time to review, but, then again, she didn't need it. She knew this marketing plan backward and forward. Mr. Kincaid was a slight hitch in the plan, but the man hadn't become president of an advertising firm without knowing his stuff. Maybe she could benefit from some guidance.

Maybe.

Okay, she would abhor his guidance, but she could play nice in pursuit of the bigger goal.

She paused for only a moment outside the conference room to smooth a hand over her hair and ensure it was in place. She twisted the knob and turned the door inward.

Male voices abruptly ceased.

"Ah, here she is now," Mr. Kincaid said.

Victoria smiled her best smile and glided into the conference room. "Sorry for the delay, gentlemen. I hope you haven't been kept waiting too long."

Mr. Kincaid was seated at the head of the conference table—her spot by rights in this current situation. She took the seat opposite Mr. Davis and his—dear God—entourage of five lawyers. She stretched her hand across the table toward Mr. Davis. "A pleasure to meet you in person, Mr. Davis."

His fingers clasped hers weakly. "Thank you for meeting us first thing in the morning. I know you're a busy woman."

She canted her head. "Never too busy for you." He released her hand, and she pressed both palms to the table. "Well, why don't I share my ideas with you? I have some great—"

"Oh, that won't be necessary." Mr. Davis smiled. "That wasn't the purpose of this meeting."

Victoria felt her brow furrowing and forcibly smoothed it out. She cast a nervous glance at Mr. Kincaid, who was making no effort to keep from looking bewildered. "It isn't?" She breathed an awkward laugh. "I confess, I thought that's why we were meeting."

Mr. Davis leaned forward. "We'll get to the marketing ideas at some point in the future. After I've decided upon an agent."

She smiled. "Of course." *What?*

One of Mr. Davis's lawyers cleared his throat. "This meeting is more of a meet and greet, Ms. Hastings," he said. "Mr. Davis has a very specific concern as we enter into this process, and he wanted to both meet you and make his concern known."

Her confusion cleared; her wariness, however, increased. "Well, I'm very glad we're meeting then. What is your concern? I'd love to put it to rest."

Mr. Davis tucked his chin down, creating a ripple of additional chins, to look at her from beneath bushy eyebrows. "Our previous marketing agent," he made an odd noise, "became an issue."

Victoria leaned forward. "How so?"

One of the lawyers placed a hand on Mr. Davis's forearm for a moment and then removed it. "Her personal matters began interfering with her professional duties."

Mr. Davis made that same, disapproving noise. "She had very loose morals. It caused quite a scandal."

One of the lawyers laughed uncomfortably. When Victoria glanced at Mr. Kincaid, his eyebrows were up at his hairline.

She smiled, though she could feel it was a bit tight. "I see."

"I know we live in Vegas, but," Mr. Davis waved a finger, "that doesn't mean I can afford another expensive mistake when someone in my employ forgets her responsibilities in favor of her vices."

*Okay*. He needed to stop talking. "Mr. Davis, I can assure you—"

"Mr. Davis will be conducting an extensive background check for both candidates he is considering," the first lawyer said. "It is part of the process, and it is non-negotiable. We will understand if you choose not to submit to this measure, and we will thank you for your time, but we will be looking elsewhere for our marketing."

Mr. Kincaid popped forward. "That will not be a problem."

*Excuse me?* She turned toward her boss. Had she imagined him giving them permission to dig into her private life? She was pretty sure she hadn't.

Where was the scrutiny of Mr. Kincaid's private life? He was, after all, the owner of Precision Media. Wouldn't Mr. Davis want to make sure he wouldn't cause a scandal?

*That's not what's going on here, and you know it.* Only feminine pronouns had left Mr. Davis's mouth during this meeting. She was being singled out for scrutiny because of her gender.

*Like this is the first time that's happened. Calm the hell down, Hastings.*

She took a deep breath. What private life did she have? What would a background check turn up? The fact that she was a widow? That she stayed at the office until all hours of the night? This could actually work in her favor. She turned back to Mr. Davis and managed to smile broadly. "That will not be a problem."

Mr. Davis returned her smile. "I'm glad to hear it. Because your proposal was quite inspiring."

"We'll get in touch with you at the conclusion of the background check," one of the lawyers said.

"And how soon will that be?" Mr. Kincaid asked.

"That depends."

"Ah," Mr. Kincaid said.

Mr. Davis pushed to his feet. "That concludes our meeting. We'll talk soon. Or, whenever."

Both Victoria and Mr. Kincaid stumbled to their feet as all six of them began filing out of the room. "Thank you for coming!" she called after their retreating backs.

But they were already gone. In the open doorway, her assistant stood with a basket of pastries in one hand and a carafe of coffee in the other. His bewildered gaze met hers.

"Thank you, Daniel. You can give those to the interns."

He was too professional to let his feelings show, but she had worked with him long enough to know that he thought this was just as weird as she did. "Yes, ma'am." He kicked the door closed behind him.

She received a hearty slap on her shoulder, and she couldn't prevent a gasp. She spun to Mr. Kincaid, who looked so pleased his chest was going to burst if he kept puffing it out. "The Ricchezza!" He slapped her shoulder again, but this time she was braced for it. "Hastings, this is a very good thing."

"Well—" She felt it necessary to be the voice of reason here. "It's not a sure thing yet."

Mr. Kincaid scoffed. "We both know you're going to ace that background check like nobody else in this business would be able to. Your life is your work."

*Ah, how comforting that he arrived at that conclusion as well.* She swallowed a sigh. "Yes, Mr. Kincaid."

He grinned. "Secure this deal, and that corner office is as good as yours."

Her entire chest lifted inside. "Yes, Mr. Kincaid." She had to bite the inside of her cheeks to keep from grinning like an idiot.

"Well, go ahead and get to work." He waved at the door. "When we hear back from them, I want everything perfect and ready to go."

"And it will be." Victoria turned to leave, and it was only at that moment she remembered that last night, she had fucked a gigolo. And this morning, she had propositioned him again.

She tripped and caught herself on the back of a chair.

"Is everything okay?" Mr. Kincaid was suddenly at her elbow, staring at her with his brows drawn.

She shoved a stray strand of hair out of her eyes and caught sight of her fingers trembling. "Certainly, it is, sir." She straightened and pulled at her jacket. "I'll just be heading to my office now."

*Oh, God. This could be bad.*

She placed a shaky hand over a queasy stomach. She heard someone call her name in greeting, and she nodded in that direction while she kept walking toward her office. Okay, Kip was discreet. Cassidy had contacted him, not her. Victoria had never contacted a prostitution business; she'd talked to Kip directly. And, luckily, he had turned down her offer of extended employment.

She entered her office, closed the door, and leaned back against it. The background check would most likely not be able to tie her to Kip in any way. This was a nonissue, and she was going to do great things for The Ricchezza when they hired her.

Everything was going to be okay.

Except, if it wasn't, and if someone found out she'd hired a gigolo, she'd just kissed—and fucked—all her dreams good-bye. For one night of pleasure. She groaned and knocked the back of her head against the door.

She'd been reckless. Hiring Kip had been stupid. She should regret it. She really should. And yet …

*Just, please … don't let anyone find out.*

# Chapter Eight

For about the twentieth time since Victoria's call this morning, Kip pulled his phone from his back pocket and unlocked it.

Then, cursing beneath his breath, he shoved it back into his pocket roughly enough that the seams would have protested if they could.

He wasn't going to take the job. Obviously, he wasn't.

He caught his hand straying to his back pocket once again.

"Stop that."

Okay, now he was talking to himself.

He rubbed his eyes with the heels of his hands and flopped down onto the sofa in his living room.

Reaching for the remote and jabbing buttons, he flipped through channels, not really seeing anything or landing on a show for more than a few seconds, before he abandoned that endeavor as well.

"This is dumb."

By giving her offer this much consideration, he was giving it the power that he was afraid of in the first place. Talk about a self-fulfilling prophecy.

So, maybe it would help to define what he was actually afraid of?

He leaned back against the sofa with a sigh. Damn it, he didn't want to examine that. He had this feeling that if he allowed himself to think about his night with Victoria and why he was so desperate not to repeat it, he'd never be able to cram those thoughts and feelings back into the box he'd been keeping them in since leaving the Desert Oasis.

And there was the crux of the problem.

*I felt something with her.*

He shook his head. Calling it *something* was a gross understatement. He'd felt … everything with her.

And he'd never felt that way with a woman before, not since his first crushes in high school before he realized how stupid it was to care about a woman. Before his parents stopped carefully hiding their disagreements from him. Before he knew what, exactly, a woman could do to a man when he was foolishly vulnerable around her.

Yes, dear old Mom had cured him of all his romantic notions, but not one of his encounters with other women had corrected the issue.

Given the chance, any woman would walk all over her man. Especially the ones who walked all over people in their professions.

Like his mother.

Like, apparently, Victoria.

Last night, he'd hoped the huge amount of money on the end table had been a fluke. The result of some careful savings. But today? When she'd called and offered him twenty thousand dollars as casually as a normal person would offer two hundred?

There was no doubt in his mind that she was a powerful woman. No other type of woman would have that kind of money. Which meant that she was powerful professionally. Which meant that power would flow over into every element of his life.

So, no, he wasn't just afraid of feeling things for Victoria. He was afraid *of* Victoria.

He frowned. Those were two very good reasons to turn her down, but by the lack of satisfaction he was feeling, there was more.

If that were all, he would be calling her right now and turning her down. There was no reason to hesitate.

And yet, here he was hesitating. So, what was the other reason?

His brows shot toward his hairline. "No," he said aloud to his empty apartment. "No, don't be this fucking pathetic."

*Twenty thousand dollars.*

The amount that would, once and for all, end any excuse he had to stall opening a business.

He'd have to start putting actions behind his plans. And if he failed . . .

He gritted his teeth. "I won't fail."

Leaning over to his left hip, he grabbed his phone from his pocket once more. This time, he got beyond unlocking it. He made it all the way to her contact information. Even pressed send.

Though he fought himself no less than five times to keep from hanging up as the phone dialed into his ear, he stuck it out.

Like a fucking man. Because that's what he was.

The phone stopped ringing.

But no one said anything on the other end. Kip frowned and pulled the phone from his ear to check that, yes, he had called the right person. He pressed it back to his ear.

"Victoria?"

"Kip?"

Her voice sounded entirely different from this morning when she had propositioned him. During that phone call, her voice had been husky. As though she were remembering in vivid detail all the things he'd done to her last night. Now, on just the single syllable of his name, she sounded as though she were asking if it was him, and hoping it wasn't.

Why the change?

Why did the thumping of his heart suddenly sting a little?

"Yes, it's me." He couldn't keep the next words inside, no matter how hard he tried. "You did ask me to call you back."

"That I did." She sighed heavily. "But, Kip—"

"I'll take it," he blurted. "I'll take the job." He shoved the words desperately from his mouth, needing to cut off whatever it was that she had been preparing to say, which he knew, instinctively, was some sort of retraction of her offer.

Which would have been perfect—freeing him from everything he feared. And, yet, his heart was pounding. His mouth was dry. He waited in the echoing silence in the wake of his nearly shouted words for what she would say, hoping against hope it would simply be acceptance.

"Shit," she muttered so quietly he knew he wasn't meant to have heard it. Louder, she said, "I really want this."

He frowned. "Then it's a good thing I said yes. Right?"

She sighed again, and this time, it was so weary, his heart ached all over again. "It's been a very trying day."

Kip glanced at the clock on his cable box. "It's only two o'clock."

"Two? Damn it." She groaned. "I forgot to eat again."

He was on his feet before he realized it, reaching for his wallet and keys. "Meet with me. In person." He shoved his phone between his shoulder and jaw. "Let's eat and chat about your day and the particulars of our deal."

She was silent on her end of the phone.

He licked his lips. "Please, honey."

He clenched his eyes closed. *Shut up, Kip. Just shut the fuck up.* Maintaining a modicum of dignity would be nice.

"All right, Kip."

There was a rustling on her end. No doubt, she was gathering that laptop bag she carried as though it were a purse. He found himself smiling as he opened his mouth to suggest a place to eat.

She beat him to it. "Let's meet at Sally's."

He tilted his head. "Sally's?"

"Do you know where it is?"

"Yeah." He laughed as though he couldn't believe what she was suggesting. "Honey, all the best restaurants are on the Strip. Sally's—"

"No Strip!"

Her words were so forceful they immediately shut him up. He could feel his molars grinding together, and his grip on his phone became painful.

"Let's not meet on the Strip," she said again, this time with a semblance of courtesy. "I just … really need a break, and the Strip's not far enough from … my office."

"Fair enough." *Bossing me around already. Are you sure you want to do this?* "Sally's it is." He could tell he was talking louder than normal, but how else was he supposed to get that inner voice to shut up?

He clicked *end*. He reached for the doorknob, but as his hand closed over it, he paused.

He brightened.

This was good, actually. Strike good. This was great! If she bossed him around—treated him like he expected her to—there would be no more risk that he would feel anything for her except the professional distance he so desperately needed.

*Do your worst, honey. I'm depending on it.*

• • •

She sat in her favorite booth at Sally's and drummed her fingers on the chipped Formica table.

Sally's was a faded and well-worn fifties diner that had been around since long before Victoria could remember. The food was greasy; the health department grade posted by the door was definitely not an *A*.

She loved this place. That it was far away from The Ricchezza, her place of work, and any place a normal person would frequent—well, those were just bonuses.

No one else was in the restaurant besides the one, tired waitress who had come to take her drink order several minutes ago. So no one was here to watch her and report back to Mr. Davis.

It was the most relaxed she'd been since taking Kip's call about a half hour ago.

Who'd have ever thought that, after his obvious reluctance this morning, he would accept her offer?

Right after she'd been informed that she would be the subject of a strenuous background check.

Fucking Murphy and his damn laws.

The tarnished brass bell hanging over the diner's door tinkled, and Victoria's gaze was on it in a shot.

As he ducked into the diner, the mid-afternoon sun shone off Kip's hair, nearly blinding her, but there was absolutely no way she could be sure that his amazing looks weren't at fault instead of the sun.

It physically hurt to look at him; an ache settled at the apex of her thighs and shot all throughout her body, making her squirm in her seat.

His blue-eyed gaze scanned the diner, and his frown deepened. She looked the diner over again, too, noticing with increased clarity how run-down it was, and she winced. She wasn't exactly proving she was a good provider, was she?

She knew the minute he felt her presence in the diner, even though he hadn't looked at her yet, because his shoulders stiffened imperceptibly beneath his light blue polo shirt. Like she was a lodestone and his gaze a magnet, he looked her way without hesitation.

He was still for a moment, and she couldn't tell what he was thinking as he simply stared at her. A muscle ticked in his jaw; his chest rose and fell. Then he smiled.

It wasn't the same smile he'd given her last night. Or at The Bar for that matter.

He walked toward her, and Victoria caught sight of the waitress stopping in her tracks and staring at Kip gape-mouthed as he made his way across the diner.

She understood the feeling, but …

*He's mine. Back off.*

The thought startled her into straightening her spine. She gripped her ice water and took a sip, nearly choking on it as her gaze focused on Kip's groin and the way it moved behind his pants as he walked.

God, the man was big. She followed the length that had been deep inside her last night as it dipped to the right and traveled several inches down his pant leg.

By the time Kip stood right in front of her, she was nearly panting with need. She pressed her thighs together, but it didn't help. "H-hi."

His smile, now that he was closer, was tight at the corners. That's what made it different from last night.

Why the change?

The way she'd barked at him on the phone. She closed her eyes. Her hands curled into fists in her lap. "Kip." She looked up at him. "Allow me to apologize for earlier. For how I spoke to you on the phone."

Something flashed in his eyes. Surprise? He shrugged with one shoulder. "It's okay."

She shook her head. "No, it's not." She gestured to the chair opposite her. "Can I explain it to you?"

He sucked his bottom lip into his mouth. A moment later, he was sitting down at the table, but not in the chair she'd pointed toward. He sat right beside her.

Immediately, she was overwhelmed by his close presence, which he made more potent by leaning toward her and threading his arm over the back of her chair. He stared into her eyes, and some of the tightness left his smile.

"Does it matter?" he asked.

Usually, explanations had no place in apologies. At least that was her personal belief. Either you thought your actions were justified and you offered an explanation, or you knew they weren't and simply offered an apology. However, in this case …

"Yes, actually."

He raised an eyebrow. "Enlighten me, then."

"It has to do with why my day was trying."

His eyes narrowed. "Does it?"

She quickly placed a hand on his forearm. "Not that I lashed out because I had a bad day. God, that would be horrible."

He shrugged. "Yes. But it would also be understandable."

She flexed her fingers against his skin. "Look, I just found out I'm going to be under a lot of scrutiny because of my job. My propositioning a"—she looked around the restaurant and then ducked toward him— "gigolo could not have been more ill-timed. *That*'s why I suggested we meet far off the beaten path."

He leaned back and blinked hard, and Victoria tensed. *Great, I just managed to offend him even more.*

"Oh." His every feature relaxed. Then tensed. Then relaxed again. "Well, that makes sense." He breathed a laugh. "It all makes sense. This is why you wanted to retract the offer?"

"It was that obvious?"

He laughed again. "You could say that."

She bristled. "Well, how about you? A girl offers you twenty thousand dollars and you're all, *hmmm, I don't know.*"

He immediately sobered. He stared at her long enough that she shifted, her gaze wanting to slide to the wall. "But I eventually said yes," he murmured.

"Eventually," she grumbled.

His fingers were suddenly atop hers where they rested on the tabletop. "Honey, I'm sorry, too." He squeezed her hand. "How about we both get a free pass on today, hmm?" His thumb traced a circle on her wrist. "Let's take that do-over we talked about on the phone this morning."

She pulled in a slow breath. Finally, she looked up at him. "I'd like that."

His smile was soft and crooked. "Victoria—" His voice was so quiet, there was no risk of them being overheard. "I'm exceptionally discreet. I'm a professional. We can do this, and no one will ever know. I promise."

And she instantaneously believed him. Because she knew by the gravity of his tone that he needed to be discreet as much for himself as for her, which was curious, but something she could trust. "Then we should do this."

He reached out and traced her jaw toward her ear with his finger. "I agree." He skimmed back down her jaw toward her chin, and as he did so, he drew her forward with the slightest pressure from his finger.

God, she wanted him to kiss her. His lips parted; she licked hers.

"Are you two ready to order?"

Victoria jumped a little in her seat, and a surge of disappointment filtered down to her gut as Kip dropped his touch from her skin and leaned back.

"Yes," he said, keeping his gaze trained on Victoria. "Honey, what will you have?"

His choice of words rocked her, and not in a good way. They were sweet. What a boyfriend would say. Or—she gulped—a husband. She turned her gaze toward the waitress, who was scowling at her and not quick enough to hide it before Victoria caught it. *Wishes Kip were hers that badly, huh?*

She couldn't blame her; she could, however, resent her for that. "Actually, we're leaving."

Kip frowned. "But you haven't eaten."

Victoria shrugged. "We'll order room service." She raised her eyebrows, asking him the only way she knew how to take her back to the hotel. To fuck her again.

His gaze roamed her face, and then he nodded. "You're right, we're leaving." His chair screeched across the pockmarked linoleum as he pushed back. He stood and reached into his back pocket, pulled out a wallet, and threw some money on the table.

"Wait." She reached for the bills. "I should—"

He captured her fingers and gave them a gentle, but definitely admonishing squeeze. "Come on. I'm starving."

The simple phrase was dripping with innuendo, and the waitress's jaw dropped.

Something surged through her chest. A feeling much, much better than the first time she'd walked into her bank with a deposit slip for $100,000 and watched the way the teller's eyes had widened. Because Kip wasn't an idiot, he knew the waitress was interested in him; because he knew how to be a gentleman, he had simply and effectively let her know he wasn't interested in anyone but Victoria.

She liked that. Liked it so much that when she rose to shaky legs, her panties were so damp she hoped it didn't show through her pants.

He tugged on their joined hands and led her across the diner and out to the parking lot. Once there, he dropped her hand. "Meet you at the same place?"

Victoria scanned the parking lot, finding her own car immediately. The only other car in the lot was also a Mercedes. *Huh.* "Did you ... walk here?"

"No." He nodded toward the other Mercedes. "Drove."

*Double huh.* She looked him over with new eyes. His line of work must be pretty damn profitable. "Yes, let's meet at the same place. I'll see if I can get the same room, but if I can't, I'll text you the new number."

"Okay." He started walking backward, keeping his eyes on her. "And Victoria?"

"Hmm?"

"I'm glad we're doing this."

It was an olive branch, compliment, and promise all rolled into one.

Her smile this time was genuine. “Me, too.” *Definitely me too.*

The ride across town took no time at all, and at the same time, seemed interminable. Kip had taken such good care of her last night, but she had visions of jumping him as soon as they were behind a closed door. Of tearing his clothes off and licking her way down his entire body.

By the time she was five minutes from the Desert Oasis, the visions were so vivid, she knew they would have to come true or the lack of fulfilled fantasy would haunt her to her grave.

Needing the distraction, she called ahead and, sure enough, the room they’d had last night was still available.

Victoria was not a sentimental woman—certainly not anymore, at least—but there was no denying a warmth surging through her as she hung up the phone through her car’s controls.

Would she be able to ensure the same room for the next couple of weeks? Why did the mere possibility make her nearly giddy in the most odd, soothing way?

She almost sped right by the hotel—which was blessedly far away from any prying eyes at The Ricchezza—but managed to tap the brakes and swing into the circle drive before missing it entirely. The valet was different from the one who had taken her car last night, and she let go a breath she hadn’t realized she’d been holding.

As soon as the valet drove off with her car, she straightened her shoulders and, with a small nod to the doorman, walked through the glass door held open for her. She marched straight toward the desk, and her luck at not being recognized promptly ran out.

“Ms. Hastings!” the clerk behind the desk called out as he spotted her. “Welcome back.”

Her smile felt tight, but she offered it nonetheless. “Yes, thank you.” She reached the desk and propped both her arms on it. “Checking in.”

The clerk's eyes widened. "Oh, I didn't realize you'd checked out. I thought—" He seemed to realize his lapse of etiquette and snapped his mouth shut. "I mean, certainly."

Victoria contained her wince but just barely. A hotel off the Strip. Checking in and out in frequent succession. Paying in cash.

The man worked in Vegas. He knew what she was up to.

He didn't meet her eyes as he typed away at his computer, and when he mumbled her total for the room and slid a paper across the stone counter for her to sign, she slid a pile of cash right back at him: enough for the room and then some.

His hand froze above it as he noticed from the fan of bills that she had definitely overpaid. She flicked a glance at his nametag. "I appreciate everything, Tony." She paused a moment. "*Everything*."

His head jerked up, and his gaze collided with hers. She pulled on all the boldness that came naturally to her in work situations. Winking at Tony, she smiled with what she hoped was a flirtatious curve of her lips.

His face relaxed. "Certainly, ma'am. We do appreciate your business."

She nodded, palmed the key card he held out to her, and turned around, shifting her laptop bag into a more comfortable position on her shoulder.

She froze.

Kip was just walking into the lobby, and as he nodded at the doorman just as she had, a lock of that thick hair fell out of place and across his brow. He raised a hand and shoved his fingers through his hair, raking it back into order.

His gaze automatically landed on her, and the easy, sexy grin that spread his lips immediately afterward made her lean back against the counter in an effort to keep from slipping to the floor.

*Thank God this is not a real relationship*. No, Kip had far too much power over her and her body to be safe for a committed relationship. She would enjoy this time with him and then—most probably—cut him loose and maintain her sanity and dignity.

Not wanting to converse in front of Tony-who-knew-everything, she pushed away from the counter and started walking his way unsteadily, her heels clicking an improvised rhythm against the marble floor.

They reached each other, and Kip surprised her by gripping her elbow and pulling her closer. He pressed a soft but lingering kiss to her cheek, and she heard him inhale slowly and deeply.

"Hello again."

His words brushed against her ear, and she shivered. He pulled back, and his grin said it all: he knew the effect he had on her.

No doubt the man planned every move accordingly. Her poor body was going to go into shock if she didn't adapt to this primitive draw she felt whenever she was around him.

"I got us a room."

He nodded. "Great."

"The same one we had last night," she blurted. She pursed her lips. *As though that matters!* Why did she say the dumbest shit around this man?

His eyes softened. "That's great," he said again. This time, however, his voice was quiet. Gentle.

He liked that they had the same room, too. Or, he was a really good actor and was making her think that …

*God, stop thinking like that!* If she constantly thought about all the ways his job trained him to make her feel things that weren't real, she would go crazy wondering what was and wasn't valid.

This wasn't a relationship. If she felt something, it was because she was paying him to make her feel something.

His hand, still cupping her elbow, squeezed. "Second thoughts?" he asked quietly.

Victoria raised her chin. "Absolutely not." *None that I'm going to be paying attention to, anyway.*

His thumb stroked the sensitive skin of her inner elbow, and her breath caught in her throat. "Then, shall we?"

She nodded dumbly. "Uh-huh."

The dimple in his left cheek flashed, but he wasn't smiling. It almost looked as though he were amused by her, but trying to hold back the feeling.

*Great.*

"Just one moment," he said. With one final squeeze to her elbow, he dropped his hand and strode to the hotel desk and Tony—the very man she'd been trying to keep Kip away from.

*Best-laid plans and all that.* She folded her arms across her chest and watched as Kip leaned in and the men carried on a hushed conversation.

She didn't like this. At all. Victoria liked being in control at every moment.

Kip straightened. The men nodded at each other, and then Kip was walking back in her direction.

She could feel by the pull of her lips that she was scowling. "What was that all about?"

He winked. "You'll see."

She narrowed her eyes at him as he took her elbow once again and steered her toward the elevator. "I feel it necessary to let you know that I don't like surprises."

He pressed the button for their floor. "Well, if that's true, it's a damn shame." He grinned in her direction, that dimple making another appearance. "I'm brilliant at surprises." He stepped into her personal space and, gripping both of her upper arms, brushed his thumbs down her biceps. "Of all kinds, honey."

Her mouth went dry. "Oh." She licked her lips and shrugged with one shoulder. "I suppose I could be persuaded to like … certain kinds of surprises."

He leaned down, and her heart galloped. Instead of a kiss, however, Kip snuggled the top of her head with his cheek and moved his hands from her arms to her back. And then, once she was firmly within his embrace, he sighed and stroked his cheek across her hair. "That's good."

*Hugging me. Holding me. Liking it so much.*

Victoria stiffened against him, and she could tell the moment he felt it, because he stiffened, too.

At that moment, the elevator chimed. Kip dropped his arms and stepped back. And, idiotically, she felt chilled and bereft as soon as he gave her the space she'd so desperately wanted.

He snagged her hand, wove their fingers together, and tugged her forward and off the elevator. "Do you have the key?"

She mutely held it up, and he plucked it from her fingers. He led them to their room, slid the key home, and opened the door. With a firm, gentle hand to her lower back, he ushered her inside.

Her arms were trembling as she stepped through the door. Her knees were so damn weak, she worried she wouldn't make it the few steps into the room. She heard the door click closed behind her.

Spinning, she dropped her laptop bag from her shoulder. It hit the ground with a thud that would have made her heart stop at a normal moment, but her heart was beating far too quickly to slow down.

With a small, desperate noise, she launched herself in Kip's direction. Her arms looped around his neck; her fingers stabbed into his hair. She crushed her breasts to his chest, and as her pelvis came flush with his, she discovered him already hard.

How long had he been hard for her? In the elevator? In the lobby? The moment he first saw her at Sally's? That's how long she'd been wet for him.

She jerked his head down and surged on her tiptoes until their mouths collided in a magnificent crash of lips and teeth and tongues.

He groaned into the kiss, his hands falling to her ass and hauling her even closer until he was grinding his erection against her belly.

Her sex throbbed painfully, and in a rush, she grew even more aroused for him, needing him between her thighs more than she needed her next breath. "Fast," she murmured.

He kissed the corner of her mouth, her cheek, her jaw. She tipped her head back and clutched him closer as he licked down her neck. "Fast, Kip." One of her hands jerked from his hair to grab his ass. She squeezed hard. "I need you."

He muttered something—she thought it might be *shit*—and next she knew, she was up in his arms.

The hotel room swayed as her equilibrium struggled to right itself. Once she realized he was carrying her to the bed, her womb fluttered even more. She wrapped her arms around his neck and leaned up to suck his earlobe into her mouth, biting down hard enough to make him grunt and squeeze her tight.

She was suddenly weightless, tossed into the air, and before she could panic, she landed with two bounces on the bed. In a flash, Kip was on top of her, shoving his hips between her legs and spreading her wide.

"Oh, God, yes." She wrapped her legs around his ass and crossed her ankles so he wouldn't get away.

But getting away seemed to be the furthest thing from his mind. He ground his hard dick against her sex and then thrust up, sending the tip of his erection right over her clit.

She cried out and arched her back. Kip nibbled his way up her neck and thrust again. Every muscle in her sex clenched, and had he been inside her, she would have squeezed him right to the edge of his own orgasm. As it was, the telltale signs of her coming apart began to show. Her aching breasts pressed into his chest, she whispered his name. "I'm going to … come." She gasped as he thrust again. "Just from this."

He kissed her jaw. "Do it, honey. Then we can do the next one slow."

"That is … a fucking brilliant"—she squeezed her eyes shut—"idea."

“That’s it, honey.”

With a wail, Victoria flew out over the edge into orgasm. She stiffened, and her lungs froze. Clutching him to her with all her strength, she writhed against his erection, wave after wave of pleasure shooting through her.

“*Fuck.*” His stiffened in her arms, and, dimly, he sounded and felt like he was coming, too. But Kip wouldn’t do that. He was a professional; he wouldn’t lose control.

He shuddered and pressed his face against her neck, and as she came down from the heights, his wild breaths wafted across her skin.

There was an abrupt, loud knock at the door. “Room service.” The words were filtered through the wood, but clear nonetheless.

Just how loud she had been seconds ago as she’d lost her fucking mind in Kip’s arms came zooming back. She moaned. “Oh, God. They heard me.”

Kip pushed up on his arms. The dazed look on his face distracted her for a moment, but not for long. “They heard me,” she said again. She covered her face with her hands. “I could just die.”

Kip wrapped his fingers around her wrist and tugged. She allowed him to pull one hand away, and the look in his eyes was … something. A cross between tenderness and lust. “If they heard you,” he said in a rumble, “then they’re so fucking jealous of me right now, they could die.”

*What?*

“Damn, Victoria.” He drew her hand to his mouth and pressed a kiss against her fingertips. “You’re so sexy, you drive me mindless.”

Okay, now she was definitely confused. This had to be part of his act, right? Yet, that look in his eyes. She didn’t know anyone who could feign those feelings.

Another knock sounded, and, if knocks could have emotions assigned to them, this one was definitely impatient. “Room service!”

Kip kissed her fingers one more time, and then he shoved from the bed. She was so relieved that he was going to the door—there was no way she could get her body to cooperate—she almost missed it as he untucked his shirt and dragged it down to cover his groin: a wet spot on the front of his pants.

Her eyes widened. He had come! Holy shit. She had made a seasoned gigolo come in his pants while they'd both been thoroughly clothed and in the span of—she glanced at the clock—three minutes.

*I might be a super hero*. A giggle burbled in her chest, and she pressed her hand across her mouth to hold it in.

Kip swung the door open—a little vehemently if she did say so—and, immediately, the hotel employee's attention shot toward the bed and landed on her. The man clutched a heavily burdened tray in two white-gloved hands, but he paid it no attention as his gaze crawled over every inch of her with such precision. She almost reached for a pillow to pull in front of her chest and hold close.

Her body was still aroused; she could feel it in every twinge of her still swollen sex and in the tight pearling of her nipples. It was, apparently, obvious to the employee as well, because his eyes became shrewd, and his look turned into something she really didn't like.

Kip stepped in front of the man, effectively cutting of his line of sight, and, despite her reaction to their embrace in the elevator five minutes ago, she wanted to hug Kip all over again. "I'll take that," he said gruffly, reaching for the tray.

The employee took a step back. "I'm supposed to deliver it—"

"Nope." Kip grabbed the handles of the tray. "You're done. Leave now." He wrested the tray from the man, and the metal dish covers clacked slightly.

"Yes, sir."

Kip kicked the door shut, and it slammed home. "Fucking pervert," he muttered, carrying the tray to the dinette and setting it down.

Victoria couldn't help it; her giggle escaped. *Fucking pervert.* This from the gigolo and his paying customer.

Kip's head snapped up, and his gaze landed on her. As soon as it did, however, his glower evaporated like magic, and a begrudging smile tugged at his lips. "Stop it. I know it's ironic."

She giggled again, but this time, it was a laugh of relief and gratitude. That guy had been creepy. And Kip had stood up for her. Again. Twice in one day.

*Damned if I don't want him again already.*

Her thoughts must have shown on her face, because, Kip's slight smile turned full-fledged. "Oh, no, you vixen. Food first." He reached out and plucked one of the metal covers from its dish.

The aroma of good food immediately wafted through the room, and Victoria's stomach growled loudly.

He chuckled. "Come on, beautiful. Get your strength up, because we have *slow* to do still."

"Oh, do we?" Her words were teasing. Flirtatious. As she rose from the bed, she couldn't remember the last time—if ever—such a tone had come from her.

Once she had taken a seat at the table, he edged out the other chair and sat as well.

It was a well-mannered move, waiting until the woman sat, and Victoria found herself suddenly curious as to where he would have learned it. In his profession or in his personal life?

*You know better!* She shook her head, dislodging the errant notion and forbidding it to return. She didn't need to know anything about Kip's personal life. It was irrelevant.

He placed a plate before her, and her stomach growled anew. He'd ordered a lunch of rich foods: some kind of bisque and a decedent sandwich that made her mouth water. She couldn't remember the last time she'd taken the time to eat a meal she actually *wanted* to eat. "Was this the surprise you were talking about?" she asked, placing her napkin on her lap.

"You haven't eaten lunch," he said, as though this were an answer.

She laughed. "I usually don't eat lunch."

His gaze snapped to hers. "Really?" He frowned. "Why on earth not?"

She shrugged. "I forget. Get caught up in work."

"That's a shame." He picked up his spoon and stirred his soup. "Where do you work?"

"Precision Media Services," she answered automatically. Her fingers froze above her own spoon.

*Personal details.* She closed her eyes, torn between begging him to forget what she'd just said and wanting him to ask her more personal details. "Kip," she said wearily.

"You're in advertising?" His voice sounded odd.

She raised her head and looked at him. "You know Precision Media Services?"

Now, his gaze skated away. "We live in Vegas. Of course I know it."

It wasn't an entirely honest answer; she could immediately tell. But they had already gotten far more personal than she had promised herself they would. "Let's talk about something else, shall we?"

His shoulders relaxed. "Please."

But, then she didn't know what to say. How did one make casual conversation with the person they were paying to fuck them?

She realized her hand was still hovering over her spoon when Kip clasped it in his. "I can see you thinking."

"Well, I am," she couldn't help but retort. She thought for a living. It was a hard thing to turn off.

"Honey, it's just conversation. If it's going to be a strain, we don't do it. Isn't that why you're paying for a lover when"—his gaze swept her —"you clearly don't have to?"

Every muscle in her clenched neck relaxed. That was exactly why she was paying him. That he said so freely and without condemnation meant more to her than she could say. "So, we'd just sit here in awkward silence?"

He took the time to draw a spoonful of soup to his mouth, swallow, and blot his lips with the napkin—again, perfect manners. His gaze was heated and never left her face. "Silence is only awkward if you make it so."

"Not in my experience." She hated silence. She could make great conversation as a professional, but that was because the conversation always revolved around her work, and she was excellent at what she did.

But, personal conversation? She was terrible at it. So she avoided it. And silence.

Okay, she avoided people.

Kip took another bite. "So, we talk." He nodded toward her spoon where it still rested beside her bowl of soup. "Eat up," he said softly.

She found herself obeying him automatically—something she would never do ordinarily, as she was used to calling the shots. As the first bite of her meal hit her belly, she realized she was ravenous, and she took several more bites before she looked up to see Kip staring at her with that damned amused dimple showing again.

She felt her cheeks heat and grew even more discomfited. Why was she always blushing?

Kip straightened the napkin in his lap and grabbed his spoon again. "What's your favorite color?"

"My—" Her spoon clanked against the side of her bowl. "Why?"

His shoe nudged against hers. "Conversation. I happen to be an expert at carrying on a conversation devoid of personal details."

She raised an eyebrow. "What if my favorite color is a deeply personal secret?"

That dimple flashed again, but this time she didn't mind. She had been trying to amuse him, and that it had worked filled her almost the same way as the several bites of delicious meal had. He sobered, and the dimple vanished. "Why, is it the color of my eyes?" he asked.

Her spoon clanged again, but she held it together. That particular clear blue was quickly making it to the top of the list, as a matter of fact. "Not everything is about you, you know." She loaded her fork with salad. "What's your favorite color?" She took her bite.

"Currently?" His shoe nudged hers again. "The pink of your sweet pussy."

Lettuce almost went flying everywhere. She swallowed hard, and her bite of salad went down as though it were a variety of tossed glass shards.

"Kip!"

"Yes?" He took a casual bite of his own salad. "Wait." He put down his fork and grew serious. "Is that your favorite color, too? We can't both have it."

*Oh, my God.* She wanted to lick that smirk he was trying to hide right off his face while straddling his lap. She looked down at her salad and carefully loaded her fork. "I don't have a favorite color, so that one's all yours."

"Don't have a—" He made a disbelieving sound in the back of his throat, and when she looked at him again, he was shaking his head. "What the actual fuck. Didn't you color as a kid? Which crayon did you fight over the most with the other kids?"

*Had* she colored as a kid? That seemed frivolous. But, kids were frivolous, right? She shrugged.

"Okay, the only right answer to that question is the macaroni and cheese crayon." He canted his head. "Obviously."

"That is not a color."

"Macaroni and cheese is everything." He placed a palm over his chest. "You hired me just in time. I have so much to teach you."

Her lips twitched. He already had taught her a lot. Like, how much she needed sex. *Good* sex.

"So, no favorite color. What about a favorite movie?" He sat back in his chair, and that was when Victoria noticed his plate and bowl were empty. She glanced down at her own plates and found them in the same condition. When had that happened?

"Um, probably a documentary?" she mumbled.

He shook his head. "This may be hopeless."

"Hey." She straightened. "Ask me about my favorite rhetorical appeal or something."

"Pathos," he said suddenly. "It's obvious." He grinned.

*Pathos?* The emotional appeal.

She hadn't thought it possible to find this man any more attractive, but then he'd gone and joked about Aristotle's rhetorical triangle.

She licked her lips, and Kip's gaze followed the progress of her tongue with rapt attention. He shoved his empty plate away. "I think it's time for dessert."

She glanced at the table and frowned. There wasn't any dessert here.

Kip reached for a small dish that had escaped her notice and removed its cover. He licked his spoon clean, his gaze locked with hers, and Victoria forgot how to breathe.

"Come here, honey."

She nearly tripped over her feet she was on them so quickly. He held a hand out to her, and she placed hers in it. He tugged her forward, and then she was sitting in his lap in a close approximation of what she'd fantasized about minutes before.

With their gazes still locked, Kip began unbuttoning her blouse. His fingertips brushed across the skin he was baring as he slowly undid each button in a way that had to be intentional. By the time he was tugging her blouse from her pants, she was tingling all over and more ready for dessert than she had ever been in her life.

He skimmed his palms up her arms, and the fine fabric of her blouse rippled between their skin, causing her nipples to pucker. When his hands reached her shoulders, he brushed her blouse off them, and it slipped down her arms and hit the floor behind her without a sound.

Kip pulled in a slow, loud breath, and then his gaze flicked down. He swore softly. “Miss prim Victoria and her lingerie.” He traced his fingers over the edge of the corset she’d hidden beneath her business attire. “You’re a walking orgasm, honey.”

As he brushed the edge of the corset again, his fingers chafed the sensitive, plumped curve of her breast, and a tiny moan split her lips. He traced the corset’s boning down to where it disappeared into her trousers. “What are you hiding under here?”

Her mouth was dry, but she still managed to say, “You have to take your shirt off to find out.”

He raised an eyebrow but didn’t take his gaze from her body. “Negotiating. I can live with that.” His hands rose to his top button, and he began unceremoniously and quickly unbuttoning his shirt.

She placed a hand over his. “Slower.”

Now his gaze found hers, and after a moment, the left side of his lips tipped up. “Yes, ma’am.”

True to his word, his movements slowed. By the time his shirt was half undone, Victoria was cursing herself and her *slower*. Her breaths thready, she shoved his hands aside and undertook the task herself. She couldn’t keep her own fingertips from his skin, so smooth and soft over such hard planes of muscle. She jerked impatiently, and the last resisting button flew off and bounced against the wall with a *pop*. She shoved the shirt from his shoulders and immediately smoothed her palms over his pecs and down the slabs of his abdomen, which dipped beneath her touch.

“Victoria, your pants.”

“Shh.” She moaned as she skated her palms back up again and over his massive shoulders down to his biceps.

If seeing was believing, touching was even more so. His body was unreal; she wanted to memorize it through her hands.

She squeezed the muscles of his upper arms, and they gave not at all beneath her fingers.

His hands landed on the tops of her thighs, and he squeezed. "You promised." His fingers traveled toward her fly.

"You can't expect me to stop touching you." She stroked the stark line of muscle between his biceps and shoulders.

"I had to stop touching you!"

Her lips curled. "Fair enough." With one hand, she led one of his to the button of her pants. Even through the corset and the fabric of her trousers, she could feel the heat of his impending touch. "Go ahead then."

She didn't have to tell him twice. For someone she was paying to romance her, he undid her pants with a speed and lack of finesse that was at odds with his job. *Thank God.*

With him distracted, she had freedom to stroke his upper body to her heart's content, but when he slid her pants down her hips as far as they would go before their position stopped them, she paused, her thumbs over his nipples, slightly anxious for his reaction.

Reverently, he stroked a thumb down a piece of elastic. "Is this a …" His gaze snapped to hers. "You're wearing a garter belt."

She knew it was ridiculous. She'd just come from work, for fuck's sake. No one wore a garter belt to work. But she hadn't had sex in so long that her lingerie had become her one and only sensual habit. She lowered her chin in the semblance of a nod.

His mouth clamped closed, and a muscle ticked in his cheek. In the next instant, he was standing.

With a squeak, Victoria wrapped her legs around his hips and cinched them tightly. One of his massive hands cradled her bottom. He snatched the dish she hadn't looked into yet with his other hand, and then he was striding across the room.

No, *striding* was too leisurely a word. One couldn't sprint with an entire other person wound about them, but he got pretty close.

His hand squeezed her ass. "Shit, this is a thong, too, isn't it?"

She buried her face in the curve of his neck and licked his collarbone instead of answering.

The clack of glass meeting wood sounded to her right, and then both of his hands were gripping her around the waist. Through the pressure he was exerting, she could tell he wanted her on her feet, but she rather liked hugging his hips with her thighs.

The skin of his stomach and back was a silky caress against the insides of her legs, and, with his current state of arousal, the deliciously firm tip of his erection was pressing right where she wanted it …

"Down, woman."

She acquiesced with only a slight grunt of irritation. "Fine, but you'd better make it up to me."

He smiled her way, but his eyes were still locked on her lowered pants. "I promise."

*Well, then.* "You want these off?" She nearly started at the sound of her own voice. *Where is this sex kitten coming from?*

"You have no idea." Kip hooked his thumbs in the waistband, and since her pants were already down around the tops of her thighs, the touch of his fingers against her ass made her shiver.

She shimmied a bit, and, amid a quiet curse, he shoved her pants down. Because of the silk stocking on her legs, the pants slid quickly to the floor. Victoria kicked them aside and glanced back up at her lover.

His mouth was agape. Literally agape.

Power unlike anything she had ever felt in a boardroom surged through her.

She stepped back, feeling the bed a few inches behind her, and, holding out her arms, spun for him on her tiptoes.

An odd noise sounded from behind her, but by the time she circled around to the front again, he was completely composed—if he'd ever truly lost his composure at all.

"Turn around again."

Victoria raised an eyebrow. It was a very clear order, and instinctively, she stiffened. Yet, the look of hunger in his eyes …

After a slight hesitation, she turned around, presenting him her back.

In seconds, there was a tugging at the laces of her corset. His breath brushed across her ears in only a moment's warning before he spoke in a low, indecent tone. "I'm taking this off, but everything below your waist stays on. You understand?"

Another order. When every inch of her tingled at the promise in his voice, however, she nodded.

The corset relaxed, but Victoria didn't find breathing any easier to come by.

His soft lips caressed the hollow beneath her ear. "Arms up, honey."

She obeyed immediately.

He drew the corset over her head, and she shivered at how good it felt to be bare.

The corset hit the floor somewhere behind them with a soft crush of bone and silk, and heat immediately covered her back.

His chest pressed against her shoulder blades, and his hands spread over her belly. "Better?" He nipped her earlobe.

She jumped, and his arms around her tightened. "Yes." Her voice was so breathy he had to have a hard time hearing her. "Yes," she said more strongly.

"Good." He skimmed his palms up her stomach and over her ribs. By the time she was arching into his touch, he was already covering her breasts with his hands and lifting them.

She moaned.

He did, too, while he pinched both her nipples. "So beautiful."

She needed to touch him, too. Reaching behind her, she found his hips with her hands, and unable to resist, she arched back even more, pressing her ass against his groin.

She was rewarded by a sharp hiss of air past her ear. The press of him was not enough. She slid her hands between their bodies, found his erection, and squeezed.

He thrust against her, and she nearly cried *yes*. But then he was gone, taking all that delicious warmth away.

"No!"

"Get on the bed, Victoria." The order was followed by an immediate slap of her ass.

She gasped and arched up to her toes, but in the next second, she was scrambling on top of the bed with a desperation that should have scared her but instead felt more natural than breathing.

By the time she lay panting on her back, Kip was reaching for the dish he'd deposited on the bedside table. He stirred whatever it held solemnly as his hot gaze poured all over her from the top of her head down to her toes and then back again. He stepped toward the bed. With one hand, he reached down and undid his pants, then shoved them and the black briefs he wore beneath over his hips and down his thighs until he could kick them away.

Her mouth went dry. She was staring, and she could tell he knew it, because, unbelievably, his erection grew even more beneath her gaze.

"Do you have a sweet tooth, Victoria?"

The gentle clacking of the spoon against the dish was starting to make her shiver. She shook her head, and her hair rustled against the pillow.

His lips hitched up on one end. "Of course you don't." He kneeled on the edge of the bed with his left knee and leaned over her. "I guess dessert is all for me, then."

The lamplight caught the rich, liquid chocolate as it spilled from the tip of the spoon back into the dish.

Her eyes widened. She'd never done something like this before. Even when they'd had a sex life, Jeremy had not been any more adventurous than making love with the lights on. "Won't that be … sticky?"

He breathed in a way that suggested he was suppressing a chuckle. "Honey, if you're thinking about how sticky it is while I'm doing this, I have bigger problems. Like the need to find a new job."

She swallowed. *If you say so.*

His eyes lit up, and now she knew for sure he was trying not to laugh at her. She tried to straighten her face—keep whatever expression he was seeing from staying around. She didn't want him laughing at her, for Christ's sake.

With his free hand, he brushed her hair from her forehead. "We'll take a shower afterward, okay?"

She nodded, and then became completely redundant when she also said, "Okay."

"Good girl."

And then, he was holding the spoon high over her bare breasts, and time slowed in a perfectly clichéd way as she watched chocolate dribble from the spoon, through the air, to land at last directly on her left nipple.

*Impeccable aim.* He had to do this often—a thought that did *not* help the anxiety climbing her throat.

"I can see you thinking again."

She wound her fingers in the sheets. "Damn it, Kip. It's what I do."

"And this"—he leaned down farther—"is what I do." His hot lips closed over the cool chocolate, enveloping her nipple in a clash of temperatures as he sucked it into his mouth. He groaned long and low, and then his tongue lapped at her. In the dim light of the lamp, she could see his throat work as he swallowed the chocolate.

And that was precisely the moment she stopped thinking so hard.

Her fingers were suddenly weaving through his hair, and she was clutching him to her breast, arching into his decadent kiss. He murmured something, but she couldn't hear him with his face pressed against her skin.

"What?" she breathed, loosening her hold slightly.

He looked up at her, his gorgeous eyes twinkling. "More chocolate."

She glanced quickly at her hands and saw they were holding him down so tightly they were blanched white. She dropped them immediately.

Kip sat up. "Liked it more than you thought you would?"

She glared. "Gloating?"

"A man's got to take his victories where he can." He reached for the dish again, and Victoria promptly forgot her pique.

This time, when he drizzled the chocolate, she arched into it, catching it with her right nipple and undulating as her nipple puckered and the gooseflesh rushed from that point and over the rest of her body.

He swore softly, and just as she was biting back her own reaction, he dove down and licked at her chocolate-covered breast as though he hadn't eaten a full meal mere minutes before. This time, she couldn't keep from swearing as well. He echoed her sentiment with a harsh groan and wrapped his arms beneath her, making her arch against his mouth even more.

Pleasure shot from her nipple straight to her sex as he sucked—first gently, but then much harder. Harder than she would have even guessed she'd like.

But like she did.

She held out as long as she could, the memory of how tightly she'd held him before stinging, but it became impossible to keep her arms at her side. She felt weightless from the pleasure of his mouth and needed to hold on to something—an anchor to keep her grounded.

She wove her fingers through his hair again, and as she tugged him closer, he moaned against her skin.

Without lifting his lips from her breast, Kip dipped his fingers in the dish—completely foregoing the spoon this time. He smeared the chocolate over her other breast, then kissed his way across her sternum, covering her wet nipple with his palm and plumping the flesh.

*Why* had she never done this before? As he slowly drove her mad with the pressure of his mouth, she leaned up and licked, then nibbled his shoulder. Delicious—just like she'd come to expect. But …

She spotted the dish, still cradled in Kip's hand, which rested on the bed. Reaching down, she dipped her fingertips in.

The chocolate was unexpectedly smooth, not sticky at all, as she smeared it over his shoulder. As she licked up the trail of syrup, his gaze found hers, his lips curving around her nipple.

*Gloating again.* She straightened, and Kip, forced to move or take a collarbone to the nose, straightened as well.

He licked chocolate from his lips, and Victoria's gut clenched. She wanted nothing more than to lie down again and let him continue driving her crazy while he ate dessert.

But that wasn't quite true. There was one thing she wanted more, and that was to remove the smug expression he wore. Get more of those uncontrolled curses. More of whatever had made him lose control before the room service delivery.

"On your back," she commanded. She took the dish of chocolate from him. "It's my turn."

He raised an eyebrow. "I thought you said you didn't have a sweet tooth."

She shrugged. "I'm coming around."

His gaze flicked down to the dish of chocolate and then back to her breasts. With an obvious look of regret, he lowered himself to the bed.

That was a reward in and of itself.

Feeling confident, she swung one leg over him and straddled his hips. Immediately, she fell in love with this position. His erection lay heavily before her on his belly, and she scooted up until her sex cradled its root.

He hissed in a breath, and his hands gripped her thighs, his fingertips digging in. She stirred the chocolate slowly and just as slowly looked over his beautiful body again, enjoying all the planes and valleys from this angle of power as though it were the first time she'd seen them.

*Where to start.* There was a buffet's worth of options before her. And to think she usually skipped dessert.

Well, she didn't necessarily want to move from his hips, so that narrowed the options down to what she could reach currently.

*What's good for the goose …*

Biting her lip to keep from smiling wickedly, she dribbled chocolate over his left nipple. Her aim was not as good as his, but she was a quick learner.

His breathing rasped through the quiet room, but it hitched into silence as she began to lean over. When she licked the chocolate away with a flat tongue, her hair rustled with the rush of air he exhaled.

His hands, still gripping her thighs, picked up the slightest tremor, but then they were moving. Tugging her thong aside.

As his fingertips brushed through her folds, she reflexively bit down on his nipple. In a panic, she loosened her bite, but his heavy groan gave her pause.

"Do it again." His voice was raspy. Rushed.

She did it again, and as she did, he thrust two fingers inside her. She cried out against his skin.

"Don't stop," he said.

She had been about to beg the same thing. Forcing all of her functioning brain cells to unite, she dribbled another spoonful of chocolate across his chest and began kissing and licking it up. At the same time, he continued to thrust his fingers and then circle his thumb over her clitoris.

She ground into his fingers as she forewent the spoon entirely and scooped chocolate up in her hand and smeared a great, long handprint down the center of his torso.

The next flick of his thumb over her clit was so good, she forgot entirely about eating the chocolate. Instead, she bonelessly flopped down on him. The fingers that were not currently driving her wild gripped her bottom. Her breasts slid through the chocolate, and the friction of his chest against hers made her pant his name.

They were definitely going to need a shower. She could not care less.

She managed to clumsily pass off the dish of chocolate to her other hand and blindly grope around until she found the side table. It was a miracle it stayed where she sat it down and did not crash to the floor.

He thrust his fingers again. "Chocolate's safe?"

She nodded.

In the next second, he flipped them. She blinked up at him as he knelt between her sprawled thighs and began rolling down his considerable length a condom that magically appeared. Her smeared handprint flexed and rolled in the lamplight, and she stared, transfixed until he blocked her view by spreading atop her.

Jerking her thong to the side, he pushed inside of her with one, long, teeth-clattering thrust.

Immediately, he stilled. "*Shit.*" He framed her face with his hands, his gaze frantically searching hers. "That was hard." He cursed beneath his breath again. "Are you okay?"

She raised her knees and canted her hips. The chocolate heated between them, and their skin slicked together. "Do it again." She reached up and bit his shoulder as hard as she could. "And don't stop."

An inhuman noise ripped from him. He rose up on his knees, clenched one of her knees to his ribs. With his free hand, he shoved her thong aside even more and found her clit with his thumb.

And then he thrust. And thrust. And—*fucking, yes*—thrust. The headboard clattered against the wall, and the dish of chocolate surrendered to gravity at last and crashed to the floor.

She barely noticed as something coiled tightly inside her. When it released, she would fly apart.

Her silk-clad thighs slid across his backside as she crossed her ankles and held on to him as best she could as he took her on an unimaginable ride.

"Victoria, honey." He gritted his teeth, and his thrusts stuttered for a second. "Come, please. *Please.*"

As though her body knew its master, an orgasm obediently ripped through her. She arched her back and screamed as her hands found her own breasts, smearing chocolate all over them.

*"Fuck."* He stilled, and her eyes flew open to watch as he threw his head back and called out her name to the ceiling. The next moment, his hips were jerking against her thighs. His chest billowed, and he gripped her thighs so hard her stockings ripped.

The way he jerked against her, the image of him in his pleasure—she tripped right over into another orgasm. As her sex clenched and fluttered along his dick, his eyes opened and he stared down at her in what could only be described as awe.

His own orgasm over, he leaned down over her and pressed the sweetest kiss to her lips as he rocked gently between her thighs, drawing her pleasure out longer than she had thought possible.

As it finally subsided, their gazes connected.

She had never felt more raw, more open in her life. His gaze searched hers for a moment, and then, cupping her jaw, he kissed her again. Slowly and leisurely, he licked into her mouth. He lowered himself until their bellies brushed, their chests met.

Tentatively, she wrapped her arms around him, her fingertips skating across his shoulders and down his back. He shuddered in her arms; laid one final, chaste kiss on her lips; and pressed his forehead to hers.

He exhaled a shaky breath. "Wow."

She brushed the tip of her nose against his. "No kidding."

He lifted his head and looked around them. Victoria did the same, and her eyes widened. The white linens were covered in chocolate. Beside the bed, the lake of syrup sank slowly into the carpet.

"We made a mess," he said, his voice filled with pride.

She felt a smile nudging her lips. "Worth it."

He looked back at her, and worry flitted behind his eyes. "I'm really glad you think so." Grasping the condom, he withdrew from her and sighed. "I've never … I don't want to be that rough with you." He wasn't meeting her gaze. "I'm so—"

She placed her fingertips over his lips, and after several moments, he finally looked at her. She smiled. "Shower with me?"

He blinked, but then his lips tipped up at one corner. "Yes, ma'am."

She could get used to him calling her that.

As he pushed off from her and held his hand out with an expression that bordered on bashful, the anticipation she felt for the coming eighteen days nearly overwhelmed her.

She placed her fingers in his, and he pulled her from the bed. Naked and holding hands, they padded barefoot into the bathroom where, by the time the mirror had fogged over with steam, Kip was already rolling on another condom and showing her the many uses of removable showerheads.

She'd never be able to look at one the same way again. And that was just fine by her.

# Chapter Nine

For at least the twentieth time that morning, Kip found himself reliving the previous night with Victoria in vivid, filthy detail.

Impossibly, each and every time they were together was better than the last. And, last night had been so good.

Victoria was the best lover he'd ever had. Him. A gigolo who made a living via sex.

Beside him, his phone chirped. He flicked a glance its way and caught sight of a calendar notification.

New client: Natalie. Tomorrow night at 9:00. Requests: tuxedo, sweet lovemaking, no cuddling after.

The grin he'd been sporting faded slowly.

*Shit.*

Unlocking his phone, he double-checked the dates, and, yep, sure enough, tonight was the last night of his and Victoria's contract together.

The breakfast he'd finished an hour or so ago began to rise and lodged in an apple-sized lump somewhere between his heart and his throat. Pushing up from the couch, he headed toward the bathroom cabinet. Maybe he had a bottle of antacids in there somewhere.

Seconds later, he slammed the medicine cabinet closed, the mirrored front rattling for long moments after.

No antacids. He wandered into the kitchen, rubbing a closed fist over that insistent lump, and peered into the fridge. Fuck, he didn't even have milk. He'd just have to muscle through.

So, tonight was his last night with Victoria. Big deal. This arrangement had always had an expiration date.

*I'm going to miss her.*

He slammed the fridge door closed even harder than he had the medicine cabinet and scrubbed a hand over his face.

He peeked through his fingers over at the clock on his microwave and saw that it was approaching lunchtime. Right this second, Victoria was at work. Was she thinking about the mere hours they had left together?

*Nah.* Not Victoria. She would be working hard. Last night, she'd told him about a new idea she'd had for a line of commercials, her eyes lighting from within as they'd tossed ideas back and forth.

*She'll forget to eat again.* She was always doing that, which meant he was always prepared with some sort of meal when they met up each night. Often, it was the only meal she ate during the day.

He drummed his fingers on the countertop, and immediately, he recognized it as an affectation of Victoria's. An adorable one. Whenever she was deep in thought, those fingers were tapping against something.

*Seeing her only once more is not going to be enough.*

He grabbed his car keys and was out the door before his smarter side could convince him otherwise. He was probably making a gigantic mistake.

*But maybe I'm not.*

He drove off the beaten path to pick up something from Sally's. Just enough for one person. He wouldn't be eating with her in the middle of the day. That would just be crazy, and also a complete violation of their soon-to-be-over agreement to keep things impersonal.

As he parked in the Precision Media Services's lot, he felt a renewed trickle of unease. This could definitely be a mistake.

He glanced at the take-out bag resting in the passenger seat. The greasy meal he'd gotten for Victoria had already tainted his

Mercedes in a way it was never going to recover from, no matter how many air fresheners he loaded on his rearview mirror. Even that thought made the corners of his lips tug up.

*What the actual fuck is wrong with me?*

Okay. Maybe he could just drop the meal off at a front desk and get out here without seeing her. Maybe he should just throw it the hell away in the nearest trashcan.

*She's hungry. You know this.*

With a groan, he got out of the car. The damn bag was in his hand as he walked past two trashcans and through the front door.

Like a lighthouse in a storm, a gleaming front desk sat immediately inside the door with a rather competent looking man sitting behind it. Kip's footsteps were a little less heavy as he made a beeline that direction.

*In and out.*

He cleared his throat, and the man's head snapped up, a welcoming smile on his lips. Kip dove right in, not waiting for any sort of greeting. "I have lunch for Victoria H-Hastings." He stuttered over her last name as his mind had to scramble through his memory to even remember it.

They'd done unmentionable things together while naked; he had trouble remembering her last name.

*What am I doing here again?*

Kip lifted the grease-saturated bag onto the front desk and rocked back on his heels, ready to flee as soon as he got the slightest indication he could.

"Certainly, sir." The man behind the desk pointed to the left. "Take the elevators up to the top floor and turn right."

Kip rubbed the back of his neck. "You don't just … ah … deliver it to her?"

The man's smile faltered for a moment but was quickly back in place. He spread his hands wide. "Not a delivery man."

"Right." Kip grabbed the bag. He looked around but saw no trashcans in the lobby, which seemed like poor building planning to him. So, look like an idiot and walk back out with Victoria's lunch after having announced that it was hers, or suck it up and deliver it. Get in and out.

"Top floor?"

The man nodded. "And to the right."

Kip offered a grimace of a smile. *Bring Victoria lunch at work.* This was the worst idea he'd had in recent memory. She was going to laugh him right back to his car.

Which wouldn't matter to him at all. Not even a little. Because his emotions were not in any way embroiled in this business arrangement. And tomorrow he had a new client. Onward and upward.

He straightened his shoulders and jabbed at the elevator button several times. As he walked aboard the elevator, someone called out, "Hold the elevator!"

Kip eyed the buttons on the control panel, and his gaze lingered longingly on the one that would close the doors. With a heavy sigh, he pressed the other one instead.

A middle-aged man in an impeccable three-piece suit stepped into the elevator, his mouth open as if to say thanks. Until he seemed to recognize Kip as someone who did not belong in the building. His mouth snapped shut, and the elevator ride up to the top floor was filled with oppressive silence and several quick, sidelong glances at the bag Kip held in his fisted hand.

As they neared the top and it became apparent that Kip and the well-dressed stranger would be getting off on the same floor, those sidelong glances became a little more penetrating.

Kip gritted his teeth and stared resolutely at the changing numbers as they neared the end of this uncomfortable ride.

The elevator ding was one of the most welcome sounds he had ever heard. Both men burst from the doors as though the elevator's fine, patterned carpet were on fire. Kip was objective enough to recognize how ridiculous they must look, and his lips twitched.

His faint smile disappeared, however, as he looked around. Which direction had the greeter said to go? His brow furrowed.

"Can I help you find someone?"

The voice came from his elbow, and though Kip hadn't heard it in all the time they'd been enclosed, he immediately knew whom it belonged to. And the helpful question contained just enough judgment to push him over the line into being officially *done*.

He turned to the man, who apparently still subscribed to the red power-tie theory, and lifted his chin. "I have lunch for Ms. Hastings."

The other man's gaze grew shrewd, and he looked Kip over again without hiding his obvious perusal. "Are you a deliveryman?"

Now he understood why the greeter in the lobby had been so incensed. This was an insult if Kip had ever heard one. He glanced down at the button-down shirt and jeans he wore. Sure, he wasn't wearing a three-piece suit, but he didn't look so bad. Kip opened his mouth. What he was going to say, he didn't know, but—

"Kip?"

Both men turned in the direction of that gorgeous, husky voice. There Victoria stood at the mouth of a hallway, a notepad clutched in one hand. Her other hand was pressed against the wall. Her eyebrows were drawn together, and her eyes were clearly confused as to what she was seeing.

"Kip, is it?" the man in the suit asked. He glanced at his watch as though Kip had already wasted too much of his time. "Sorry for the less-than-warm greeting. We have some highly confidential projects underway, you understand."

Victoria walked toward them as though in a daze. She stopped several feet away and frowned. "What are you doing here?"

*Making a mistake. Obviously.* Kip shifted his weight and could find nothing to say. Was it too bad an idea to shove the take-out bag her direction and then sprint away?

"Why don't you introduce us, Victoria?"

She snapped to attention; it was obvious this was her boss.

That she had reasons to request his discretion became suddenly clear. As did the fact that he was an ass. There was nothing he could say or do to salvage this. He'd fucked things up but good. Without a word, Kip extended the bag toward Victoria. "I'm just a friend."

Her lips pursed, and as she accepted the bag from Sally's, her boss turned his attention toward her. With her boss's back turned, Kip mouthed, *I'm sorry*.

A muscle ticked in her jaw in response.

"A friend?" her boss asked.

"Yes." Kip cleared his throat. "One who is currently late." He glanced down at his own wristwatch but knew it lacked the power of when her boss had done it. "I have to run."

And with his boss and her boss staring at Kip's back, he retreated, cursing internally with every step.

*Fucking had to see her one extra time.* Brilliant. Now, he'd managed to ensure he'd never see her again whatsoever.

He stepped into the elevator still waiting for him as though it knew it would be needed, and he couldn't resist drinking her in as the doors closed. Because he was certainly fired after such a stunt.

Maybe, if he were lucky, she would fire him in person.

*If I am lucky?* The elevator doors closed, and Kip covered his eyes with one hand as he sank back to the lobby. God, he had it bad. What kind of gigolo found himself hoping his current client would fire him face to face just so he could see her one more time?

*One who has crossed all the lines.*

# Chapter Ten

"Victoria?"

The question in her boss's face was undeniable. The heavy scent of salt and grease floated up from the bag she held in her hands, and her stomach heaved a rumble of appreciation.

What the hell had Kip been doing at Precision Media? It was, in fact, the question Mr. Kincaid was asking her without putting it in words.

She was currently the subject of a background check that, were it very thorough, would open her and Precision Media Services up to a rejection neither of them could afford. But, both she and Mr. Kincaid seemed to know any further questions would be entirely inappropriate for a boss and his employee.

Thank God.

She took a step back. "I'll be eating lunch in my office."

He looked as though he wanted to protest, but he didn't.

By the time she closed herself in her office, her blood felt like it was percolating. She dropped the Sally's bag on her desk, where it emitted a *plop*. He could have ruined everything!

In a way, he had ruined everything. Because there was certainly no way she could meet with him tonight, their last night together, now.

And their working relationship had come to mean a great deal to her. More than almost anything in her life, as a matter of fact. Only her desire to achieve her goal of representing a major casino meant anything more to her. Every time today she'd remembered tonight was "it," her mind had blanked, sweat popping out on her upper lip, her hands turning clammy.

The only thing that had gotten her through the day was knowing she'd get to see him one last time tonight.

She sank down in her chair. *And he'd ruined it!*

She snatched the bag and peered inside. She groaned. Her favorite. Naturally.

Damn, he made her happy. Really, truly happy. And now she had to tell him he was fired, and the very thought almost made her appetite vanish entirely.

But the smell of the greasy cheesesteak sandwich would not be ignored. She took her first sloppy bite, leaning far over the paper bag so it could catch the pieces of meat that fell from the sandwich.

She chewed and couldn't prevent a moan. "Goddamn it, Kip."

*I don't want to fire him.* In the dim recesses of her mind, a thought echoed back: *Maybe you don't have to.*

Kip had introduced himself as a friend. It was false, obviously. They had no relationship between them other than that of employer and employee. But perhaps she could convince Mr. Kincaid that Kip was a friend. If he even asked again.

She and Kip were officially over after tonight. He would not show up at Precision Media in the future. He'd have to be an idiot to do that, and he certainly wasn't. And Mr. Kincaid viewed matters of a personal nature with trepidation.

This could be okay.

But that wasn't going to keep her from giving Kip a piece of her mind.

She took another bite of her sandwich, and, with her other hand, reached for her cell. With one clunky thumb, she typed out a message to meet in their room at the same time tonight.

Something fluttered in her belly. It was not excitement at seeing Kip after nearly convincing herself that she never would again.

No, it was not that.

The rest of the day crawled by, and though Victoria had heaps of work to do on the new idea she and Kip had developed last night, she found herself unable to concentrate on the simplest of tasks. She checked the clock at embarrassingly short intervals.

Kip never responded to her text.

For the first time since the incident, as she had taken to calling it in her mind, she reflected on her own behavior during the confrontation with Kip and Mr. Kincaid.

She hadn't behaved very well.

Yes, sometimes her introversive tendencies and also the—she mentally flinched—pain of her past made her a reluctant member of society. But at least she could always say that she was kind.

Well, she couldn't say that anymore, now, could she?

She drummed her fingers against her desk and fought to swallow past the lump in her throat. Kip had done something undeniably sweet bringing her a meal from her favorite restaurant—one he, incidentally, hated with a passion.

He'd braved the notoriously sassy greeter in the lobby and the cold reception of Mr. Kincaid and the even more dismissive reception she herself had given him. What's more, he had done so with more manners and composure than any of them had managed to scrape together.

When she thought about the stiff set of his shoulders as he'd walked to the elevator after introducing himself as her friend, she wanted to weep. She wouldn't treat the lowliest intern at Precision Media the way she'd treated Kip today, and the interns didn't do for her what he did.

No one did what Kip did.

She swallowed. *No one makes me feel the way Kip does.*

Physically. Yes, just physically.

At last, it was an acceptable time to leave the office. Well, not acceptable by Victoria's normal standards, but a person with an understanding of work hours would not find her departure unacceptable.

What she was going to do in the hotel room for the three hours until the time Kip would arrive, she didn't know. But she couldn't stand to stay in her office for one minute longer, which was odd, as her office was one of the few places of solace Victoria had. Along with her home and …

Victoria started. She had mentally added the hotel room at the Desert Oasis to the list of places she felt truly at peace.

*Ridiculous.*

She'd only known the hotel room—and the man in it, for that matter—for just over two weeks. It had taken her a year to be at home in her office. Around that length for her house as well.

It seemed as though every traffic light in Sin City was determined to switch to red as she headed over to the hotel. As her frustration mounted, she had to remind herself nearly every minute that she was still two and a half hours early. That there was no reason to rush.

In fact, Kip might not come at all, and that would be only what she deserved.

The clerk behind the desk gave her a knowing nod as she strolled to the elevators. By the time she got to the right floor, she was finding it hard to catch a breath that was deep enough to keep her from feeling slightly dizzy.

She couldn't figure this out—why she was so affected. It defied explanation. Her fingers trembled as she inserted the key card. She pushed the door inward, stepped over the threshold, and froze.

Kip was already spinning around from where he stood by the window. Their gazes connected at once.

For the first time that day, everything within her calmed immediately beneath the balm of that blue gaze.

They took simultaneous steps toward each other. "I'm sorry." The words left their lips at the same time. In the next moment, they met in the center of the room. As the door clicked closed behind her, his arms encircled her.

She took a deep breath—the first of many. Her heart rate began to slow, and she had not even realized it was racing prior to stepping into this room and seeing him here waiting for her.

"I never should have come to your work." His words fluttered the hair at the crown of her head.

She shook her head, brushing her face against his shirt. "I shouldn't have treated you that way."

He pulled back. "What do you mean?" He looked truly confused. "I messed up here."

Her gaze searched his, and she realized he believed everything he said. That he deserved to be treated the way she had treated him. As though he were nobody. As though she were better than him. She frowned. "I … think I'm getting mad again."

He nodded. "Say whatever you need to say."

"Kip!" She shoved him away with two hands against his chest. "No one is allowed to treat you the way you were treated today." She poked him in the chest. "Not me. Not anybody."

He rubbed at the spot she had poked. "Um …"

"I could see it in your face! You thought you didn't deserve to be there, and it makes me sick."

"Wait." He tilted he head. "You're not mad at me?"

She huffed and crossed her arms, feeling suddenly cold. "I'm mad at me."

He shook his head. "Well, I'm not."

"You should be."

"Victoria, you stressed to me that we have to be discreet. I showed up at your work."

"Well, yes, but—"

"That was dumb. Really, really dumb." He stepped toward her again. "You set boundaries, and I crossed them."

Well, when he put it that way. She shook her head again. “That still doesn’t excuse—”

He placed a finger over her lips. “I don’t think either of us is going to win this argument.”

She felt her brows pull together. “We’re arguing?”

He breathed a laugh. “Yes. Can’t you tell?”

“I …” She swallowed. “I don’t argue.” Not for years. Jeremy had been so very sick. She’d voluntarily walked on eggshells to make life as smooth as possible for him. Did she like her life there at the end of his? No. Did that mean she could confide that in Jeremy, or for that matter, anyone?

*Definitely no.*

He cocked one eyebrow. “Let’s just admit we both made a mistake—though, it pains me to compromise.”

She considered him for a moment, and then smiled and dipped a nod. “All right then.” Her gaze connected with his and held. “I’m sorry.”

His lips quirked. He raised a hand, then brushed his fingers along her cheek until he cupped her there with his palm. “I’m sorry.”

She licked her lips. “Did we just make up?”

A gentle shake of his head. “Not yet.”

And then he kissed her.

He’d moved so quickly, she hadn’t seen it coming, but her lips were ready for him in a way that could only be described as instinctual, parting beneath his. Her tongue darted out, meeting his in the middle, anticipating the move that had become second nature to them in the last two and a half weeks.

Funny, she’d been married to Jeremy for years, and they’d never perfected the physical ebb and flow that she and Kip had down almost immediately.

*What does that mean?*

Nothing! It meant nothing.

As he kissed her deeper, wrapping his arms around her and pulling her in to his firm chest, her heart began to pound. Oddly, though, it wasn't from being close to Kip, which never failed to get her body's most passionate response.

It was from the way her mind was racing.

If Kip were to be believed, they'd had their first argument. They were making up.

It did not feel like a working relationship right now. And that was when the truth hit her: it hadn't ever felt like a working relationship.

At least not for her. Had it for him? God, maybe it was a good thing this was ending tonight.

Kip bit her bottom lip and licked away the sting. "You're thinking again."

Guilty. She sighed and pulled back. Questions rioted within her, and as she stared up at him, she knew one of those questions was going to burst out, God help them both. Her lips parted; she braced.

"What made you become a gigolo?"

She wanted to slap a hand over her mouth as Kip's eyes widened, but damn it, she wanted to know the answer too badly to take it back. And it was a way less embarrassing question than some of the others that had been brewing in her panic. His hands fell from her body, and she nearly groaned.

He puffed a breath, his cheeks billowing for a second. "An accident."

She tilted her head. "Wait. An … accident made you a gigolo? Like, 'Oops, I'm accidentally fucking you for money'?"

When his head tipped back and a full-bodied laugh poured out of him, she grew even more confused. He lowered his head and looked at her again. "Actually, yeah. Almost exactly like that. Minus the fucking."

"Okay, you've lost me."

He gave her a half smile and held out his hand. "Come here."

His hand was warm and comforting as he tugged her across the hotel room, climbed up on the bed, and pulled her onto the mattress after him. He settled them against the headboard and then arranged her across his chest, wrapping his arms around her.

Cuddling her.

They'd never done this before. Though after sex there had been a few tender kisses—more so lately, as a matter of fact—they'd never simply lain around and held each other.

She willed her body to stiffen. To pull away. But she knew it was a lost cause as soon as she had the thought. Her body—traitor that it was—loved this. She nestled her cheek against his shoulder, and her arm drifted across his stomach. She could feel his heartbeat against the inside of her forearm, steady and strong.

"I don't tell people this story." His words rumbled through her.

She closed her eyes. "I'm sorry. I didn't mean to—"

"I was seventeen."

"*What*?" She nearly screeched the word, and as she tried to shoot upright, his arms tightened around her.

"Calm down." He sounded amused. "It's not a sad story."

She gritted her teeth. "That's a pretty damn sad beginning."

"She was seventeen, too."

She paused. "Oh." Her brow furrowed. "Where the fuck does a seventeen-year-old girl get that kind of money?"

He shook her shoulder. "Are you going to let me tell the story?"

Her lips twitched. She raised her arm and waved him on.

"Thank you." He shifted beneath her, and she felt his chin press into the top of her head. "I took her to prom our junior year of high school." He breathed a laugh. "Had a great time, actually. She was hilarious and this amazing dancer."

*This isn't a sad story?* There was a shade of nostalgia in his voice that led her to believe otherwise.

He blew out a breath. "Anyway, I took her home, and I was all excited the way high school boys get, wondering if I was going to get laid or not. We pulled up in front of her house, she turned toward me, and I'm like *this is it*! Thought she was going to kiss me or suggest we climb into the back seat. But"—his shoulder shifted beneath her in a shrug—"she paid me instead."

"What?" Victoria rolled so she was lying across him more and could prop her chin on a hand she spread over his heart. "Why?"

He was looking up at the ceiling, and he frowned. "I can guess, but I don't know for sure. She wasn't … *popular* is a word you could use. I was, though that was entirely an accident, too, and I didn't care about it at all." He looked down at her, and his lips curved on one side. "I know enough about how women think of themselves now to guess that she probably thought she wasn't pretty enough. She was … a little bigger? I thought she was gorgeous," he added quickly. "God, she had this rack I just wanted to bury my face in."

Victoria felt a sudden and irrational surge of jealousy toward this nameless, faceless seventeen-year-old with a great rack.

"I'd thought I had a real date to prom, right up until she slipped fifty bucks into my hand."

She felt a pang in her heart. *Not a sad story, my ass.*

"Anyway, she told some friends, and next thing I knew, I was going out a lot. But I didn't sleep with anyone for money until college." He shifted a bit beneath her. If she thought it possible for Kip to be embarrassed, she would have sworn that he was feeling the emotion currently. His heart rate had steadily increased, and he seemed to be avoiding meeting her gaze. "I didn't want to lose my virginity on the job, and it wasn't until after high school that I actually had some real dates, so …" He shrugged.

She felt her jaw drop. She couldn't imagine anyone more sexually experienced than Kip, and it sounded like he was a late bloomer. "How old were you when you—" She snapped her mouth shut.

He answered her anyway. "Nineteen." He gave her a long look, and his lips quirked. "I made up for lost time quickly, though."

He would have had to. "Wait." She had a sudden feeling of dread. "How old are you now?"

"I'm twenty-three. Why?"

She stiffened. "Twenty—" *Shit*! "Kip!" She jerked upright, and though he tried to hold her close, she persisted until he reluctantly let her rise.

"What's wrong?" He looked sincerely confused.

She threw her hands up in the air. "I'm thirty-three! A full decade older than you." Oh, God, she'd robbed the cradle. Contributed to the delinquency of a—Well, Kip was pretty delinquent already, and he definitely wasn't a minor. But, still. "Oh, this is terrible."

"You can't be serious." He sat up, too. "Honey, an age difference doesn't matter."

Her shoulders sagged. Yeah, she was making a big deal out of their ages, when, just like he said, it shouldn't blip on her radar. For one, she was never going to see him again in a few hours. But most important, she was paying him for sex; he was accommodating her. What did age have to do with it? She felt like an idiot.

"What did I say?"

The soft question made her open eyes she hadn't realized she'd closed. She frowned.

"I said something that made you sad." He leaned in and traced a finger down the curve of her mouth. "I saw it right here."

"Was probably just a wrinkle."

He chuckled but grew serious again quickly. "Tell me why you got sad."

"I'm not sad."

He tilted his head. "Victoria."

She huffed. "I'm not excited about being ten years older than my lover, okay?"

"Did you know I was ten years younger before I told you?"

She swallowed. "No."

“It’s when one of us acts so immature that everyone knows without being told that it’s an issue.” He scooted closer to her. “And even then, that’s private and nobody’s fucking business. That’s what I meant when I said age doesn’t matter. I didn’t mean it didn’t matter because you’re paying me.”

His words were nearly a physical blow. She’d been that obvious? “I didn’t think you did.”

He gripped her chin between thumb and crooked finger and raised her face toward his. “Liar.”

She’d kept her eyes lowered, but now her gaze jerked up and locked with his. If his eyes had contained anything other than amusement, she’d have been pissed, but as she could see the laugh he was holding back bouncing in his blue eyes, she had no choice but to bat his hand away with a smile. “Fine.”

“You’re admitting I’m right.”

“Nope.”

“Victoria.”

The way he said her name was grave. “What?”

“When we’re together, I’m not thinking about the money.”

She longed to say something back. Something pithy and quick. Something that didn’t feel as heavy as his words made her feel, because—

“I’m not thinking about the money either.”

He snagged her hand and gave it a little tug. Reluctantly, her gaze met his. He grinned. “I certainly hope you’re not, or I’m not doing it right.”

This got a small, answering smile. God, he was so good at this. At everything, really. He seemed at ease every second they were together, no matter what they were doing, which was something she had to work very hard at. And even with all that work, she was not always successful.

“Why are you doing this?”

His fingers tensed against hers, but only for a second.

Though he could have, Kip didn't pretend to have misunderstood her question. Didn't take the easy way out. "I want the money."

He drove a Mercedes. He always dressed well, even when delivering greasy diner food. He didn't appear to need the money. "But, why?"

His shoulders straightened; his chin lifted. "I'm going to start my own business."

Now he was speaking her language. She leaned forward and tightened her grip on his hand. "In what?"

His eyes darted away from hers. "In whatever I want."

Okay, that was … "What do you want?"

He was silent for a moment. "Hey, I'm kind of hungry. Want to get something to eat?"

Never once in the admittedly short time they'd known each other had Kip dodged her. She absorbed the fact that he had just done so in a second of shock before she tugged on his hand. "Kip—"

"Don't." He finally did look at her again, but his blue eyes were pleading. "Please?"

By some sort of accident, she had managed to find Kip's weakness. She hadn't thought he possessed one, but here it was, staring her straight in the face through his puppy dog eyes. Her heart ached in a way it never had. She cleared her throat.

"How much money do you need?"

He pressed his lips together. Was he going to answer her at all? She had no right to this line of personal questioning, and she fully expected him to call her on it.

"About twenty thousand more," he said.

At first, she was shocked he'd answered her. But then her mind made the connection, and a different feeling took place in her chest. One she didn't like very much. "Well, then, you're almost there."

He looked down at their hands, which were resting on his knee. "Pretty damn close. Yeah."

She wanted to touch him. Her fingertips ached to stroke his jaw, but he felt so fragile to her right now, she wasn't sure he'd not shatter if she tried it. "But you don't know what you want to do."

It wasn't a question. Kip didn't reply.

"Kip." He looked at her warily. She could understand why. The guy's big life plan … well, "That's not a plan."

He dropped her hand as though she'd scalded him. "I know that," he gritted through tight lips.

"But it easily could be."

He froze in the process of leaving the bed, and the thundercloud that had crossed his expression froze, too. He blinked. "What?"

"Let's think about this for a second." Her heart started racing, as it always did when she perched on the edge of some excellent work. "Twenty thousand alone is pretty decent, but I'm guessing you have more saved?"

After a slight hesitation, he jerked a nod.

"That's really good." She tapped her teeth with her fingers. "*Really* good. You have a great starting budget for advertising." She tilted her head as she looked at him and narrowed her eyes. "You're incredibly charming, but most businessmen are. No, your real talent is finding what someone wants and giving it to them. That's rare."

He looked as though she'd hit him in the face with a board.

"Would you want to still work with women, or do you want to branch out?"

She waited for him to answer, but he simply stared at her. "Ummm," he said.

"Because there are lots of options for either. Especially in Vegas. And especially since you're not a one-trick pony. Let's see—funny, well-educated, experienced, personable, good taste. God, you could do anything, really." She lurched from the bed and started toward her laptop bag. "I have some ideas we could look over, see if anything strikes your fancy." She reached into her bag and found her thumb drive. When she spun around again, however, she collided with a wall.

A warm, muscled wall she'd grown increasingly familiar with over the last weeks. She removed her face from his pecs and wrinkled her stinging nose. She blinked up at him and stilled.

The way he was looking at her right now—Kip had a lot of expressions, but she'd never seen this one: a mixture of hungry and sated all at once.

Her lips parted. "Are you o—"

His mouth cut off her words. With a growl, he thrust his tongue into her mouth and jerked her body against his.

She gasped; he used the opportunity to deepen the kiss. His fingers were in her hair, and she felt her bun loosening. Wisps of her careful hairdo began to brush her collarbone and shoulders while he gripped her head and tilted it so he could kiss her deeper still.

With a moan, she dropped the thumb drive, not caring where it landed, and fisted both hands in Kip's shirt. He ground his erection into her belly, and she ground right back against him, whimpers slipping out of the small breaks in their kiss.

He began walking forward, pressing her back. Her ass met the wall, and he kept coming, crowding into her and pushing his front against hers so that she could feel every tense inch of him. His kiss grew wild, and she could barely hold on as he nipped and licked with a passion he hadn't shown her until this moment.

And then his kiss was gone. She was gasping, staring at the space that had held him moments before. Dizzy with lust, she gazed down to find Kip on his knees. He tugged frantically at her fly, and, so on board with the direction this was going, Victoria canted her hips, bringing her ass away from the wall so that he could tug her pants down.

He hissed shortly at the sight of her red, high-cut lace panties, but, unlike his usual routine, he tugged them down, too, with barely a glance.

She kicked one leg out of her pants, and he dragged her panties down far enough to get the same leg out of them as well, but just as she was getting ready to remove her other leg, he grasped her bare knee and directed it over his shoulder.

Her calf trailed down his back, and his muscles rippled against it as he leaned in and nipped at her bare mound.

She jerked; he gripped her thigh with sprawled fingers and squeezed until she couldn't move again. Then he licked, his tongue darting between the lips of her sex and finding her clit in a firm undulation that left her gasping all over again.

"*Kip*."

He shoved closer, his shoulders forcing her captured leg wide and opening her completely to him. To his mouth. He scraped his teeth against her lips, and she shuddered. Her fingers found his hair and held on tight, drawing him closer.

The hand that held her leg steady against his shoulder disappeared, and she flexed her thigh to keep it right where she needed it, whimpering a little in distress at the thought that maybe he was stopping. Getting ready to rise to his feet.

Instead, he spread her lips with both thumbs and licked her with the flat of his tongue from her opening to her clit, where his tongue then darted a circle. And another.

"Shit." Her hands jerked in his hair, and she knew she had to be hurting him, but he never stopped. He closed his lips over her clitoris and one of his broad fingers eased inside her.

Victoria's hips arced, and she threw her head back as pleasure radiated from what he was doing to her, shooting throughout her entire body. Another finger eased in next to the first, and Kip began drawing on her clit with firm sucks from his lips. All the while, he flicked that tongue over her again and again.

In seconds, it was over. Her body stiffened. A moan turned into a cry, and she arched back, grinding her clit against his face as he thrust his fingers inside her once, twice, countless times.

He groaned against her skin, and as her orgasm began to abate, she grew overly sensitive. Every lash of his tongue now felt like ten. She tugged at his hair, but he didn't move. She moaned again, this time with a little distress at the edges of the sound. He said nothing but shook his head against her, picking up the pace of his licks so that Victoria couldn't gain a breath.

She sucked in air that didn't seem to find its way to her lungs, and Kip wedged a third finger inside of her. He began lapping at her clit—quick, broad licks that seemed to cover every inch of her.

And then, his pinky stretched. Brushed against her back entrance. Just that—a brush and nothing more.

But it was everything.

The orgasm stormed through her, taking her by surprise and sweeping aside all thought, all inhibition until she was shoving against his hand as he penetrated her. Grinding desperately against him as she keened toward the ceiling. She screamed his name, and he nipped at her clit in response, sending shooting sparks through the powerful waves of her orgasm.

Almost as though he knew her body better than she, he slowed the thrusts of his fingers, the flicks of his tongue, as those waves began to abate until they were gently rolling through her, just barely kissing the shores of her nerve endings.

She shook so badly from the pleasure she wasn't sure she could stand if he moved. But he didn't. Instead, he gently withdrew his fingers from her, brushing the tips over flesh swollen from what he'd done to her. He pressed a soft, tender kiss to her clit; then, with a sigh, he palmed her thigh again, and, holding it tightly, rested his cheek against its soft inner skin.

He glanced up at her, rubbing his day's growth of beard against her leg. His lips were swollen and shiny, and as she watched, he licked them clean, making something clench low in her belly all over again, as though her body had anything more to give to this man.

Who was she kidding? It'd give Kip whatever he wanted.

She braced her hands on the wall behind her and tried to catch her thundering heart so she could slow it down. When she had enough breath, she dared to speak.

"Your turn."

# Chapter Eleven

Kip was so hard inside his pants it was difficult to think of anything else. But he was somehow managing it. To a fantastic degree.

As the soft, warm skin of her inner thigh cradled his cheek, he stared up at her and the way her lips were still pursed after her statement, and all he could do was think.

Think about all the things she'd said before he'd flown across the room and pinned her against the wall. Think about the way his heart ached even more than his cock at present, and *that* was really saying something.

Think about the way she'd tasted as he'd licked her to orgasm twice. The way he didn't feel life was so hopeless and scary because she believed in him.

She believed in him.

His fingers tightened on her thigh.

"Kip?" She pulled one shaky hand from the wall and ran her fingers through his hair. He turned into the touch, forcing himself to keep his eyes open when they fluttered. "Don't you want me to—?"

He kissed her fingers and shook his head. If she touched him right now, his going off like a rocket was the least embarrassing thing that could happen. The back of his throat felt full of words that—surely not—had the shape of …

He jerked to his feet, dropping her leg without ceremony. Victoria swayed and grappled at the wall, and, feeling like a heel, Kip gripped her shoulders and steadied her.

And again, those words crowded the back of his mouth.

*I love you.*

He clenched his teeth. *You are an ass!* He schooled himself to keep his grip light when his fingers wanted to tighten.

Two and a half weeks.

Two and a half weeks he'd known this woman. He'd never said those words before, and he was certainly not going to say them now, hours away from telling her good-bye.

*But I feel them.* God, how he felt them. No one had ever, in his life, said the kind of things to him that Victoria had minutes ago. No one had thought he was worth them.

Surely that was all that was going on here. Like a dog who had been whipped for years finding kindness for the first time. That was it. He didn't—he swallowed—love Victoria.

That was impossible. He wasn't that stupid.

But the way that the light bounced off her loosened hair and reflected in her enormous, brown eyes … maybe he wanted to be that stupid.

Fuck, she was so beautiful he hurt from it. Suddenly, he didn't have to fight his hands to keep them gentle. He wanted to touch her softly. Reverently. He brushed his thumbs across her collarbone, and she relaxed into the simple touch, smiling with a gentle curve of her lips. Technically, he could call it a night right now. He'd pleasured her; she was satisfied. He could shake her hand and walk away. Their agreement would be over.

*No. Need more time.*

He swallowed. "Will you show me your ideas?"

Her gentle smile took on a bit more brilliance. "Of course. But …"

Kip braced himself.

"I think we should go get something to eat while we do it," she finished.

He was so relieved that she hadn't blown him off that it took a moment for him to understand what she'd said. "Go out?"

She laughed. "Yeah. Like a restaurant?"

He felt his brow furrow. "With me?"

Her smile fell, and a flash of sadness passed through her vivid eyes. "With you. We're friends, right? Friends eat out together."

"But what if—"

"Friends eat out together," she said more firmly this time. "And if we don't leave this room soon, I can guarantee we won't get any work done."

Huh. Sure enough, he was lazily thrusting his erection against her soft belly. With a surprised laugh, he stilled his hips. "Point taken."

"Grab my laptop bag." She bent down and pushed her leg back through her panties and trousers. "And do you see the thumb drive anywhere? I dropped it."

He spotted it on the lush carpet almost right away. He stooped to scoop it up and then held it to the light, trying to decipher what was written on the label. Hopes and Dreams.

"You're going to show me what's on this?"

She plucked it from his hand. "Well, not everything." She winked. "Just the good stuff."

Her hopes and dreams meeting his hopes and dreams. Why did the thought of that not send him running from the room? Why did it make him want to hold her? Kiss her hair?

*I love you.*

He pressed his lips together to capture some sort of noise. Victoria was finger combing her hair—which he'd managed to mess up spectacularly, he was proud to say—and trying to subdue it into a ponytail.

He'd never seen her wear a ponytail before. She pulled it high, wisps of hair falling down and framing her face. He swallowed hard.

Fuck, she was beautiful.

"Ready to go?" she asked.

"Where?"

She laughed. "To eat, Kip."

Oh, yeah. He quickly located her laptop bag on the chair to his right and snatched it for her. "Sure." *Please don't regret this.*

Nothing bad was going to happen. Right? A simple meal with a woman he was having very unprofessional feelings for who thought he could do stuff. Real, meaningful stuff.

"Lead the way, honey."

As they walked toward the elevators, he ached to hold her hand like they were fifteen. Luckily, when they got on the elevator, someone was already on it, so he couldn't make a bigger ass out of himself by kissing the curve of her neck all the way to the lobby.

Damn, he had it bad.

*Get it together!*

They walked off the elevator together, and Kip, figuring they would simply eat in the hotel restaurant, stared at it in confusion as Victoria walked past it and continued through the revolving glass doors to the curb. He had to hoof it to catch up.

"Where are we going?"

She grinned up at him. "There's a great falafel place just down the block."

His brows shot up. He knew immediately which place she was talking about, and calling it a restaurant was optimistic. So was hole in the wall. "You do realize you're a big girl and can eat big girl food, right?"

She wrinkled her nose, and his heart stuttered. "Falafels are big girl food. Snob."

Well. That was a first. "Snob?"

"You heard me. Talking bad about my taste," she muttered. "I'm with *you*, I might add."

That desire to hold her hand became nigh impossible to bank. "Well, your taste there is faultless."

She stopped in front of the "restaurant." "I think so, too."

*God.* If his heart kept panging like this, he was going to have to see a doctor. It couldn't be normal. He tugged open the door, and she slipped past him into the dingy, greasy interior. Spices filled the air, and, despite everything, his stomach growled.

She turned twinkling eyes his way. "Heard that."

He smirked. "I've already eaten, thank you."

How she still managed to blush each time he teased her, he'd never know, but he was more than addicted to the pink tinge that covered her cheeks, throat, and—he knew—breasts. He flicked a glance at her chest and forced his gaze back up.

The woman had some fantastic breasts. He couldn't wait to become reacquainted with them.

She marched straight up to the counter, and the employee behind it smiled with recognition.

*Victoria Hastings, patron saint of dives.* His cheeks stung as he fought back a smile.

She looked at him over her shoulder, and even that drove lust straight to his groin. The curve of her neck, the tender skin under her jaw—she was speaking.

He'd heard nothing. "What was that?"

She gave him the look that deserved. "Want me to order for you?"

Considering he had no idea what a falafel even was? "Yep."

Victoria leaned over the counter and began ordering, but, again, Kip heard nothing, because the position she was in forced that gorgeous ass out, straining the seat of her pants. He knew her lacy lingerie was so thin it wouldn't leave a panty line, but that didn't keep him from tracing with his gaze the rise of her ass where he knew the lace cut over silky skin.

She spun suddenly and caught him ogling her—again.

He could safely say he'd never had this problem with another client. Hell, with another woman, period and full stop.

She walked his way, and the sway of her hips, the way she licked lips that were still swollen from his kiss—even that made the front of his pants tight. She stepped into his personal space, rose to her tiptoes, and whispered in his ear, "We'll get no work done if you keep that up."

And then, she bit his ear, and he made the most horrifying, desperate noise that echoed loudly in the empty restaurant.

She giggled as she fell back on her heels. "I cannot wait to get you alone again."

He reached for her hand. "Don't fight the feeling." He was more than ready to tug her out of the restaurant and race back to their room.

She tugged back. "This is important." He looked at her, and her soft brown eyes sucked him in. "You're important."

"Fuck."

She raised her eyebrows. He cleared his throat and nodded toward a booth in the corner. "That work for you?"

She narrowed her eyes, and for a moment, he worried she wasn't going to let him get away without an explanation. Finally, she nodded and started walking toward the table herself.

*Phew.*

She scooted across the cracked, plastic seat and patted the space right next to her.

"Gladly." He took it, pressing his hip against hers under the guise of leaning over to get her laptop out of its bag. He handed it to her silently and watched as she fired it up and plugged in the Hopes and Dreams thumb drive the way a dealer over on the Strip dealt blackjack.

Something about the thumb drive stuck in his chest; he couldn't pinpoint why.

When a window automatically popped up on her screen, he couldn't help reading the file names over her shoulder as she scrolled through them. Hopefully, he wasn't far overstepping his bounds. "Ricchezza?" He pointed at the screen. It was the file name at the top, and, unlike all the other file names, was all caps. "If your hopes and dreams are The Ricchezza, honey, I'll take you right now."

His heart thawed of all tension when she laughed instead of swatting him and telling him to mind his own business. "No, not *going* there. It's—" She stopped and looked at him. He could see her throat work around a harsh swallow. "Do you … want to see?"

Even an idiot would be able to tell that what she'd just offered to do was not normal for her. *Tread lightly*. "Very much."

She double-clicked on the file, and a new window bloomed. She began chattering immediately, jabbing her finger against the laptop screen as she pointed out item after item in what was an absolutely brilliant marketing campaign for the famous casino.

Kip had majored in marketing—it was the only way his parents would pay for college—and he had his mother's natural knack for it. Had grown up cutting his teeth on it.

Victoria's plan was unlike any he'd ever seen. A mix of relying on The Ricchezza's already sterling ethos while taking the casino in new directions. It was going to put her on the map in the marketing industry.

The whole reason he was a gigolo was because his parents had cut him off when he refused to go into advertising like his mother expected of him. But the very thought of being like his mother turned Kip's stomach. If he'd known advertising could be like this? He'd have jumped into the profession with both feet.

As her excited explanations began to taper off, her anxious stare burned his profile. He flicked a quick glance her way; she was chewing on her bottom lip.

He turned bodily toward her. "Victoria." He ducked his head to make sure their gazes were locked and level. "This is incredible."

She blushed again, but for the first time since they'd met, it was for a reason other than sex.

"They're going to snap this up like crazy." He snapped his fingers for effect. "So, what's next?"

She tilted her head. "Next?"

"Yeah. After they hire you. What else is on the thumb drive? Dream house? Dream vacation?"

She puckered her lips as though the words he'd uttered had no meaning in the English language.

And, suddenly, the reason he'd been wary about her Hopes and Dreams thumb drive surfaced. *She has no hopes and dreams.*

This—a marketing plan—would not satisfy the woman he was getting to know. Victoria not only deserved the world, but she also wanted it. It was obvious in everything she did.

It was, apparently, not obvious to her.

He saw the exact moment she realized she didn't have a life blueprint beyond winning The Ricchezza. Her jaw clenched, then something resembling panic flashed through her eyes.

Instinctually, he reached for her hand. Stroked his thumb across her delicate knuckles. "Victoria—"

"Ready to see some business ideas?" she blurted. She jerked her hand from his and began clicking on files.

"Um." His empty hand hovered awkwardly between them, and he quickly placed it on the tabletop. "Yeah, sure."

When she started blinking rapidly at the screen and her mouse hand shook a few times, Kip thought his heart was going to fight its way up and out of his throat to get to her. He gently laid his hand over hers, quelling the shaking the only way he knew how. He gathered all his courage. "You help me figure out mine, I help you figure out yours?"

The words were too quiet, too timid; what if she hadn't been able to hear them and he'd have to find the courage to say them again? Her hand was so warm, so slight beneath his. A fierce protectiveness he'd never felt before surged through him.

After an interminable silence, she slowly turned her head toward his. Her eyes seemed impossibly bigger and sparkled like gems with—he realized with a gut wrench—unshed tears. She stared at him for several seconds. Finally, "Okay."

His chest puffed so big, one would have thought she'd just handed him an Olympic medal for best move in an awkward situation. "Okay," he repeated softly.

There was a loud *clack*, and both Kip and Victoria jumped. His gaze swiveled around to find an equally startled restaurant employee staring at them. "Um," she said, "your order is ready."

Sure enough, there was a tray loaded with food. The source of the *clack* apparently. "Thank you." When he looked back up, the employee was glancing back and forth between Kip and Victoria, her brown eyes lighting up and a smile beginning to dawn. *Great.* So, he looked as besotted as he felt. *Just great.*

"Enjoy," she said in a lascivious tone before turning and walking back to the counter.

After an interminable, awkward moment when they just sat silently next to each other staring at their food, she reached forward and snagged a falafel. Kip automatically followed suit, but when the spicy, flavorful bite he took registered with his brain, his eyes widened. "This is good!"

She laughed around a bite of food, and, just like that, all the awkwardness vanished. "I told you."

He narrowed his eyes and looked at her sideways. "Now I'm actually going to have to eat something from Sally's, aren't I?"

She raised her brows. "You mean, you haven't yet?"

"No! What am I, crazy?"

"Yes." She grinned at him.

He grinned back, and the urge to touch her nearly strangled him in its intensity. He reached out and tucked a strand of hair behind her ear.

She tilted her head into the simple touch and leaned forward, almost as though she wanted him to kiss her.

And, God, he wanted that, too.

Her eyes were wide when he met her in the middle, and they paused, their lips just a breath apart. His fingertips still on her cheek, he brushed down that soft skin until he could slip a finger under her chin and tilt it up. Then he brushed his lips over hers.

It was a simple, chaste kiss. The most innocent he'd ever given. It rocked him with lust. He forced himself to back up, to lower his hand, because if he didn't, he was going to push her into the back of the booth and press his body into hers, their meal entirely forgotten.

She stared up at him with foggy eyes, and he was struck anew by both her beauty and the urge to smile. *Not bad for a simple kiss.* He had to distract them both. "How about those business ideas, hmm?"

She blinked once. Twice. "Oh, yes." She looked down at the keyboard, and after a moment, straightened. "Right, business ideas."

This time, there was no stopping his grin. Victoria clicked on some files, took a bite of her falafel, and then launched into business, slipping seamlessly from one type of woman to another in the span of a hot second.

A very hot second.

As Kip scooted in close—for the sole purpose of seeing the screen clearly, of course—he became even more undeniably aroused by the brain this woman possessed. These ideas for his future business were stunning in both their intelligence and possibility of success. Personal concierge, social media coordinator, graphic design, event planner.

His own brain started firing, and suddenly, his fuzzy future looked a lot clearer. Not only didn't he hate any of these potentials, but he could also see himself loving any one of them. Could see the life he'd always dreamed of coming into focus.

Things really started clicking, though, when he fired out advertising ideas of his own for some of these businesses. Cross promotions he could work out with limo services in the area. An interactive website. He was shocked when, more than once, she said, "Oh, that's *good*!" And then her fingers would fly across the keyboard, and there his idea was, nestled in among hers.

She wouldn't do that just to humor him, would she? She had to think his advertising ideas were really good. Right?

*Oh, God.* He was shocked by how much that meant to him. By how much this work fulfilled him.

*Maybe I made a mistake rejecting advertising?*

He shoved the thought away, not ready for it to ruin what was turning out to be one of his favorite evenings ever.

They finished their meal but continued to sit companionably hip to hip and go through everything Victoria could put in front of him, bandying advertising ideas back and forth. Kip hadn't been aware of the passing time until lights began flicking off in the kitchen behind stainless steel swinging doors.

He glanced at the clock in the bottom right corner of the laptop; it was nearly eleven.

"Is it really that late?" Victoria asked.

"Yeah, I think so." Fuck. The night was almost over. He stretched, and the muscles in his shoulders and neck twinged, making him wince. If he hurt there from bending over the laptop …

He reached out and kneaded the base of her neck, and her head dropped forward. She moaned, and Kip swallowed hard. "Need a backrub?" *Please say yes. Please say yes.*

"God, yes."

*Yes!* Kip nodded toward the laptop. "Save your thoughts, honey."

Victoria clicked the mouse several times and then closed the laptop. Taking that as his cue, he gathered her computer and slipped it into the bag she always carried. Then, he scooted from the booth and held out a hand to her.

Almost shyly, she placed her fingers in his. As they began walking toward the door of the restaurant, the same woman who had delivered their food hours ago hustled their way, a key ring jostling in her hand. With a sly smile, she unlocked the door for them—they'd been so engrossed in each other they'd missed her locking it, apparently—and then held the door open as they entered the night. "Have a good evening, you two," she called.

*Oh, I plan on it.* Kip drew her to his side amid the clatter of the door being locked once more behind them. He dropped her hand and wrapped his arm around her shoulders instead. She fit perfectly in the notch of his side, and as they walked toward the hotel, the lights from the Strip several miles away cast the sky in an eerie and magical glow.

"I love those lights," she sighed.

*I love you.* Kip sighed, resigned. He was going to have to swallow those words at a continual pace tonight, it seemed, until he came to his senses.

He didn't notice the desk clerk or anyone else—if they even passed others—as they made their way to their room. All he could think about was that he was finally going to be able to put his hands on her again.

*Finally.* As though they hadn't been nearly naked with his fingers inside her just hours ago. Doing something he'd never allowed himself to do with another client. Something that, with anyone other than Victoria, would have been risky, what with the act's inherent intimacy that could surpass intercourse in the right situation.

He definitely didn't suffer from any feelings of regret.

He closed the bedroom door behind them and flipped on the light switch right beside it. She turned, and her greedy gaze roved all over him, stopping at—what he knew now after many nights—were her favorites: the hollow of his throat, his chest, his thighs. Then, back up, and up, and up her gaze went again until it met his.

Slowly, she raised her hand and pulled her ponytail free. Thick, honey hair tumbled down around her shoulders, whispering against the soft skin covering her clavicle—one of his favorite spots. One he wanted to be licking and biting right this second.

He pushed away from the door, and her pupils expanded, gobbling up that sweet, rich brown as he strode toward her. Needing the control it would buy him, he would undress himself, first. He knew the moment she was naked, he was going to have the fight of his life ahead of him to keep calm and make sure this was slow. Sweet.

Because, for some reason, he wanted slow and sweet more than he wanted anything in the world right now.

When he popped the button beneath his throat, Victoria's lips parted. Her gaze darted to his fingers and held, then followed them as they made their way down the rest of his buttons. He half expected her to brush his hands away and do it herself—something she'd done each time they'd been together, as though she couldn't wait to see him. But, against all his expectations, she simply watched raptly.

Maybe it was the same for her, the barely contained control. Maybe she was as conflicted as he was, and this was one way she was holding on to her restraint. He could hope at least. And he really liked the idea of her seething beneath the surface, needing him more than she knew how to handle.

He shrugged the shirt from his shoulders. Her doe-eyed gaze followed it to the floor, and by the time it rose again, his fingers were working at his belt buckle.

The slow, steady rise and fall of her breasts began to accelerate. His fingers stuttered at his zipper, his focus too embroiled with what he knew lay beneath her blouse. He rallied and shucked his pants, his erection springing free.

A soft noise slipped through her parted lips, and he heard it with an echoing clench in his gut. His erection bobbed; her throat did as well.

And, still, she didn't touch him with anything other than her gaze.

He stepped toward her, and the crown of his cock brushed against the soft satin of her blouse, momentarily distracting him with a shock of soft pleasure. He wanted to thrust there, feel her warm skin beneath cool, silky fabric. Instead, he raised hands that trembled slightly, making slow, clumsy work of her small, pearl buttons.

He was growing obsessed with her buttons. Each blouse she wore had them. Tiny, delicate. Hiding such wicked feminine decadence. For the rest of his life, Kip knew he would picture these buttons when he thought about the most arousing sights he'd ever seen. He untucked her blouse, then smoothed his palms over her shoulders, pushing the blouse down.

He'd seen her red lace thong before dinner; he had *not* seen the matching red lace bra. It was so sheer, he could see her mouthwatering, rose-colored nipples beneath. They pressed into the lace, straining it to miraculous lengths. The bra pushed her full breasts up to nearly the spilling point.

With a harsh swallow, he unhooked the clasp between her breasts, freeing them to his gaze.

"Oh, Christ." His erection kicked again, this time brushing against the soft skin of her belly instead of her blouse. It left a trail of pre-cum behind, the tip of him sliding against her. He muttered her name—how many times, he wasn't sure, but hopefully it was just once—and then cupped her breasts, savoring the soft scrape of her nipples against his palms.

His control shuddered.

He needed it too desperately to concede it now. He allowed himself only one gentle squeeze before he dropped his hands to her pants along with his gaze. If he looked at her breasts any longer, he was a goner.

Her stomach dipped as his fingertips brushed against it, and her breath fanned across his chest, quick and erratic.

He knelt and pulled her pants and underwear with him, skimming his fingers down the fronts of her thighs as he did so until he got to her knees. Once there, he stroked the sensitive back of her knee, raising first one and then the other as he took off the last of her clothes.

Then, he stood once more, allowing himself the unmitigated pleasure of looking at Victoria Hastings completely bare to him. He held stock still as his gaze hungrily devoured her, but not even that stillness lasted long. His hand found his cock, and without his permission, gave a stroke that curled his toes into the carpet.

He stopped himself, pulling his hand away and extending it toward her. With no sound other than her harsh breathing, Victoria again placed her hand in his. He swallowed hard as he led her over to the full-length mirror in the dressing area.

God, he wanted to look at her, to look his fill. But with her completely naked, with him completely naked. With the closeness he was feeling. With three enormous words clawing to get out of him.

He needed a little distance.

He stopped them beside the vanity. Her back was to the mirror, and she gazed up at him with complete and utter trust—a gift he knew she hadn't bestowed on any man in a long time. It touched him deeply. With gentle hands, he grasped her shoulders and turned her until she faced the mirror as well.

Their gazes connected through the glass, and, just like he'd hoped, the intensity was less. Still more powerful than he'd ever felt with someone else, but manageable. If he took her here, in front of this mirror, he could have his soft and sweet. Would be able to give that to her instead of the frantic fucking they'd had every night since they'd met.

As he held her gaze, he threaded his hands through the space between her arms and hips, skimming his fingers across that delicate nip of her waist and to her stomach. Like a dream, she leaned back against him, capturing his throbbing erection in the small of her back and resting her head against his chest.

He skated his fingers up to her delicate ribs, counting each one he passed, and—finally—he cupped her breasts once more. This time, he couldn't stop from groaning. Gave himself up to it, his hips thrusting, grinding his dick against her.

She moaned, too, arching her back into the touch, pressing herself further into his palms. He squeezed, and she moaned again. When he pinched her nipples, she cried out, and for a moment, he worried he'd been the same rough Kip he'd always been with her. Worried, even, that he'd hurt her. But her head rocked back and forth against his chest. She raised her own hands and covered his with them, and then she forced him to pinch her again, more firmly this time.

He bit out a curse. "Victoria." He plumped her breasts. Pinched and teased her nipples. Within seconds, she was squirming against him. He relinquished one of her breasts. Wrapping his arm around her ribs in an embrace, he palmed her right breast with his left hand. With his now free hand, he circled her navel and then ventured down to her sex. Her arousal slicked his fingers, and, with a groan, he pressed a kiss to her shoulder.

"Please, Kip," she moaned.

*Yes. Anything you ask.*

With his foot, he snagged the small, upholstered bench from the vanity. It traveled across the floor with a very unsuave screech. Once he had it where he wanted it, he leaned down. Grasping her behind the knee, he raised her leg until she planted her foot on the bench.

In the mirror, paradise opened for him. “Fuck.” He used his fingers to spread her farther. *So soft and pink. So mine.*

Just for tonight.

She moaned again and chased his touch with a small, frantic bucking of her hips. With a soft nip to the back of her neck, Kip eased his hips back. Bending his knees, he grasped his erection, directed it just where he wanted it, and …

Her eyes widened as he slid into her. That brown gaze of hers narrowed in the mirror, and she watched as her body took every inch of him into her. “Kip.” His name was desperate and barely audible.

The soft, silken clasp of her sex around his wrenched a groan from him, and then he froze. It was too good. Too silken.

“Condom,” he bit out from between tight lips. He couldn’t move, because if he did, he wasn’t going to have the strength to pull out of her.

She shook her head, her hair catching against his rough jaw. “On the pill.” She pulled in a ragged breath. “Clean.”

In an ordinary situation, with all his mental faculties firing, Kip would have pulled out, gotten a condom, and arranged for them to exchange medical histories outside a sexual situation. He would never, never take a woman’s word for it, nor would he expect her to take his. But with Victoria?

“Me, too.” He shook with the effort of holding still as their gazes connected once again in the mirror.

“Then fuck me.” She rocked back against him and he bit back a groan. “God, please fuck me.”

This time, he couldn’t bite back the groan, and when it rumbled up from his chest, it carried surrender. He thrust up into her, and pleasure lit all throughout his body.

He couldn’t remember the last time he’d gone without a condom. It certainly hadn’t been in a professional capacity, which meant it had been years. And whomever it had been with, it dimmed to nothing in comparison to the feel of Victoria around him, squeezing him with her body, drawing him deeper than he'd thought he could go.

He thrust again, and she moaned. Then she brought her arms up, filling his palm with her breast even more, and wrapped them around the back of his neck.

Her fingers played with the hair at the base of his hairline, and she rocked back on him, grinding against him the only way she could in this position.

The sight of all that pink, swollen flesh in the mirror made Kip's balls ache and semen climb his shaft within seconds. He wound his arm over her propped up leg and found her clit with his fingers. Pressing two over it, he circled firmly.

Her sex clenched in response, and he nipped her shoulder, trying desperately to delay the inevitable for minutes, even seconds more. "Victoria," he groaned. He rubbed her clit again. And again. And then, praise God, her sex clenched and began undulating against him.

"Kip!"

He raised his head, catching sight of her rapturous face in the mirror. Her eyes were closed, her lips parted. Her breasts heaved and her stomach quivered. His name left her lips over and over.

He tightened the arm beneath her breasts, needing to be as close to her as possible. He pumped into her once, twice, and then froze as pleasure cascaded through him. He groaned her name as he began to jet inside her.

*I love you.*

Had he said the words out loud? "Oh, God." He forced his head up from where his forehead was pressed into her shoulder, scanning Victoria's face for any signs of horror.

Her eyes were still closed. Her upthrust breasts still bobbed against his arm. She moaned softly as her orgasm abated.

She showed no signs of hearing the words that had been screaming inside his skull as he'd emptied himself inside her.

Her knee buckled, and she slouched against him. Because he held her around the ribs, all he had to do to keep her from slinking to the ground was tighten his hold. His sweat-slicked chest slid across her back, and when he peered at her closer in the mirror, he could see a fine sheen of perspiration on her as well.

That pulled him from his funk with a small smile. *Job well done.*

Though, he frowned again, it had definitely not felt like a job. Hell, it hadn't felt like a job since night one. And now, it was over.

To shut out his thoughts, he slowly pulled from the warm clench of her sex, unable to stop from groaning as he did so. There was one more thing he could do to delay the inevitable. One last, desperate bid for a few more minutes together. She gasped as he scooped her up in his arms and walked the few feet to the massive glass shower. Switching her weight to one arm, he reached in and started the spray, turning the dial three quarters of the way to hot.

It was too soon for the water to have heated up, but he nevertheless carried Victoria inside the shower, turning his back to the water so the ice-cold hit him instead of her. It was a much-needed slap of reality, and as goose bumps crawled all over his body and his nipples grew so hard they could cut diamonds, he gritted his teeth and welcomed it.

Victoria sighed and nestled her cheek against his chest. Despite the cold water, he felt warmed from the inside out.

When the water finally did warm up, Kip turned and sat on the bench, settling her across his thighs. He glanced down at her. She hadn't moved at all since he'd scooped her into his arms. Her eyes were still closed, and now her thick eyelashes were dotted with droplets of spray from the showerhead, lending her an otherworldly quality that made him want to sit and stare at her even more than he normally did. She was so still she might be asleep.

At the thought, he cradled her closer, racked with the most absurd urge to rock her. Instead of that idiocy, he smoothed a palm over her hair, wetting it. Then, he reached over and snagged a bottle of shampoo and set about the unmistakable but unexpected pleasure of washing a woman's hair.

It was a bit awkward with only one truly free hand, but as he scraped his fingertips across her scalp, she moaned deeply and snuggled in against him even closer, so …

Awkward be damned, he'd wash her hair all night long if that's what she wanted.

However, with a sigh, her eyelids fluttered open. He smiled down at her, and when she smiled back, he realized he'd never seen her so utterly relaxed.

*He'd* done that to her. For her.

Something surged in his chest. He sat a little straighter.

"Want me to wash yours, too?"

Her hands on him again? "Yep."

She breathed a laugh, and then she straightened. He immediately regretted his quick agreement if it meant she was leaving his arms. But then, things got even better. She turned toward him, and in a short series of moves, ended up straddling his lap, her knees planted on the tile bench at either side of his hips.

He gulped and immediately shot hard as titanium. She dipped a glance down at the erection now pressing into her inner thigh, and she wore a sly grin.

But she didn't do anything else. Didn't take him inside her, like he was half hoping she would. Didn't make any sort of comment. Instead, she simply began washing his hair.

Despite the fact that this made her breasts bob right in front of his face—his mouth, for God's sake—he didn't wish she'd chosen a different action than what she had.

*The first time a woman's touched me in years without sexual intent.*

Why did that rock him to the core? Why did the simple act of her washing his hair mean almost more to him than the hours he'd spent with this same woman in a knot of sweaty sheets? Why did his hands go to her waist and squeeze, just because he wanted to hold on to her? Feel her beneath his hands without having her body beneath his?

"Your hair is so thick."

He blinked up at her. "What?"

She smirked again, and, swear to God, he wanted to kiss that smirk right off her face. What had she said? "Oh." His hair. "Right." He stroked up her back and liked it so much, he decided to stroke back down, too. So soft and silky. He did it again.

She moved slightly out of the way so the spray could hit his hair and rinse out the shampoo, and her shifted balance did amazing things to her breasts, which he had quickly grown obsessed with.

To keep his hands behaving, he reached for the bar of soap to his left. A perfect excuse to keep touching her, and a purpose that would hopefully keep his hands occupied. He started by soaping up her back, since his hands were already there. Far too soon, that task was accomplished, and he had to move his hands to much more treacherous ground.

As he washed her arms—a safe enough place to start—she sighed again and settled her bottom more firmly against his thighs.

*I could get used to this*. He washed her breasts next, and—damn him—he lingered. There was no way to avoid it. But just as her breathing started to hitch every other breath, and just as her skin started to pinken across the top of her chest, he forced his hands to safer ground, sweeping the soap across her belly and then thighs.

Last, he washed her gently between her legs—something he'd never had to do before with another client, thanks to his fastidious condom use. He braced for regret to course through him. He had violated a personal code of ethics, after all.

But as he washed his semen from Victoria's pink, still-swollen flesh, he felt nothing but a completion that was as terrifying as it was gratifying.

By the time she was clean, she was also nodding, her eyes drifting open and closed in longer blinks. He held her against his chest, quickly rinsed himself off as best he could around her, and then carried her to the bed, snatching two fluffy towels on the way.

Propping her in one arm again, he spread one towel and then gently lowered Victoria to the bed atop it. She immediately spread out like the world's most adorable, naked starfish, and Kip had to bite his lip to keep from chuckling and waking her up. He soaked up the rest of the water dotting her skin with the spare towel, and when she was dry, wrapped it around his waist.

He pulled the covers up to her chin, spread the wet hair he'd washed across her pillow. And then he stepped back.

This was always when he left. Hell, with another client, he'd have been out the door as soon as they'd finished.

He located his clothes with his eyes. They were in the same heap where he'd discarded them before taking Victoria's clothes off her as soon as they got into the hotel room.

Ten steps away at most.

And, look there, his keys were on the table beside the door.

*Get dressed. Get out. Go home.*

Which is why he stared in horrified fascination at his hand as it drew down the covers beside Victoria.

*What are you doing?*

His body answered by sliding between the sheets until he was lying right next to her outstretched hand.

As though his body were a magnet for hers, her hand groped for him, found his shoulder. Next he knew, she was sliding across the bed in her sleep and curling against him.

And he loved the way it felt.

With a final sigh of resignation, Kip removed his towel and dropped it beside the bed. Then he slid his arm beneath her and hauled her close. Her cheek came to rest on the pad of his chest, her arm draped across his ribs, and her knee drew up and over his thighs until the heat of her sex branded his hip.

After only a slight hesitation, he reached over and clicked off the lamp beside them, pitching the hotel room into darkness.

Only then, when he couldn't see himself breaking another of his ironclad rules, did he relax.

Unmatched comfort and peace rolled through him, and as his eyelids grew heavy, his final thought was a promise to himself:

*I'll leave before she wakes up. She'll never have to know I did this, and I can pretend I was never this stupid.*

*I'll leave … before she…*

Sleep took him over.

# Chapter Twelve

The first thought Victoria had as she came to wakefulness was the words she thought she'd heard Kip whisper to her last night as he came.

*I love you.*

It was a damn good fantasy. But a fantasy nonetheless. He'd never say something like that.

Still ... *I love you.* Those words—the ones he'd never said—had sounded divine.

She opened her eyes with a smile on her lips. A smile that quickly faded. *Last night was the last night.*

Oh, damn. That hurt.

"You are a bed hog."

*What?* Her head swiveled to the left—toward the sound of the voice she'd just been fantasizing about.

Kip sat on the edge of the bed, fully clothed—more's the pity—and holding two paper coffee cups.

He was still here? Did that mean something?

*Oh, God, what did it mean?*

Amid the cacophony of her internal thoughts, what came out of her mouth was, "You brought coffee?"

*That's right, Victoria. Go for what matters.*

"And croissants." He nodded to the bag on the side table as he extended a cup her way. "It's black, but I had them leave room at the top and brought back the typical stuff. I didn't know how you take it. I got espresso and milk if you like that better."

His words were quick—almost on the verge of babbling—and it was very un-Kip-like.

She bit back a smile. "I take it black."

He shook his head, biting back his own smile. "Of course you do. I'll remember that."

Like he was ever going to be bringing her coffee in bed again?

Her heart leapt. *Holy fuck, do you* want *him to bring you coffee in bed again*?

While she had to admit that him bringing her coffee every damn day sounded pretty great, she snatched the cup of coffee from his hand with a bit more force than was necessary.

A flicker of doubt lit through his eyes and was gone. But she'd seen it. He was as unsure about what he was doing here the morning after as she was.

With both her hands wrapped around the cup, she glanced back and forth between her coffee cup and the brown pastry bag on the nightstand as her stomach rumbled.

Next she knew, Kip was plucking a flaky croissant from the bag. "Let me," he said softly, extending the pastry toward her lips.

How he managed to make even those two simple words sound like sex personified, she didn't know, but her lady parts perked up immediately.

*This morning-after business does have some potential bonuses.*

Warm croissant touched her lips. She took her first bite, and her eyes slid closed. Somehow, it tasted better than normal.

He exhaled loudly. She opened her eyes to find he wasn't quite looking her way as he set her pastry down on the side table. "Well, I'm going to head out."

"Oh." She picked at the sleeve around her coffee cup. "Okay."

He stared at her hands and jerked a nod. "Okay." Then, he pushed to his feet, rocking a bit when he got there. "Victoria … this has been …" He shoved a hand through his hair. "Pretty incredible," he finished softly.

Her bite of croissant seemed to stick in her throat. She cleared it. "Yeah. It has been." Oh, God. Did her eyes sting?

Then, she straightened. "Oh!" Sliding out of bed, she raced to her laptop bag. "I can't believe I forgot." She balanced her coffee and fished around in her bag until she found the cashier's check she'd had prepared yesterday for the remaining balance of their agreement. This had to be why he'd stayed.

That her stomach sank because he hadn't stayed simply because he wanted to had to be an anomaly.

Spinning around, she thrust the check out between them.

His gaze landed on it, and his eyes widened. "Huh."

*Huh?* What did that mean? That he hadn't remembered the money either? Wait, he had stayed just for this reason. Right?

The check, which she'd thrust toward him perfectly straight, suddenly wilted and bent over her fingers. She cleared her throat and waved it a bit.

Jerking forward, almost as though he'd forgotten he needed to move, he reached out and gently slid the check from her fingers. "Thank you," he said softly, folding the check without looking at it and putting it in his back pocket.

He turned toward the door, then paused. "Oh, yeah." He turned back to her. "I should … kiss you." He raised his eyebrows. "Right?"

How this situation managed to become so awkward was a mystery. "You don't have to."

"No … I want to." Then he leaned down and pressed a soft, espresso kiss to her lips.

*Mmm, delicious.* The awkwardness faded away, but she could feel it perched in the wings, ready to make a reappearance at any moment. To keep it at bay, she wanted to grab his shirt and pull him down for another. Alas, her hands were occupied with scalding coffee, and he was leaving. *Needed* to leave.

He stood straight and shoved a hand through his hair. "I'll … uh … see you later, then." Immediately, he winced. "I mean—"

She nodded. "I know what you mean." She licked her lips. "Take care of yourself, Kip."

He gave her a half smile and then beat feet toward the door as though his loafers were on fire. When he escaped into the hall, closing the door firmly behind him, Victoria didn't know whether to frown or snuggle into the pillows that would probably still smell like him.

So, she opted for a third option: getting her ass out of this hotel for the last time and forcing herself to go home and get ready for work. She'd neglected some of her other clients lately as she'd worked on The Ricchezza campaign. She owed them more than that and was prepared to rectify matters right away.

She was distracted the entire time she went through the motions of getting ready. All the way up to the office building, she nursed the coffee Kip had gotten her, and then, even though it was empty, she carried the cup with her to her office, tracing her fingertip over Kip's name.

*Like a fucking eighth grader with a massive crush.*

"Ugh." She dropped the cup into the trashcan by her desk.

"Hastings!"

Victoria's head jerked up. Mr. Kincaid was standing in the open door of her office, glowering her direction. She flicked a quick glance at the clock on her desk. *Not late.* "Is … everything okay?"

"Conference room, now!" He stalked down the hallway.

It never failed. Whenever someone talked to her like this, she got the same, sick feeling in her chest that she'd gotten since elementary school: the *I'm in trouble* feeling.

She just couldn't think of what she'd done. Was he mad about her other clients' neglect? She was fixing that!

She straightened her blouse, smoothed a hand over her hair, and followed the wake of Mr. Kincaid's palpable wrath to the conference room.

He was already sitting at the head of the table, the phone conference speaker several inches in front of him. He gestured at the chair to his right, and she obediently moved toward it and took a seat. She couldn't get any words out past the lump in her throat.

Mr. Kincaid pressed a button on the speaker. "Go ahead and patch the call through."

"Yes, sir," came the immediate reply.

When the light on the speaker flicked to green, Mr. Kincaid leaned forward. "Good morning. I have Ms. Hastings here with me. What can we do for you?"

The deference in his tone. Her brows shot toward her hairline. He never talked like that unless the client was really …

The sick feeling in her stomach got worse, and then, everything was confirmed.

"Ms. Hastings, this is Mr. Davis's personal secretary."

"Oh," she replied, like an idiot. "Good morning."

"Yes," the secretary said. "I'm sorry to make this so short, but I have to sit in on a conference call in a few moments." She cleared her throat. "You were spotted with a man at a local eatery last night." Victoria's blood stilled. She'd been spotted with Kip last night. Just what had they done in that booth at the restaurant? She racked her brain as the secretary continued with, "Mr. Davis has expressed his—"

She struck out on pure instinct. "Oh, Kip?" For some reason, Victoria laughed. "Yes, I was out with my significant other last night. The local falafel restaurant, right?"

In her peripheral vision, she saw Mr. Kincaid jerk back his head and snap his attention her way.

"That's wonderful!" the secretary said with absolutely no pause beforehand. "That's exactly what we thought, which is why I'm calling."

Wait, the secretary wasn't calling to tell her they knew all about her dirty little secret and she was so, so up shit's creek? "It … is?"

"Mr. Davis," the secretary continued, "would like to invite you and your young man to dine with Mrs. Davis and himself tonight. A get-to-know-you, if you will."

Victoria momentarily closed her eyes. So, they weren't calling to fire her because she'd been spotted with a prostitute. They were calling to invite her and her significant other over for dinner.

A significant other they only thought she had because she'd assumed the worst and opened her big mouth.

*Fuck.*

She blinked her eyes open and cast a wary glance her boss's direction. She'd really done it now.

*Say yes!* Mr. Kincaid mouthed.

*As though I would say anything else.* "Certainly!" Her voice cracked, but she forged on. "What a delightful invitation. Kip and I would be happy to join you."

"Someone will be waiting for you at the main entrance to The Ricchezza to direct you to our private dining." The next second, there was a click, and then the dial tone.

She turned toward Mr. Kincaid reluctantly. *Here comes the barrage of questions.*

He was staring at her as though she were a puzzle he couldn't figure out. "Will these dinner plans be a problem for you to uphold?"

She frowned, but then his meaning became clear. He hadn't believed her when she'd said Kip was her boyfriend. Lord knows what he thought instead, but the fact that it couldn't be worse than the truth stung a bit. "You met Kip yesterday." Her tone was defensive, but she couldn't help herself. "Shook his hand, don't you remember?"

Now Mr. Kincaid frowned. "That … boy you kicked out of the building and refused to introduce me to. He's your boyfriend?"

Victoria winced. "Kip is not a boy." *That's what I decided to argue?* The word vomit continued. "He's a gentleman, and my only hesitation about tonight is introducing him to Mr. Davis. Not the other way around." *What the* fuck *did I just say?*

Mr. Kincaid's eyes widened. "Well, I'll be damned. You definitely sounded like a girlfriend just then."

*I did?* That was … concerning. And there was the word *girlfriend*, dropped like a fucking grenade into their conversation. "This evening will be perfect." She looked him directly in the eye and faked all the confidence she didn't feel. "I won't let you down."

For the first time that morning, Mr. Kincaid's eyes softened. "I suspect you won't."

Victoria nodded, then turned and walked out of the conference room. Her ankles wobbled more than usual in her modest-height heels. By the time she got to her office and closed the door—something she rarely did—more than just her legs were trembling. Her fingers shook as she reached for her phone. The fact that his number was at the top of her most used contacts made the swishing feeling in her stomach grow worse. This was horrible. They'd been so awkward this morning as they ended things, and now she'd gone and done this …

He answered on the first ring. "Victoria?"

The confusion in his voice was glaring. He may be her most used number, but that was attributed entirely to texting. She hadn't called him in the morning since the one after their first night together. "Kip." Her voice cracked. "I fucked up."

There was a pause on his end of the phone. "Honey, I sincerely doubt that."

She covered her eyes with one trembling hand. "I told my boss you're my boyfriend."

"Oh."

"It's worse."

He laughed. "That's not exactly horri—"

She blurted it all out, shoving words from her mouth as though they were rats fleeing a sinking ship. "I told the owner of The

Ricchezza the same thing, and now we're supposed to have dinner with him and his wife tonight, and they think we've been dating for months and that you're my significant other."

Her breaths were billowing in and out, creating a horrible, desperate static over the awkwardly silent line between them. "Oh, God, say something."

"Are you asking me out?"

The amusement in his tone was palpable, and even so, she found it impossible to believe what she was hearing. "Are you … laughing?"

And then he did. Laugh. Hard. "This is you fucking up? Shit, you would lose your mind if I told you about my college years."

Her brow furrowed. "Kip!" But then her lips twitched. "This is serious!" A giggle burbled from her lips, and next she knew, she was laughing just as hard as she was. How in the world had she thought things had turned so awkward between them this morning? She must have been imagining it.

Her laughter rolled around the room. Her office was not soundproof. No doubt everyone at Precision Media thought she'd cracked. She brushed a tear from the corner of her eye and collapsed into her chair with a groan, smoothing a palm over her aching belly. She couldn't remember the last time she'd laughed that hard. "You're not mad?"

"That you didn't tell two powerful men who could destroy whatever business I choose to run with before it starts that I'm a gigolo? Oh, yeah, I'm furious." He chuckled.

*Oh, wow.* He was right. If he wanted to break into the small business world, he wouldn't be able to be honest about his past. Ever. The thought made her swallow hard. She wanted to reach through the phone and touch him.

She clenched her fingers in her lap. "I hate to ask this of you, but—"

"Victoria."

The soft utterance of her name across the line was louder than a crash of lightning.

All the humor had left his voice. She licked suddenly dry lips. "Yes?"

"I … have another client tonight. I'm sor—" He cleared his throat. "I never cancel on clients."

"Oh." Her cheeks filled with heat. And, hello again, awkward. "I shouldn't have assumed. Of course, you would have …"

Another client. Another woman who would be running her fingers through that thick hair of his—the very hair she'd tenderly washed last night. Another woman who would see and kiss and lick every inch of Kip's skin. The dip of his collarbone where he was particularly ticklish. The underside of his dick, right close to the crown, that when she stroked it with the pad of her thumb never failed to make his eyes roll back in his head …

Just this morning he'd been in her bed. Something clawed its way up her throat. It was either going to be a scream, or—

"I'll buy you out," she blurted. "You know. Whatever she's paying"—she waved a hand through the air—"I'll double it."

Silence filled the line.

"Kip?" Her fingers clenched the phone. "You there?"

"Buy me out," he said quickly. "Wow, that's very generous."

She frowned. He didn't sound like he thought it was very generous. Nor did she feel like she was being generous. For only the second time since she'd met him, the money between them felt huge. Like it was the most important player. The only other time that had happened had been this morning. She placed a palm over her woozy stomach. "Did I … say something—"

"No." He sighed. "Honey, of course not."

"Okay. Umm … Me buying you out—Is that something you'd be interested in?"

There was another pause.

*Oh, dear God.* He was going to say no. Her fingers tightened on the phone.

"Victoria, it's not all about the money. I have a professional reputation to uphold."

"Yeah, but not for much longer. Right? With the money I paid you this morning, you're nearly ready to quit." Her voice was tinged with the slightest hint of desperation. She bit her lip to keep from spewing more words. She'd insulted him. Talking about money like this—it just felt … wrong. "I'm sorry. Kip …" She sighed. "I'm sorry. This just means a lot to me, and—"

"I know it does," he said quietly. "I'll do it. Of course, I'll do it. Just text me the details."

Victoria's head reeled back. "Oh!" She practically yelled the word and cringed. "Oh, right." Where she'd expected relief, ice instead filled her veins. "Right."

"See you soon, honey." The endearment lacked the usual warmth.

"See you—" The phone call cut out. "Soon."

Victoria set the phone down gently on her desk, then scooted it away with a nudge of her fingertips. She was going to cry. She could feel it in that tight, suffocating sting behind her eyes and nose.

Her phone rang, and she hated herself for the way she snatched it up. Her shoulders fell when she saw Cassidy's name on the caller ID. "Hello?" She sniffed.

Instead of the psychotic stream of words that usually met her ear when she answered a call from Cassidy, there was nothing.

Victoria pulled the phone from her ear and saw that the call was active. She pressed the phone to her ear again. "Cassidy?"

"Okay, what's wrong?"

Victoria sighed. *Nothing.* The word never made it out of her mouth.

"Okay." There was a clatter from Cassidy's side, almost as though she'd thrown down a game controller. "I'm picking you up for lunch right now."

Victoria exhaled. "It's barely ten o'clock."

"Brunch then."

Victoria leaned forward, propped her elbow on her desk, and pinched the bridge of her nose. "Yes, please."

"On my way."

The feeling that she was going to cry didn't abate for the twenty minutes it took her sister-in-law to get to the office. And it didn't go away as they drove to Sally's, sat in their favorite booth, and ordered enough calories to fill a week.

As she sipped her sweet tea, she eyed the stack of napkins. She could have one in her hand at a moment's notice if any of the tears she was fighting broke free.

Cassidy sat back in the booth. "What'd the gigolo do?"

Victoria's head snapped up. "Do?"

"Do I need to kill him?"

Victoria, against all odds, chuckled. But then she looked closer at her and saw that Cassidy was, for all appearances, serious. "No killing hookers!"

Cassidy narrowed her eyes. "You're no fun."

"He didn't do anything. I promise."

"Uh-huh."

"It's my fault actually."

"The fuck did you just say?" Cassidy leaned forward. "Did he tell you that? I hate when men say that!"

Victoria's lips twitched. "Hear it a lot, do you?"

"As a matter of fact, no. I don't make mistakes with men."

"Oh, yeah. I mean, clearly." God, she loved her sister. The tightness behind Victoria's eyes finally eased. "But this really was my fault."

"We'll see about that." Cassidy paused as their food was delivered, a gigantic greasy burger set in front of each of them. "So tell me what 'you' did." She dropped her air quotes and popped a fry into her mouth.

"I—" *Such an idiot.* "I … fell for him."

Cassidy's mouth dropped open.

"Maybe," Victoria said quickly. "Actually, probably not. No." She stuffed a fry into her mouth.

Cassidy's open mouth slowly closed, and her lips tipped up at the edges. "You slut!"

"*What?*" Victoria looked around the abandoned restaurant. "Shh!"

"You love him!"

*No way!* But what came out of her mouth instead was, "How does that make me a slut?"

"Sluts are always falling in love with one guy and getting married and having babies."

"Oh, my God!" She jabbed a fry Cassidy's direction. "There is no love, and certainly no marriage and babies."

"Really?" Cassidy raised her brows. "There's no love?"

"Cassidy, be realistic. It's been two and a half weeks."

"I'm not hearing a no." She reached toward the ketchup. "And nearly three weeks is plenty of time."

"No. It's actually not."

"Every guy I've fallen in love with, I've fallen in less than two weeks."

Victoria rolled her eyes. "You've never been in love."

"That's beside the point." She poured ketchup on her burger. "The point is, what are you going to do about it?" She took a big, sloppy bite, and, as she chewed, she gazed pointedly at Victoria.

Some of that sadness edged back in. "What is there to do?"

"How 'bout everything?" Cassidy asked around her bite of burger. "The possibilities are endless."

"There's a ten-year age difference between us. He's a gigolo. I only know him because I regularly pay him for sex." Victoria laughed helplessly and spread her hands out. "There's no happy ending here." She'd pointedly left off any mention of Jeremy and the haunting memories that made her flinch from any thought of a relationship.

"Well, not with that attitude, there isn't." There was a glint in Cassidy's eyes. She knew Victoria hadn't mentioned Jeremy on purpose. Knew that Victoria wasn't over everything that had happened by a long shot. And she wasn't going to let her get away with it.

*Go on the offensive.* If there was one thing that would make Cassidy defensive… "Oh, my God." Victoria leaned toward Cassidy. "You're a romantic."

Cassidy's eyes narrowed. "You shut your filthy mouth."

"I can't believe I didn't know this." As Cassidy's cheeks pinkened, it felt good to tease her, even if it was just a ploy.

"You're not fighting fair."

Victoria smiled. "I'm not fighting at all."

"I'm pretty sure you're fighting your feelings."

*Guilty.* "Cassidy … I don't know what to do." The confession itself felt dangerous, but she also knew there was no more danger of either of them mentioning Jeremy's name and bringing up a tidal wave a pain Victoria barely kept at bay on a regular day.

Cassidy chewed for a second, then set her burger down on her plate. "So, don't do anything just yet." She folded her arms on the table. "You're right, two and a half weeks is soon. But it's not impossible. Why don't you just see how this plays out?"

Victoria pressed her fingertip into the tines of the fork beside her plate. "Last night, our agreement ended. Today he had an appointment with another client"

Cassidy wrinkled her nose, and sympathy flitted through her green eyes. "Yeah, that sucks. But appointments can be canceled."

Victoria breathed a laugh. He had canceled it. *After I threw money at him.* Her laugh died a sad death. She forged ahead before

Cassidy could notice. "A romantic and an optimist. It's like I'm meeting you for the first time."

"Well, you keep that shit to yourself. I have a reputation to protect. And, Tori?" Cassidy laid a hand over Victoria's arm and squeezed. "Promise me you'll at least give this a chance."

Victoria shook her head. "Cassidy, I don't see a future for us."

Cassidy shrugged. "I do. Borrow my glasses."

"The rose-colored ones?"

"Fuck you."

# Chapter Thirteen

Kip lifted his chin and watched his fingers in the mirror as they tied a double Windsor knot. The same mirror in which he'd watched his fingers do much more pleasant things last night. A night that felt so much farther away than a mere twenty-four hours.

Kip had several suits in his closet at home—an occupational necessity—but this one was his favorite, so it was the one he brought to the hotel room to change into for dinner with Victoria tonight.

Because he was a fucking idiot who cared more than he should for a mere client. A client who, apparently, saw dollar signs when she thought of him.

He slipped into his suit jacket and jerked the sleeves down until they covered his French cuffs, trying to force himself into a semblance of a good mood before Victoria arrived, because he did have a price, as evidenced by his being here tonight, and she didn't deserve his pissiness and …

He wanted to enjoy tonight with her. Because it was probably going to be the only night he got to be someone Victoria introduced to people she respected instead of—

His phone buzzed again. One of his regulars—the second time she'd called today—and he hovered his finger over the green button on his screen. It hovered there until the call went through to voicemail. A minute later, he got the notification she'd left a second message.

He'd never checked the first.

But if Victoria asked tonight, he'd lie and say he'd set up more clients for after tonight. He'd lie with everything inside of him, because that offer of buying him out had …

*Fuck.* It had destroyed him. And he'd strike back the only way he knew how.

But there was one thing Kip knew for sure. Victoria may not want him in any capacity other than their arrangement, but he was never taking a client again. And not just because he didn't have to, due to starting his business.

Given a couple more hours, he probably would have canceled tonight's new client anyway, even without Victoria's phone call. He'd never be able to do this with anyone else again. Ever. For the first time in his life, he'd had sex that meant something. Completely by accident, but it had happened nonetheless. He didn't want to go back to the meaningless kind again.

The sound of the hotel door opening made him spin around, and he wobbled as he caught sight of Victoria standing limned in the hotel hallway light. She was wearing a black cocktail dress that hugged every single one of his favorite curves. Her hair was down tonight, taking him by surprise. It curled in loose waves around her face and shoulders, leading his gaze to her cleavage, set to breathtaking display by the best fucking dress he'd ever seen. The hem was daringly high on her thighs, and he followed long, long legs down to peep-toe black stilettos.

"Holy hell," he breathed. Everything—all the hurt, confusion, and angst—disappeared at the sight of her, and he was just so damn happy to see her that walking over to take her hands in his became the only thing he cared about.

Her brown eyes looked up at him. "You're so handsome," she whispered.

"I'd better be if I'm going to keep up with this." Kip held their linked hands out to the sides and took unmitigated pleasure in looking her over again. "I'm not going to want you to take this off tonight."

Her lips parted, and her sweet, pink tongue darted out and along her bottom lip. "Sounds promising."

He eyed her red lipstick with regret. "I want to kiss you so bad."

She breathed a laugh. "Don't you dare. It took me forever to get this on right."

He brushed away a stray bit of red with the edge of his thumb, something in his chest getting tight. "Well, you nailed it."

She pulled in a slow breath. "I'm so nervous." He saw her throat work around a swallow. "About dinner. I'm terrible in social situations. Put me in a boardroom and I dominate, but dinner?"

His brain fritzed out for a moment, catching on the word *dominate* and hanging there while possibilities of her demonstrating said dominance danced in his head. Handcuffs would definitely be involved.

He cleared his throat and shoved the images aside. He could revisit them later. "Well, dinner is my specialty. I've got your back" He turned to the side and offered her his arm. "Ready to go?"

She slipped her hand into the crook of his elbow, and he took that as a *yes* even though her lips hadn't moved, her pulse was visibly racing in her throat, and her already huge eyes were larger than normal.

Victoria was rarely composed in bed, but in every other situation—except for the lock-herself-in-the-bathroom incident, of course—she was unflappable. He used her grip on his arm to pull her closer. Their hips bumped into each other as they walked, so instead of walking in a line, they weaved a bit. Kip didn't care. The thought of Victoria in a panic did something to his chest that was tight and uncomfortable, and he was going to do whatever he could to make sure her panic over tonight was unfounded.

When they passed the desk in the lobby, the employees who were used to seeing them daily at this point all seemed to gawk at the couple who rarely left the room at night now strolling across the marble in semi-formal wear.

Victoria ducked even closer to him. “They’re staring.”

He placed a hand over hers in the bend of his arm and squeezed. “Well, yeah. You did look in the mirror before we left, right?”

She sniffed, but that blush he loved swept up her chest and throat to her cheeks.

When they got outside, there was an awkward moment when Kip automatically started leading her to his car, and she did the same toward hers. Their arms jerked a bit, her hand sliding from under his at the pressure of separating bodies.

She looked up at him, her brow furrowed, and he realized what he’d done.

*Damn it.* He’d gone into date mode, even though he hadn’t been on an actual date in recent memory. Even though Victoria had just reminded him of his place in her life earlier today. He’d been ready to escort her to his car and drive her around as though he had the right to.

He cleared his throat and reached for her hand again. “Sorry. Thought your car was over here.”

Her brow smoothed out. “Oh. Nope.” She tugged at his arm. “This way.”

Kip smoothed a hand down the front of his jacket as he followed her lead. When he opened the driver’s side door for her and handed her in, he couldn’t resist pressing a brief kiss to the back of her hand before closing the door for her and making the trek around the trunk to his side of the car. He gripped the handle but paused to draw a deep breath before opening the door and sinking into the buttery, leather seats.

*Head in the game.*

"So, when you told them about our relationship, what specifics did you give?"

Victoria pulled out onto the street, a small line appearing between her eyebrows, making him want to smooth a thumb over it. "Specifics?"

"How we met. How long we've been together."

"Oh." She flicked a quick glance his way as she made a right-hand turn. "No specifics. Just that we've been together for months." She smiled sheepishly. "Plural."

He raised an eyebrow. "We're going to need backstory."

"Shit." She clenched the steering wheel. "We will, won't we? Ah, God, why didn't I think of that?" She looked at the dashboard. "We're going to be there in five minutes."

For someone who was so afraid of potentially awkward situations, she sure got herself into them with a frequency that was … endearing. He reached over and placed a palm on her thigh. When his fingers—without his express permission—flexed into the supple flesh, he forced himself to behave. "Relax, honey." His fingers squeezed again, damn them, and things got uncomfortably tight behind his fly. "Let's say, ten months, okay?" He shifted in his seat, hoping to give his pinched dick some relief. "Respectable without them expecting a ring on your finger. And we met at—"

"Church!" she blurted.

Kip reeled back. "Church?"

"He's a Republican! I don't know!"

He was starting to get a glimpse into how they'd landed in this situation to start with. Under-Pressure-Victoria was a powder keg of bad ideas and loose lips. It was fucking amazing. "Honey, the way I'll be looking at you tonight, there's no way they'll believe we met in a place of worship."

"Kip, be serious. We're almost there."

"The man owns a casino, Victoria. He makes a living off of vice. Just"—he squeezed her thigh again—"relax. You don't have to be perfect."

She muttered something that sounded like *yeah, right*. "How about … charity work?"

He smiled at her. "That's good. Needs to be something we know enough about to carry on conversation, though. How about volunteering at the children's hospital?"

She shook her head. "I don't know anything about that."

He shrugged. "That's okay. I do, so just follow my lead."

She looked at him hard as she pulled up to The Ricchezza. "You know about it?"

Kip straightened his sleeves. "Volunteer twice a month."

As her mouth dropped open, Kip turned and exited the car, trying valiantly to keep the surge of victory at bay. It didn't matter that he'd surprised her. All that mattered was pulling this off.

A casino employee held Victoria's door open for her, and she wobbled as she got to her feet. Every protective instinct Kip had flared to life, and he found himself hustling around the car to grip her elbow.

He pulled her against his chest for just long enough to whisper in her ear, "It will all be okay. I promise, I won't let you fail tonight."

She relaxed against him and exhaled, her warm, sweet breath seeping through the fine fabric of his dress shirt. She straightened, and as her warmth receded, Kip's nipples tightened.

If only his body weren't so responsive to hers. Maybe then he'd have half a hope of getting out of this night entirely intact.

He turned and tucked her hand into the crook of his arm. "Just trust me." He lowered his voice. "Follow my lead and know I'll agree with whatever you say. Even if you blurt out that we met in fucking Sunday school, okay?"

She drew in a shaky breath and nodded. She glanced up at him. "Thank you, Kip.

He smiled softly. "Anything."

Which was an asinine thing to say, as it both didn't fit the context of what she'd said and was completely inappropriate for a working relationship. *Damn*.

One of the many doormen held a glass and gold door for them, and Kip ushered Victoria into a land of opulent chaos. The dinging of slot machines echoed from every corner, and gold dripped from the ceiling. The scent of cheap but copious liquor was stringent enough to sting his nose.

Beside him, Victoria's gaze drank in everything. She stilled completely, and he could practically see the wheels turning in her head as ideas cropped up like dandelions.

She wanted this so badly. She deserved this account. He was going to make sure she got it.

"Ms. Hastings."

They turned to find a woman wearing a floor-length, sequined ball gown smiling in their direction. She was beautiful in the conspicuously perfect way that seemed to negate the very word *beautiful* itself. Every hair was in place; her makeup was flawless. Men stared in stupefied wonder as she walked past them toward Kip and Victoria with a vacantly welcoming expression. If Victoria hadn't stressed Mr. Davis's conservative side, Kip would have pegged this woman as one of his own profession.

He cast a quick glance at Victoria; her brown gaze swept the other woman from perfectly manicured toes to perfectly styled hair, and her tongue darted out and along both lips before disappearing back inside her mouth.

Kip drew his elbow close to his body, pinning Victoria's hand against his ribs to remind her that he was here with her.

The beauty queen stopped right in front of them and smiled dazzlingly. All she was missing were the roses and the wave. "I'm Tiffany. Mr. Davis requested I escort you to the dining room."

*Naturally, your name is Tiffany.* Kip waited a moment for Victoria to say something along the lines of *great.* He waited another moment. Finally, he flicked a glance in her direction. Her face had paled considerably since Tiffany had begun walking their way. Kip leapt into the silence. "That would be great, Miss—?"

Rule number one of keeping your client happy: never call another woman by her first name when you're with the client.

"Oh, just Tiffany." Smile.

*So much for rule number one.* He felt Victoria tense against him. He placed a hand over hers and squeezed her fingers. "Lead the way."

With another of those brilliant smiles, Tiffany turned and began walking through the casino, leaving gaping mouths in her wake.

Automatically, Victoria started to follow her, but when Kip stayed where he was, she tugged to a halt. He brought the fingers he was holding up to his lips and brushed a kiss across them. It worked: Victoria focused on him. He nipped the knuckle of her middle finger, and her pupils flared. "I've got you," he whispered.

Her lips pressed together, and she swallowed hard before jerking a nod.

He tucked her hand back in the crook of his arm and started walking in Tiffany's path. When he dragged his gaze away from Victoria a few seconds later, it was to find Tiffany waiting for them several feet away.

She smiled, but this time, it seemed genuine. "You two are so sweet. I can tell you're in love even from across a casino."

Victoria's fingers jerked. Kip covered them with his hand. "Guilty." He winked.

Victoria's death grip on his biceps relaxed as Tiffany led them through the maze of the casino, designed to keep people and their money inside, until they reached a door marked Private. A few more twists and one elevator ride later, they arrived at what had to be the most luxurious dining hall this side of the Atlantic Ocean.

An enormous chandelier presided over a table dripping with crystal and gold place settings. Fresh, opulent flower arrangements dotted every available surface on and around a table that could easily seat twenty.

Tonight, however, it was only set for four.

Victoria and Kip stood silent in the doorway, and he looked behind him for Tiffany, hoping she would tell them to take a seat, but she was nowhere to be found. She'd slipped away, abandoning them to a situation nearly everyone would find intimidating.

*Which is probably what Davis intends.* Kip straightened his shoulders. "Come on, honey." He led Victoria to the table, and—blessings abound—spotted name cards immediately.

He pulled out the chair for her; she took it without a word. Tension radiated from her, and he briefly pressed a thumb into the muscle between her neck and shoulder, rubbing a circle.

She tipped her head back, and her gaze met his. His fingers stilled against her skin. The tip of her tongue darted out and swept along her top lip—the second time she'd done this very same thing in a short span of time—and he felt an answering clench in his gut. Reaching out, he hooked her chin and brushed his thumb across her bottom lip. Her exhalation of breath wafted over his thumb, tempting it to come closer.

There was a sudden flurry of noise, and as Kip's and Victoria's heads jerked toward it, Mr. Davis and, one would presume, Mrs. Davis entered and bustled toward the table.

Mrs. Davis was already talking as she entered. "… forgive us for being so late—" She halted and blinked at them.

That was when Kip realized he was still gripping Victoria's shoulder with one hand and with the thumb of the other was stroking her lip. With her seated position and upturned face, they looked—

He felt his lips stretching with a smile. *We look wicked.* As though any second, he was preparing to slide something between those lips, be it his thumb or what lay behind his fly, which was a very convenient amount of space away from her mouth.

Victoria's cheeks turned burgundy as she, too, realized the picture they made.

Kip withdrew his hands, but he did so leisurely and with a regret he didn't have to feign.

"Mr. Davis," Victoria said, jerking to her feet. "Thank you so much for inviting us."

The greeting whipped Mrs. Davis into motion again. She grabbed the arm of her husband, who was silently studying Victoria and Kip with a shrewd eye, and pulled him to the table. "We're just so glad for the chance to get to know you more!" she said genuinely.

And with that, he decided he liked Mrs. Davis. She reminded him of his mom—if his mom were even partly human. They were about the same age and both dressed to kill—Mrs. Davis wearing a gorgeous, golden cocktail dress with her graying blond hair pulled back into a chignon—but Mrs. Davis seemed soft and gentle, whereas Kip's mother was all hard edges and business. Much like, actually, Mr. Davis, who took his seat before his wife took hers and tugged at his bowtie as though it were strangling him.

Kip began to circle the table and hold out Mrs. Davis's chair for her in light of her husband's lack of manners, but one of the tuxedoed employees, who had magically appeared at the same time as the Davises, got there almost too quickly for the human eye to track.

Mrs. Davis took her seat. "Thank you, George."

Kip sat and snagged Victoria's hand from its nervous fiddling with the countless pieces of silverware next to her plate. He squeezed her fingers and rested their joined hands on the tablecloth between their place settings.

Mr. Davis's eyes narrowed in on their hands for a moment, but then his attention returned to their faces. "I'm glad that you both could make it on such short notice."

Kip waited a second for Victoria to speak, but when she didn't, he launched into the void again. "We had plans together tonight anyway. A change in venue, especially"—he grinned at Mrs. Davis—"such a favorable one, was not a problem."

He nudged Victoria's foot with his own. She jumped. "Yes," she squeaked. "Not a problem." Then she straightened and seemed to grab hold of her nerves, making Kip's chest swell. "Kip knows work is a priority." She turned to him and looked at him so adoringly that he felt it down to his toes.

*Doesn't feel like an act.* He winked at Victoria while internally schooling his stomach to stop rioting.

"Well, aren't you two just the cutest," Mrs. Davis said. Her warm gaze was on them both, and she was wearing a soft smile.

She was already in the bag.

Mr. Davis's face was impressively devoid of any indication of what he was thinking or feeling.

*A poker player.* Made sense, considering the profession the man had gone into.

Kip happened to be an excellent poker player. In fact … "Mr. Davis." He pulled the napkin from his plate and laid it across his lap. "Tell me, were you as nervous during The Ricchezza's televised poker tournament last week as I was?" Kip reached around the glass of white wine to snag the red. "I still think that man was bluffing."

Mr. Davis straightened, the first flicker of life crossing his face. "A poker player, are you?" His voice carried the faintest hint of Southern accent and was followed by a hearty chuckle. "Yes, I was. And they cleaned up the cards before I could check, but"—he leaned forward—"I think he was bluffing, too."

They were going to be okay. Victoria must have felt it also, because the death grip she had on his hand loosened.

Kip held his wine up in a salute to the man. "Wish I could have played. It's been too long since I've had a chance to play a challenging opponent, if I'm being honest."

"Well!" Mr. Davis edged his chair back. "We can fix that tonight!"

Mrs. Davis placed a hand over her husband's. "Not until after dinner, dear."

The old man's smile deflated so quickly that, if they'd been in a different circumstance, Kip would have been unable to contain a chuckle. "Yes, of course." Mr. Davis scooted back up to the table and gave a nod toward something or someone behind Kip.

As though the move had been previously orchestrated, several servers entered the room, bearing platters of food in a scene straight out of *Downton Abbey*.

He could feel Victoria tensing up next to him again as a servant, dressed far better than any of the people seated at the table, began serving her cuts of meat.

So he draped his arm across the back of her chair and brushed her shoulder with his fingertips. He could feel Mr. Davis's gaze, but it wasn't as piercing as it had been before they'd connected over cards. "Mr. Davis, Victoria has been working so hard on your campaign." Kip squeezed her shoulder. "Even I'm excited about her ideas, they're so creative." He leaned over and bumped Victoria's shoulder with his. "I know tonight's not about business," he said, "but I just had to throw that out there." He shrugged. "I'm proud of her."

And it was true. More than that, though, he was struck by a deep yearning in his gut that he was doing this *with* her. Not here as her date and social buffer. He wanted to be sharing these ideas of hers. Putting his input to use. For the first time in his life, he was chomping at the bit to do advertising.

Victoria's shoulders shifted beneath his arm, and he was dying to look back at her, but he had to focus. Tonight, his job was all about Mr. and Mrs. Davis, no matter how much he wished it was about just him and Victoria and a bed. Or a wall. Or a mirror ...

• • •

*I'm proud of her.*

Kip and the Davises continued to chat, but all Victoria heard was that phrase over and over in her head. Whenever Kip glanced at her, she nodded, and the conversation continued to flow.

Kip was proud of her.

She couldn't remember ever being more affected by a group of words in her life. Not even *I love you*, which she'd heard plenty from Jeremy, even as their marriage has started to disintegrate.

Though—she glanced at Kip—she suspected hearing those words from Kip's lips might give her a coronary.

*Don't think about that!*

He looked at her again, and when she nodded this time, his lips twitched and he gave the slightest shake of his head—one no one would notice but herself.

*Shit*. She'd missed something. Just as she was about to say *I'm sorry*, Mrs. Davis repeated the question she'd obviously daydreamed through.

"Kip was telling us how you met at church, dear."

Victoria's eyebrows popped right toward her hairline. "He was." She turned toward Kip. "At church."

His lips twitched again, and undisguised amusement lit his blue eyes.

And, suddenly, Victoria's nerves disappeared. She didn't know how he'd done it, but he'd managed to shrink down this massive room filled with countless servants and the Davises to just the two of them.

She wanted to kiss that smirk right off his lips. Something bubbled in her chest. She nibbled her bottom lip for a second to keep the laugh inside. Once she had control, she said, "That's right, but it wasn't until we found out we volunteered at the same hospital that we really started to talk."

Out of the corner of her eye, she saw the Davises straighten and look at each other, but she couldn't bring herself to look away from Kip, whose smirk had softened.

"I'll never forget seeing her sitting on the ground playing *Sorry!* surrounded by kids," Kip said softly. "Knew right that second that she was the one for me."

Victoria's heart thudded, then seemed to stutter to a stop. She warmed from her toes to her shoulders, with a few places in between heating to extreme temperatures. And throbbing.

She knew what he just said wasn't true, but the way he said it. The way he looked at her while he did …

Someone needed to tell her body that it wasn't true. Her heart as well. Because they seemed to remember that moment he just talked about with perfect clarity.

Kip's arm was still around her, and his thumb started stroking tiny circles on the bare skin of her shoulder.

*What am I doing here?* Because whatever it was, it was interfering with her leaving this room right away and taking Kip somewhere private so he could look at her like that while they were both naked. And sweaty.

Reality bitch slapped her. This dinner was the linchpin in her biggest dream ever. There was nothing—*nothing*—more important than impressing the man sitting across the table from her. Not the man beside her. Not even close.

Victoria sat forward a bit until Kip's thumb was no longer able to stroke—and therefore, distract—her. She smiled at Mr. Davis as she reached for her white wine glass and took a sip. She'd gone with the white because it was chilled.

She needed to cool the fuck down.

She was dying inside to ask Mr. Davis questions that would help her put the final touches on her campaign. This was the first time they'd had a length of time together, and the passing opportunity to pick his brain was skating by her almost painfully.

Kip removed his arm from the back of her chair and began eating his meal, carrying on a conversation with both Mr. and Mrs. Davis while she retreated into her mind. Victoria blinked down at her plate filled with lobster tail and a filet that should make her mouth water. Instead she was too shocked at how distracted she'd managed to become by Kip to even think of enjoying it.

She heard her name and jerked her head up. Mrs. Davis was leaning toward her across the table.

*Damn it.* She'd missed another question, hadn't she? She flicked a glance at Kip and Mr. Davis, but they were quietly conversing with each other. She heard the word *poker* several times in quick succession.

"Victoria," Mrs. Davis said, drawing her attention back to her. "I can see your mind working a mile a minute."

Victoria grimaced. "Sorry."

Mrs. Davis waved a hand in the air. "No, don't apologize. I'm used to it with this one." She nodded toward her husband. "So." Mrs. Davis scooped up a spoon of peas. "Just how uncomfortable are you?"

Victoria stilled. "Um, come again?" She looked at Mr. Davis again, the beginnings of panic stirring in her gut. Was she that obviously out of her element?

"Don't worry," Mrs. Davis said. "He won't hear a word we say right now unless it has to do with cards." She smiled. "I like you." She pointed with her spoon to Kip, who was blithely carrying on his own conversation. "I like you both, actually, so I'll be rooting for you. But I can tell this is just about the last thing you would choose to do on your night off."

She didn't know what to concentrate on first: the fact that Mrs. Davis was in her corner or that her social awkwardness could very easily have killed this deal if she hadn't lucked out to the degree she had.

She took another sip of wine. "Thank you?" She shook her head. "I mean thank you," she said more definitively. "I don't know what I've done to deserve your support, but I'm grateful for it nonetheless."

Mrs. Davis leaned back in her seat and seemed to study Victoria. Finally, she said, "The good thing about good things is that we never deserve them. That's why they're good." She nodded toward Kip, and her smile pushed away decades. "Am I right?"

Victoria looked at Kip, drinking in his profile. "You're right," she whispered.

Mrs. Davis shrugged. "It happens every once in a while. Should we pull the men back into our conversation?"

Huh. She'd actually enjoyed the past several minutes of quiet conversation with a woman who was far more human than Victoria could have guessed thirty or so minutes ago. "I suppose so."

Then with a skill Victoria immediately envied, Mrs. Davis took the reins of the conversation back in a firm hold and led them all through a shockingly pleasant social get-together.

After the third course, Kip's arm was around her again, his thumb stroking her shoulder once more and stoking a fire that she knew he would happily and proficiently bank later this evening.

Kip deserved someone who would be willing to look past meeting as client and gigolo. She was not that person. But Kip was hers for these few hours. And she was not going to take that for granted.

# Chapter Fourteen

She had been very un-Victoria-like the whole ride home, talking a mile a minute about how successful the evening had been. She could hear the giddiness in her tone and see how out of character she was acting in the deepness of Kip's dimple as he let her talk and talk and talk.

"Can you believe how that ended?" she practically squealed. "I couldn't have asked for better!"

Mr. Davis had told her he'd thoroughly enjoyed the evening. Then he'd invited her to a final meeting on Monday morning in which she and Masterson would both present their pitches back to back, but he "had a feeling about who he would choose."

And then he'd *winked* at her!

She'd done it.

Oh, it wasn't official. Not yet. But, she couldn't see this ending any other way than Mr. Davis offering her the job.

Victoria finally took a pause from speaking as they walked from the car to the hotel room, but once they got into the quiet of the elevator, she couldn't refrain from speaking again.

"Seriously, Kip, I can't thank you enough for tonight."

He smiled absently and snagged her hand, running his thumb over her fingertips and focusing on them with admirable determination.

"I couldn't have done this without you!" The elevator dinged and the doors opened. Victoria tugged Kip into the hall and toward their room. "I don't know how you got Mr. Davis to like you after about five minutes. I'm pretty sure he has people who have tried five years to get that to happen."

Kip slid the key card into their door and held it open for her. She breezed past him, drawing her next breath for a stream of words, but when she spun around, she crashed right into his chest, and in the next moment, his lips captured hers.

Distantly, she heard the click of the door as it closed, but by that time, Kip's fingers were in her hair, destroying her carefully put-together style. With a groan, he tilted her head, deepening the kiss. All her giddiness funneled into this merging of mouths. Fisting Kip's dinner jacket, Victoria pulled him close, grinding her breasts against his chest.

That got his hands to leave her hair alone—not that she'd minded. He grabbed her ass with both hands and hauled her up. She obediently wrapped her legs around his hips as he walked them across the room while she nipped along the edge of his jaw with her teeth.

He didn't take her to a wall or even to the mirror like he had last night. It was the soft cushion of the mattress that met her back. Her thighs cradled his body as he followed her down and leisurely returned to their kiss, licking his way inside her mouth and covering her breasts with his palms.

He pulled from the kiss for a mere moment. "You would have done fine without me, honey." He pressed a light kiss to her lips.

She shook her head. "No—"

He bit her bottom lip. "Don't think I didn't notice you and Mrs. Davis talking."

That giddiness bubbled again. "I did. I talked to her." She said it as though it were the biggest deal of the evening and not something most people did regularly.

"I know." His lips were curved the next time he pressed them against hers.

He didn't back away again, instead, thrusting his tongue into her mouth and grinding his erection into her belly.

She dug her nails into the fine fabric of his suit coat, spiraling into the space he always managed to take her with the press of his body against hers. She began thrusting her hips against his rhythmically, a promise of how she was going to move with him inside her. God, she loved this.

Loved *him*.

Her thrusts lost their rhythm.

What had she just thought? Surely, it had not involved the word *love*. The one she'd assured Cassidy, just hours ago, was not involved in any way.

No! Her nails curled into claws against his dinner jacket. She could not love Kip. She couldn't love anyone! She *would* not. Not only had she promised herself she would never enter another disastrous relationship after Jeremy, but also, if she fell in love with Kip, everything she'd worked toward would be for nothing. She was already neglecting clients. Was perched right on the edge of achieving a goal that would require even more of her time.

She couldn't do this.

Her eyes started to sting, and, no longer able to distract herself from these ugly thoughts, she pulled from the kiss. She stared up at him, and his eyes widened.

Great. That meant she did have tears in her eyes.

"Victoria?"

The way he said her name—both promise and supplication—made that hated *l*-word flit through her mind again. Her bottom lip trembled. This was bad. Scratch that. This was hopeless. "What am I going to do when you leave?"

She gasped. She should have never said those words out loud. And as Kip's gaze took in her tears, her obvious anguish, there was no mistaking a quick flash of hope as it passed through those blue eyes. For a moment more, he didn't say or do anything, and she felt her own flare of hope. Perhaps he would ignore what she'd said. Perhaps they could continue as they had been.

In the next second, though, his eyes softened. He licked at his lips in what could only be described as nervousness.

As he opened his mouth to speak, Victoria's stomach lurched.

"What if—" He licked his lips again. "What if I didn't … leave?"

His gaze darted away from hers on the last word, as though he couldn't bear to see her reaction. Which was just as well, because react is exactly what she did.

Her eyes popped wide, allowing one of the tears that had been swimming there to escape down her cheek. She pulled one of her hands from Kip's back and covered her open mouth with trembling fingers.

*Oh, no.* It was worse than she'd thought. Not only was she falling for Kip, apparently, he was falling for her as well. This was a disaster.

*Okay, calm down.* She'd misheard him. Had to have. All a misunderstanding.

And then she laughed. A short, hysterical laugh.

Kip flinched, and that was when she knew she hadn't misheard him. He shifted off her and sat up, rubbing a hand roughly down his face.

"Wait." Victoria sat up, too. "Did you say what I think you said?" she asked, still clinging to the asinine hope that they were preparing to resolve a big mix-up.

"Forget it." His words were clipped. He sat on the edge of the bed, staring at the wall. A muscle ticked in his jaw.

All hope died.

She shifted her gaze from his profile to his back, unable to look at him a moment longer. "Kip, we can't be together." His back stiffened at her words, and panic clawed up her throat. He was going to argue with her. Try to persuade her.

*Don't ask me to be together!* She wanted it too badly.

*And why* can't *you be together?* The question plowed through her mind, knocking aside thoughts of Jeremy. The memories of how bad it had been for them as they'd tried to navigate his depression and failed spectacularly. She clung to those memories. To the promises she'd made herself that she'd never again have to go through what she had with Jeremy.

*But Kip is not Jeremy.*

The thought was clear. Bold.

Blood cold terror streaked down her spine as her body relaxed, for all intents and purposes appearing to accept the comparison of Kip to Jeremy as irrefutable fact. To accept Kip.

*This can't be happening*!

Reality. She needed a dose of reality, and so did he. Her mouth was opening before she could stop it, knowing, even as she wet her lips, that she was about to do something she'd regret. "We can't be together," she stated again. "It's impossible! You're a hook—" She caught the word back a moment too late.

Kip jerked straight, his gaze swinging around to collide with hers. For the first time, the blue of his eyes was cold when he looked at her. "Finish it." He ground the words out from between clenched teeth.

Sudden anger spiked through her, flushing her first hot and then cold. Anger she needed. She embraced it, letting all the ugliness she was feeling surge up her throat and out of her mouth. "Kip, you're a gigolo. What, should I pretend you're not?"

Kip got slowly to his feet. His jacket was rumpled from the way she'd jerked it around in her fists just moments before, but he still straightened it in what could only be described as a dignified manner before turning to face her. "I'm a lot of things actually. Funny that you see only that one part."

His words destroyed her, because they gave her every bit of proof she needed to confirm that her own callous words had destroyed him. She didn't see just that. Wanted to make him understand that this moment.

She curled her hands into fists. *It's best this way.* If she drove him away, this would all end tonight. Victoria threw her hands up in the air. "Kip. Be real. It's a big part."

"It is a big part. Present tense, huh?" He shoved his hands through his hair in the first slip of his façade and the first peek she got to the true anger he was hiding beneath it. "Even after all our plans. All I'm going to do in the future. The fact that you're the last goddamn client I'll ever have." His voice rose. "I'll always just be *the hooker,* won't I?"

His last client? *No! I can't hear this!* She jerked to her feet. "And I'll always be the girl who drove her husband to suicide. We don't get to shed our past, Kip, no matter how much we want to." She jabbed a finger in his direction. "And don't pretend this was anything other than it was. I don't even know your real name, for Christ's sake. We are not in a relationship; this was never anything but business."

A muscle flexed in his jaw, and his nostrils flared as he pulled in a long, slow breath. He looked like she'd just slapped him.

Funny, she felt like she'd just slapped him. Her anger abated in a sudden rush, leaving her feeling hollow. Empty. In its wake, she longed to reach out to him. To smooth a hand over his tense shoulders. To say she was sorry.

But there was no *sorry*. There was only necessity.

So softly, she barely heard him, Kip said, "I've never once thought about you only in the light of your past." His blue eyes connected with her. "Thought of you as his. Not once."

*I've thought of you as mine. As the present.*

She heard the words as loudly as though he'd spoken them. Felt the condemnation she fully deserved.

As Kip turned from her and walked to the door, tears tumbled down her cheeks. With his back turned, she allowed herself to reach out to him.

He shut the door resolutely behind him.

# Chapter Fifteen

*Knock, knock, knock.*

Victoria groaned and rolled over, burying her face in her pillow. "Go away."

Was her pillow … wet?

She pulled back and blinked down at the white pillowcase. *Yep*. Wet and streaked with mascara.

"Ah, fuck." She'd cried in her sleep.

There was a noise at her front door again, but it wasn't a knock this time. Instead, the very distinct sound of someone using a key to get into her apartment reached her in muffled clicks of gears.

*Cassidy*. They were supposed to meet this morning and head to the farmer's market. But that had been before Victoria had changed those plans to lying around in bed all day eating ice cream, without telling Cassidy.

Once Cassidy saw her pillow, she would be relentless.

She heard the door open at last, and in a very mature move, stuffed her pillow beneath her bed. She jerked upright again and shoved her hair out of her eyes just in time to see Cassidy sail through the open bedroom door, holding two coffees.

Cassidy froze, blinked twice, and said, "Shit, your face."

Victoria rolled her eyes. *So much for hiding the evidence*. "Good morning to you, too."

Cassidy gestured toward her with one of the coffee cups. "No, seriously. What the hell happened to your face, because I'm guessing gang fight or … Wait." She crossed the distance of the room in seconds. "Were you crying?"

And—just perfect—two more tears made treks through what was apparently epic makeup marks all over her face.

"Oh, honey." Cassidy plopped down on the bed beside her, the coffee sloshing ominously in the cups, and leaned her shoulder against Victoria's. "What happened?"

Victoria hiccupped. "Nothing."

"Ah." Cassidy shook her head and sighed. "So it wasn't the gigolo who did something this time. It was you."

"I said something really terrible, and he walked out, and now I'll probably never see him again!" Victoria wailed.

"Okay." The mattress jiggled as Cassidy turned to face her. "First things first: caffeinate." She thrust one of the coffee cups Victoria's way. "And then we have got to wash that face before we head to the farmer's market."

She took the coffee and sniffed. "I don't want to go to the farmer's market."

"And I don't fucking care. We're going. Because it's one thing to cry all night, but it's another thing entirely to wear sweats for four weeks solid and gain ten pounds from Ben and Jerry's, which, clearly, is where this is headed." Cassidy nudged the coffee toward Victoria's mouth, and she took an obliging sip, feeling the slightest bit more human as the brew made its way to her gut. "We're going to talk this out and find a way for you to get your man, all while buying organic strawberries. This is the best plan ever. Embrace it."

When Cassidy tugged her from the bed and toward the bathroom, Victoria followed, but she made sure to glare the whole way so Cassidy would know she protested.

Cassidy ignored her.

Thirty minutes later, carrying her second coffee of the morning, dressed in an actual cute outfit, and tearstain free, Victoria was beginning to see the wisdom of getting out of the house.

"So," Cassidy said, trailing her fingers through several daisy blooms at the flower stand. "What happened?"

"Kip …" Victoria swallowed. "Said he wanted to stay."

Cassidy's eyes brightened. "What? That's great!"

She shook her head.

Cassidy's smile crashed. "Oh, crap. What did you say to him?"

She sipped her coffee and took her time swallowing it.

"Victoria?"

She cleared her throat. "Let's just say the important word was *hooker*."

Cassidy gasped. "You twat!"

Victoria groaned. "I know."

"I told you they like to be called gigolos."

"Cassidy, that's not the issue and you know it."

"Well, what did he say when you apologized?"

Victoria took another leisurely sip of her coffee and started walking quickly to a stand of produce.

"Victoria Hastings!"

She stopped and spun to face her sister-in-law. "Okay, fine, I didn't apologize. But that's because I don't apologize for saying things that are true, and one of us needed to be remembering it!"

"Tori, only massive dickholes think it's okay to say something hurtful just because it's 'true.'" Cassidy jabbed her air quotes Victoria's way as though they were weapons. "And I thought he was opening his own business. He's not even in the profession anymore."

"*I'm* paying him."

"And judging him for it, too. It's a twofer. He's so lucky."

Victoria's coffee sloshed in her stomach. Judging him? "Well, that ugly word puts some perspective in the mix."

"It's not the only ugly word in the mix," Cassidy mumbled. "I can't believe you called him a hooker."

"Just—" Victoria sighed. "Stop reminding me for one second?"

"That's a big *nope*. Someone has to. Might as well be me." Cassidy put her hand on Victoria's arm. They both stopped walking, and Victoria braced herself as she met Cassidy's gaze. "And don't pretend this has nothing to do with Jeremy."

Victoria winced. Immediately, her throat clogged with more tears. "Please don't," she whispered. They couldn't talk truth right now. She wouldn't be able to handle it.

Cassidy narrowed her eyes, capturing Victoria's gaze. "Kip is not Jeremy, honey. Hell, at the end, *Jeremy* was not Jeremy. You can't keep expecting misery around every corner."

The very same words she'd thought herself last night. Victoria shook her head. *Stop. Now!*

Cassidy sighed, a look of resignation entering her eyes. "Okay, we'll table this for now." She raised her eyebrows. "For now."

Victoria bobbed her head. "Yes."

Cassidy shook her head, and Victoria knew she was safe. The mood immediately lightened.

Cassidy nudged Victoria's shoulder with her own, and they started walking again. "Look, Tori, you know I love you. That's why I have to tell you these things. Kip?" Cassidy shrugged. "We don't know if anyone loves him. If he has anyone to tell him when he messed up or when someone he cares about messed up. So, I kind of have to look out for him, too. Especially since he's probably going to be my brother someday."

"Whoa!" Victoria's arm jerked and a splash of coffee scalded her forearm. "Ow! Son of a bitch! Why would you say that?"

"What, too soon?"

Victoria stalked toward the vegetable stand, shaking out her stinging arm along the way. *Too soon*. More apt than Cassidy knew. How could Cassidy talk about a new brother when she'd lost one? Because of Victoria no less!

She wasn't looking where she was going and plowed right into someone.

She reflexively tightened her grip on her coffee cup, so she and the stranger were spared an additional scalding. She stumbled back a step and raised her head, an apology already on her lips.

But then she froze.

*You!* She just kept herself from spitting the word, but her mind sure screamed it loud and clear. Victoria had managed to run into Georgiana Masterson. "The Master."

Tens of thousands of people in this city, and she'd bumped into the one she never enjoyed seeing. Figured.

As she watched recognition flash on The Master's face, Victoria fought the desire to narrow her eyes at the woman.

The Master did not choose to fight that battle, apparently, because soon, the woman's blue eyes were squinty and thoroughly disapproving.

Victoria's chest panged. Those blue eyes. Even in someone as hateful as The Master, the blue eyes made her think of Kip. They were even the same shape.

*Damn her*!

She felt Cassidy come up behind her. "Who's this?"

Before Victoria could even struggle over whether she should do the socially acceptable thing and introduce her nemesis to her sister, Masterson stepped closer. There was something menacing about it, and she found herself taking a step back, bumping into Cassidy in the process.

"I heard about your dinner last night," Masterson said in a low voice.

Victoria tipped up her chin. "Don't sweat it, Masterson. You can't win them all."

The Master smiled slowly and in a way that did not denote amusement. "You haven't won anything, yet. How have you felt about your life choices lately, Hastings?" She tilted her head. "Anything untoward that you might come to regret?"

The hair on the back of Victoria's neck stood on end.

"Seriously," Cassidy said from over Victoria's shoulder. "Who is this slag?"

"Mother?"

All three of their heads swiveled around toward that deep, male voice. A voice Victoria recognized at once.

Sure enough, Kip the Gigolo rounded the corner of the vegetable stand.

The sight of him shot straight to her heart, which started beating hard enough that it was actually painful. *What is he doing here?*

Cassidy asked the same question in a whisper, and Victoria momentarily jolted. How in the hell did Cassidy know Kip? But, then, she would, wouldn't she? She'd hired Kip to start with. There would have been a picture at the very least.

Victoria hated her hope that Kip had sought her out to make up.

"Ah," Kip said to The Master. "There you are, Mother."

*Thud.* Victoria's speeding heart abruptly stopped.

It was at precisely that moment—when there was no way in hell Victoria was disguising what she was feeling—that Kip seemed to see her for the first time.

He stuttered to a stop at Masterson's side. In his hand was a burlap shopping bag filled to the brim with produce. Their gazes connected, and now with him standing side by side with Georgiana Masterson, she could see that the shape of their eyes was, in fact, identical.

Because The Master was her lover's mother. The lover whom she had shared all of her secret advertising plans with. For the client over which his mother and she currently competed.

*Oh, God, I'm going to be sick.*

Victoria opened her mouth. To say what, she didn't know, but Kip beat her to the punch.

He tilted his head toward The Master. "Who is this?" he asked conversationally, smiling Victoria's direction.

*What is he—?* Were they going to pretend they didn't know each other? What the fuck was going on!

While social niceties had been a struggle for Victoria moments earlier, The Master did not suffer from the same conflict, apparently. "Kipling, this is a competitor of mine: Victoria Hastings. Hastings," she said, waving a hand in Victoria's direction and then back at *Kipling fucking Masterson*, "my son."

"Oh, shit," Cassidy mumbled. Victoria was pretty numb, but she was able to feel Cassidy's hand on her arm nonetheless. "Nice to meet you both, but we have to go."

Victoria tried to speak but ended up grunting instead.

With that, Cassidy began ushering her away. "Forget everything nice I said about him earlier. He is a hooker!"

"What just happened?"

"Well, sweetie, I think you just got the shaft, and not in the way you paid for."

"Oh, God, his mother!" She jerked to a stop. "Cassidy, I told him everything!"

"Victoria!"

*Kip?* They turned, and, sure enough, there he was, streaking across the parking lot to get to her.

• • •

"Victoria!" he yelled again. Not that he needed to. She and the woman she was with had stopped the first time he'd shouted at them. They were both standing next to her silver Mercedes and glaring daggers his way.

The daggers gave him pause.

She had, just the night before, shown him exactly what she thought of him, and it wasn't an opinion he was willing to accept from anyone, much less the woman he had considered a relationship with.

But the way she'd looked at him when he'd found out who his mother was—like she was utterly devastated—he couldn't ignore that. His heart wouldn't let him.

Why she cared who his mother was, he hadn't a clue.

He stopped running while he was still several feet away, so that by the time he was approaching them, it was at a wary walk. "Victoria?"

Something within her seemed to snap. "How could you not tell me The Master is your mother?" she hissed.

Kip's head drew back. "The Master?"

"Kip! You've seen every single advertising plan I have for The Ricchezza. Even if you didn't tell Masterson what you've seen, at the very least, any decent person would have warned me he was related to my biggest competition before I gave away my biggest dream to him!"

*Oh. Holy shit.* Victoria was competing for The Ricchezza against his mother. *No, they can't be similar.* The women had nothing in common! He wouldn't be so stupid as to throw his heart at the feet of another heartless woman.

"Victoria, there's something you need to know about my mother and me." *She has destroyed every shred of confidence I have. And you seem to be molding yourself in her footsteps.* He shook his head, displacing the errant thought. "We don't talk. I had no idea that she was who you were competing against for the account."

Victoria snorted a laugh. "How much of what comes out of your mouth is a lie, *Kipling*?"

And that's when he got angry. "Why would you care who I am? All I am to you is your hooker!" He shoved a hand through his hair and tried to calm down. "You know what? I'm tired of this. Do you know how I would have known you and my mother were out for the same client? If you would have fucking opened up to me. Even once. But every time shit got personal, you bailed." He couldn't deny it anymore. Not with such blatant evidence. The similarities between Victoria and his mother were glaring. Two days ago, he would have never thought Victoria was the type of person to climb over others in pursuit of success. Now?

"You know what?" she hissed, leaning in. "You and The Master can have those old, tired plans. I'll spend every moment between now and Monday morning revamping everything, and by the time I present them against your mother in that boardroom, she won't know what hit her."

And, like an idiot, the first thing Kip wanted to say was, *No, don't change those plans! You worked so hard on them!* Instead, he leaned back and completely detached himself. *Yep. Just like my mother.* "I guess you've got to do what you've got to do." His tone was the same dead tone he used every time he talked with his family.

Her warm brown eyes hardened. "Yes, I do."

Despite her revealing her true colors, Kip found himself regarding Victoria with pride. She was incredible. Resilient. Bitter. "Good-bye, Victoria. I wish you the best." He meant it. The discovery felt groundbreaking. Freeing. Maybe he was ready to move on. From his mother. His family. Anyone—he met Victoria's gaze—like them.

She didn't say good-bye back. Instead, she spun on her heel, flopped into the driver's seat, and slammed the door behind her.

The woman she was with shifted awkwardly from foot to foot for a moment before saying, "Well, this was fun." She smiled sadly at Kip. "I'll see you around, I guess."

With that, she walked around to the passenger's seat and got into the car.

"No, you won't be seeing me around," he whispered. *I never have to see them again.*

Oddly, the thought did not comfort him as he'd intended.

# Chapter Sixteen

Victoria blinked blearily at the changing red numbers of The Ricchezza elevator. It had been a whirlwind these past forty-eight sleepless, frenzied, work-filled hours, but she was here, and she was confident.

She could sleep later. After she'd signed The Ricchezza.

Unfortunately, she'd been unable to save the crying for later. Her fingers delicately prodded the swollen skin beneath her eyes. It felt like her makeup was still intact. She glanced at the mirror on the ceiling of the elevator. *Yep*. The dark circles and baggy skin were covered up.

She'd devoted too many precious minutes this weekend to mourning both Kip's betrayal and—because her heart liked to be contradictory—his sudden absence in her life. Luckily, her dream had not suffered twice because of him.

Her new plans kicked her old plans' ass.

When the elevator dinged, Victoria jerked upright, surprised to find she'd nodded off somewhere between checking her makeup and arriving at the business suite of The Ricchezza.

Yes, sleep definitely needed to happen soon.

When the elevator doors opened, she found none other than Just Tiffany sitting at a reception desk situated directly opposite the bank of elevators. Tiffany's head rose from where it was bent over the desk as she typed away. She smiled.

Victoria pulled in a fortifying breath, smoothed her hand down her business suit jacket, and walked toward the desk, gripping her folio between her arm and side hard enough to crack a rib.

"Ms. Hastings," Tiffany said. "What a pleasure to see you again."

Well, at least she'd recognized her. That had to be a good sign, right? "For me, too." Victoria smiled and hoped she was awake enough to make it vivid and sincere instead of a grimace.

"Ms. Masterson has already arrived and is setting up in the boardroom." Tiffany floated up from her seat. "I can take you there now."

*Of course, Masterson beat me here.* "That would be great, thank you."

With each step down the hallway, Victoria's minimal nerves dissipated. She was as ready for this meeting as she'd been for anything in her life. Mr. Davis had already hinted he was going with her. This was a formality.

Tiffany stopped beside an open door and gestured for Victoria to proceed inside. "May I get you anything? Coffee? Water?"

She straightened her shoulders. "No, thank you."

With a final nod, Just Tiffany was gone, swaying her way back down the hallway.

Victoria walked into the room and spotted The Master immediately. She was standing by an easel holding some projected numbers and clicking away at a laptop attached to a projector by a cord. She didn't even bother looking up.

*Fine by me.* Victoria laid her portfolio on the magnificent mahogany table and began to pull out her own easel.

"Oh, I wouldn't do that if I were you."

Victoria paused, coached herself not to overreact, and raised her head. "Excuse me?" *Bravo, Victoria! You sounded semi-normal!*

The Master nodded toward Victoria's still-collapsed easel. "Bother setting up. There won't be a need."

As quickly as Victoria's nerves had disappeared, they were even quicker on the rebound. She suddenly remembered something grief, frenzied work, and lack of sleep had not-so-conveniently erased from her short-term memory: the cryptic comment Masterson had made before Kip showed up at the vegetable stall. Something about Victoria's choices.

*Oh, so many shits*. This was bad. *Please don't know what I think you know*. Masterson's smile was predatory, and Victoria's heart sank to her gut. Her rival knew Victoria had hired a gigolo.

*Ouch*. She palmed the ache in her chest. Who knew she'd actually been harboring hope that Kip hadn't been playing her the whole time? That pipe dream was over. The only way Masterson would know about Victoria's indiscretion would be if Kip had told her. And if that were the case, it was probable that The Master had been in on it from the start. That it had been some sort of subterfuge. A plan.

How … horrifying. And fucking painful.

He'd never wanted her after all. And she'd never forgive herself if her ill-advised business agreement with Kip cost her the only thing in life she cared about.

Against all odds, she was able to put her game face on. "I'm not sure I follow."

Instead of an answer, Georgiana Masterson merely cocked an eyebrow.

It was the exact same expression Kip favored. Victoria looked away and swallowed hard.

For the first time since Friday, her confidence not only wavered, it shattered. Her hands shook as she set the easel on the tabletop.

"Ah, you're both early."

Out of the corner of her eye, Victoria saw Masterson look toward the door and Mr. Davis. Victoria stared at her closed folio. Odds were, she'd never get a chance to open it.

Bracing herself, she finally looked up. Several people filed into the room after Mr. Davis, and they began taking seats, with Mr.

Davis, naturally, in the place of power at the head of the table on the far end of the room.

He looked at her and smiled. She needed to say something. What would stop Masterson's bombshell of information in its tracks?

She came up empty. Mr. Davis's smile slipped. "Miss Hastings," he said, "are you all right?"

Victoria bit her bottom lip.

"Actually," Masterson said, "I have something that may interest you before we begin our pitches."

*And here we go.*

Mr. Davis glanced Masterson's way and then slowly dragged his gaze back to Victoria. She saw the moment he realized something was going on flicker in his eyes. "Okay," he said, his gaze bearing the weight of an anvil as it remained on her.

Someone got up and closed the door.

The Master stood front and center and pressed her palms onto the tabletop. "Mr. Davis, sir—"

How absurd for The Master to call someone younger than her *sir*. But, hell, Victoria was a suck-up, too, for ingratiating herself to this man.

"—and I'm sure your background check was thorough, but our firm also employs a private investigator, and he turned up something I think you should know."

After a brief pause, Mr. Davis said, "I'm listening."

*Wait, a private investigator?* So, not Kip? Another lie, perhaps?

The Master squared her shoulders. "For the past month, Ms. Hastings has employed the services of a paid male prostitute."

There were several audible gasps in the room, and Victoria, oddly enough, found herself fighting the urge to roll her eyes. This wasn't Victorian England. These were grown-ass men who worked at a casino. It's not like they'd never heard the word *prostitute* before.

But none of this made sense. This woman now tucking nonexistent stray strands into her oh-so-proper bun would never open herself up to the possibility that Victoria would tell Davis that the prostitute she'd hired was, in fact, Masterson's son. Mr. Davis would no doubt find that just as incriminating as the act of hiring one. Which meant …

Georgiana Masterson did not know that the gigolo Victoria had hired was her own son.

"Oh, my God," Victoria muttered.

Masterson's lips spread with a cocky smile. How sad. The Master had someone like Kip in her life, and she'd alienated him to such a point that she didn't know what he did for a living.

What an unimaginable loss.

*Well, not that unimaginable, is it?* Victoria, too, had alienated him. Had allowed fear and the past to keep her from happiness. Kip, who was nothing like her husband, would have made her happy. For the rest of their lives.

*I'm a fucking idiot.*

Mr. Davis glared at her, drawing her from her thoughts. "Miss Hastings," he grumbled, "what do you have to say to these charges?"

And this would be when the old Victoria Hastings did whatever it took to secure her dream. Threw Masterson under the bus, and in the process Kip, who would never be able to make it in his legitimate business if it got out, especially in this circle of vipers, that he'd been a gigolo.

There was no way she was going to do that. Pressing her lips tightly together, Victoria said nothing.

"Young lady—" Mr. Davis began.

*Um, say what?* And she'd wanted to work for this prick?

"—I cannot believe you would have dared to expose this casino to another scandal so shortly after the first. It is completely unconscionable."

"I agree," piped in The Master.

"And I assume this was the man you brought to dinner to meet my wife?" Mr. Davis's face was an impressive shade of red.

"Mr. Davis," Victoria raised her chin, "I don't regret any of my choices." It wasn't entirely true. She just didn't regret the ones he was accusing her of.

Mr. Davis blustered over that for a moment. "Well, you'll regret them soon enough. Needless to say, The Ricchezza will not be hiring you or Precision Media Services."

"If that's what your heart is telling you to do, you should do it," she said. "And so should I."

Mr. Davis's brows drew together at that, but she didn't wait for him to say anything else. She gathered her folio and easel, and, turning toward the door, stopped for a moment beside The Master. "Congratulations, Georgiana," she said softly. "I hope this is everything you dreamed of."

As for Victoria, it no longer was. It seemed her dream had morphed sideways on her when she wasn't looking.

Unfortunately, she had more than likely made sure she'd never get that dream either. After the way she'd treated Kip, she didn't deserve it. Didn't deserve him.

Now, she just had to find a way to live with that.

# Chapter Seventeen

The weekend had been interminable, and this week wasn't shaping up to be any better. Not only had he been cruelly reminded of his place in life, he'd had to spend Saturday morning with his mother, who, for some godforsaken reason, had insisted he escort her to the farmer's market when his father couldn't make it. Then, after Victoria had turned into a stranger and broken his heart into a million pieces, he'd been expected at the usual weekly Sunday dinner. He hadn't yet shored up the courage to cut ties with his family, though he was working on it and expected to do so any day now.

So why—dear God, why—was he at his parents' house again this Monday night? He hadn't spent this much time at his childhood home since he'd had the option not to.

His mother had demanded his presence, saying dinner tonight was a special occasion. And here he was, half hoping he'd be able to cut ties tonight. But the other half of him was here because if his mother was happy and celebrating today, that meant Victoria wasn't.

And, glutton for punishment that he was, he wanted to know the details. Even though he didn't have a right to anymore—had never had the right to, apparently—against all reason, he was worried about Victoria.

There were flutes of champagne at all three of their place settings, and Kip had already drained his twice. Why didn't he chug champagne like water at every family gathering? He was finding his parents' company moderately tolerable, and everything was slightly fuzzy. In other words: an improvement over the past three days. He was even eating his dessert, and, honestly, eyeing his father's, too, even though as a rule he avoided sweets to keep his body fat down.

And then his mother had to open her mouth. Well, damn.

"I've asked for us to meet tonight," she said, "to celebrate a momentous occasion."

The flourless chocolate cake he'd been inhaling now seemed to stick in his throat. With a grimace, Kip set his fork beside his plate. *Way to ruin a perfectly good chocolate binge, Mother.*

Kip's father smiled wanly, and then they both looked at Kip. Was he supposed to react to his mother's statement in some way? He cleared his throat, but the chocolate cake wasn't budging. "Oh, really?" His voice scraped its way out of his mouth.

"I've had a victory." His mother smoothed a hand over her hair. "Well, I've had two victories, rather."

*Ah, Victoria, I'm so sorry, honey.* He couldn't prevent the surge of misplaced sympathy. Couldn't bring himself to think Victoria deserved her own bit of misery. Damn it, she'd worked so hard for this. His mother had, too, but this had been Victoria's dream.

"I got The Ricchezza account!"

"Congratulations, dear." His father reached over and patted the back of Mother's hand.

Something twisted sharply in Kip's chest. "Oh, really?" he said again.

"But"—his mother smiled, and that was rare enough that his interest was piqued despite himself—"that's not even the best part. I permanently eliminated a source of—I can say it now since it no longer applies—the most stringent competition I've ever encountered in my profession." She turned to him. "Kipling, you actually met her on Saturday morning."

"Um …" *What?* Eliminated? Kip straightened in his seat, and his buzz sloughed off in the span of one second. "Do you mean Victoria?"

His mother waved a dismissive hand. "Yes. Hastings. Anyway." She leaned toward Kip and his father, and a gleam Kip didn't like lit her blue eyes. "She had been sleeping with a paid prostitute."

Everything Kip had eaten roiled in his stomach, and he pressed a fist against his mouth.

"Can you imagine?" His mother straightened. "Of all the things to do when your life is under scrutiny." She reached for her champagne flute and raised it. "I was obligated, naturally, to let Mr. Davis know since our integrity was such a matter of importance to him."

"Oh, fuck."

His mother's jaw dropped. "Kipling!"

"What happened next?" His voice was alarmingly loud. When his fingers started to ache, he realized he was gripping the table with all his strength.

His mother blinked several times. "What needed to happen. He hired me instead, and I will no longer have to worry about Miss Hastings as a source of competition."

"You mean …" He tried to catch a breath. "She didn't say anything? Didn't try to make excuses?"

Her mother laughed. "Really, Kipling. What excuses would she be able to make?"

He made an odd noise—something between a laugh and a grunt—and both of his parents looked at him as though he'd suddenly stripped naked right in front of them.

*Why?* Why would Victoria have protected him? One sentence—that's all it would have taken to turn the tables and secure her biggest goal. Sure, it could have destroyed his chances to have a legitimate business, one he still hadn't managed to choose despite all the good options he had before him, but she'd more than made it clear that she didn't care about him. Hadn't she? So why would she do it?

Goddamn it, *why*?

*Because, you fucking idiot, she loves you, too.*

The idea hit him like a plank to the face, and in the next second, he was grinning so broadly his cheeks hurt. He'd been wrong. So wrong.

Victoria Hastings was nothing like Georgiana Masterson.

He laughed again.

"Kipling?" His mother tilted her head and flicked a quick glance at his father. "Are you well?"

Kip shook his head. "I really wish you hadn't done that to Victoria."

His father's lips parted, and Mother sat back in her chair. "What are you talking about?" she asked.

"Mother"—Kip placed his palms on the table and pushed to his feet—"I am the prostitute Victoria was sleeping with. Me."

Her mouth dropped open.

"And things are going to be very awkward in the future because, one, you did something horrible to your future daughter-in-law, and, two, I'll be amending that horrible thing by telling Mr. Davis the truth about my identity."

His mother's mouth moved several times as though she were trying to speak, but no sound came out.

"Wait," his father said. "You sleep with women for money?" He sounded intrigued by the idea, not appalled.

Kip smiled at him. "Not anymore, I don't. But, yes, I did. Victoria was a client, but now she's much more." *I hope.*

God, he still couldn't believe she had put him above her greatest desire.

"Daughter-in-law?" his mother finally managed to say. "Kipling, what in the world—"

"I'll be unavailable for a time." He straightened his cuffs and pushed his chair into the table. "I'll be starting my own business"—probably in advertising, the only thing besides Victoria that seemed to make his heart beat faster despite desperate attempts to resist the pull—"and settling down with the woman I love. When you're ready to meet her—and apologize, of course—please let me know."

"Kipling!"

He turned to leave the room, and he'd been planning not to look back, but he caught the sight of a grin on his father's face. Kip paused, and their gazes connected.

His father winked at him.

When Kip walked out of the dining room, he was smiling, too.

He jogged down the front steps to his car, got in as quickly as he could, and tore down the long driveway.

He pointed his car in the direction of the Strip. Twenty minutes later, he was walking back to his car where it was parked in The Ricchezza parking structure.

"Just a minor setback," he told himself.

He'd been told that Mr. Davis was not in the office. It probably wasn't true, but at least Kip had tried. He'd have hated himself if he'd skipped the most obvious way of contacting the man when it could have worked.

He needed to think, but his empty apartment didn't seem inviting, so he drove to the only place he could think of: Sally's. God help him, he was seeking solace at the world's most disgusting diner. There were only two other cars parked in the lot. Neither of them were Victoria's. Though he hadn't come here looking for her, he still felt a keen sting.

The dull, throbbing ache of missing her he'd experienced all weekend had become a sudden and insistent roar the moment his mother had dropped her bombshell.

*Need her bad.* He just wanted to hug her, for God's sake. Bury his nose in her hair and breathe her in. Watch a movie marathon on the couch together.

The bell over the entrance to Sally's tinkled as he walked in. He saw a couple in the booth where Victoria and he last sat, so, with another healthy dose of disappointment, Kip turned to find a different seat.

But, then, he turned slowly back toward the couple.

They were kissing so hard he doubted they were breathing. He felt like an absolute creeper staring at them now, but—

Yep, his eyes had not deceived him. That was Mr. Davis, owner of The Ricchezza casino, making out in the corner booth of a seedy diner. And the woman on the other side of that kiss?

Not Mrs. Davis.

Kip wanted to grab a passing server and ask *Are you seeing this?* but he refrained. This couldn't be happening. He didn't have this good of luck.

And yet, after a couple of seconds, a slow smile spread his lips, and he took his time walking over to the booth.

He stopped about a foot away, mostly because the sounds the two were making were ridiculous to the nth degree, and laughing out loud was a real possibility. He waited for them to notice they had an audience, but it soon became apparent that was not going to happen.

Kip cleared his throat.

The kissing stopped abruptly. The two stared up at him, and Kip caught his first glance of the woman's face …

Just Tiffany.

He felt a pang in his chest for Mrs. Davis, who was a truly lovely woman—one whom he genuinely liked.

Mr. Davis had begun staring at Kip with a scowl, but as soon as Kip's identity registered, his eyes widened and his kiss-bruised lips parted.

"Nice to see you again, Mr. Davis," he said with a jaunty little salute. "Hello, not-Mrs.-Davis."

"Ah, shit," Tiffany muttered.

Kip pointed to the spot beside her in the circular booth. "Mind if I—?"

Tiffany gave him an *Are you serious?* look but did end up scooting closer to Mr. Davis and making room for him.

"Thank you. Now, here's the thing. I'm of the mindset that people's private lives are none of anyone else's damn business. But," Kip smiled at Mr. Davis, "seeing as how that is not an opinion we share …"

Mr. Davis straightened his tie, pulling at it a bit in the process. "What is it you want?"

Kip sobered. "Nothing you can give me, unfortunately. However, I do have some information for you."

Mr. Davis frowned. This was obviously not going the way he expected it to, being as how he was a massive asshole who liked to manipulate people. "Okay," he said slowly.

Kip leaned back in the booth. He was going to enjoy this. "Georgiana Masterson is my mother."

Tiffany had already grown bored and was examining her manicure, but Mr. Davis's eyebrows popped toward his hairline. "Oh, really?"

"Yes, really." He leaned forward. "I thought you might want to know that before hiring someone who doesn't even know what's going on in her own family." Kip narrowed his eyes. "And speaking of women not knowing what's going on in their own families …"

Mr. Davis's face grew red. It was a good thing he didn't know that Kip probably couldn't look Mrs. Davis in the eye and break her heart. "I think I understand," Mr. Davis grumbled.

"Actually, I don't think you do." Kip's voice cooled. "Mrs. Davis is a wonderful woman. If you understood that, we wouldn't even be chatting right now."

*Fucking hypocrite.* Even though he didn't say the words out loud, Mr. Davis had understood them nonetheless.

"Welp." Kip knocked his knuckles on the table. Mr. Davis and Tiffany both jumped. "I think I'm going to take my scandalous, hooker ass home." He got to his feet and nodded at both of them. "Y'all enjoy your adultery, now."

He walked out of Sally's biting back a grin.

# Chapter Eighteen

Victoria scraped the bottom of her pint of Chubby Hubby ice cream, then shoved the watery spoonful she'd managed to collect into her mouth, staring listlessly at the part of *Gone With the Wind* when Melanie died.

Unlike every other time she'd attempted this cure for a bad day, it wasn't working on the ache in her chest.

An ache associated entirely with losing Kip, not with losing The Ricchezza account. Whenever she thought about her actions in the boardroom of The Ricchezza, she felt …

Worthy of the good things that happened to her, even if she hadn't appreciated them at the time, and she felt she was better than the bad things that marred her past.

Her cell started ringing somewhere in the apartment, the ringtone muffled. Victoria glanced around and didn't see it. She was getting ready to let it go to voicemail, but maybe it was Kip calling to tell her he loved her and wanted to have her babies.

She launched into motion, digging through the couch cushions and eventually finding it on the last ring, stuffed between a cushion and the arm.

Her hope plummeted as she checked out the caller ID.

*Well, it's already in my hand. Might as well.*

She pushed the green button. "Hello, Mr. Kincaid." Damn, she was not looking forward to this conversation.

"Congratulations, Hastings!" Mr. Kincaid boomed so loudly Victoria had to momentarily pull the phone from her ear.

"Umm." *What?*

"Just got off the phone with Mr. Davis a moment ago. Why wouldn't you call me this morning to tell me you got the contract?"

Victoria frowned. "I … got the contract?"

"As if you didn't know." Mr. Kincaid chuckled. "I already have them working on the nameplate for your corner office. You can start moving in tomorrow morning."

Her lips parted. "Are you—are you promoting me?"

"Of course, I am! God, Davis faxed over the contract, and not even I could believe the kind of deal you're getting. This is going to mean big things for us at Precision Media Services, and we have you to thank for it."

Victoria was speechless on the outside, but her mind was running at breakneck pace. *What had happened?*

There was only one thing that could have changed Mr. Davis's mind: the very secret Victoria had kept from him to protect Kip. Which meant—

She sank down onto the couch, covering her lips with her fingers. Kip had to have … No, he would have—

*He sacrificed his dream to give me mine.*

An unimaginable warmth began in her gut and quickly spread throughout her chest and limbs until Victoria was smiling from it.

"Victoria?" Mr. Kincaid's chuckle this time was a little awkward. "You still there?"

She nodded, which was ridiculous, so she forced herself to open her mouth. "I quit."

There was absolute silence on the other line and in her apartment. She waited for the panic, but it didn't come. Instead, she scooped up another bite of Chubby Hubby. For the first time since cracking open the pint, the ice cream had a delicious flavor: victory.

"I'm sorry," Mr. Kincaid said, "I thought I heard you say *I quit*." Another awkward chuckle.

Victoria straightened. "I did say that."

"But …"

"Mr. Kincaid, the scrutiny put on my private life these past few weeks has been unacceptable. I'm a human woman; that earns me a modicum of respect. I didn't receive any. I won't be working for Mr. Davis, and for your role in supporting his inappropriate monitoring of my private life, I will not be working for you anymore either."

"Victoria," Mr. Kincaid spluttered, "this is a massive mistake."

She paused for a moment to examine what she was feeling. She shook her head. "I don't think it is, actually."

"You'll never work in advertising in this city again."

Victoria pursed her lips. "Kind of like how businesswomen all across the city would withdraw their accounts from Precision Media if they knew you held them to a different moral code than their male counterparts?"

Technically, it had been Mr. Davis who had held her to a different standard, but the powerful women she worked with daily wouldn't quibble over the difference. Mr. Kincaid had supported it, and that would lose him business if it got out.

He was smart enough to know that.

"I—" Mr. Kincaid cleared his throat. "Is that a threat?"

"In all fairness, Mr. Kincaid, you did threaten me first. I was trying to keep this amicable."

"Amicable," Mr. Kincaid muttered, as though he didn't know the meaning of the word.

"In that vein, I'll be taking my accounts with me. For when I open my own firm."

Holy shit, she was on a roll!

"No, I can't let you do tha—"

"I wasn't asking. We both know that my clients work with me, not Precision Media. If I leave, they will leave, too. This way you get to pretend it was intentional."

"You're kind of ..."

*Awesome?* She smiled to herself. She was being awesome, though it was highly unlikely that was the adjective Mr. Kincaid was thinking of.

"Cutthroat," he finished eventually.

"If I were a man, you'd call me something like ambitious, but I'll take cutthroat, Mr. Kincaid." Victoria pushed to her feet, suddenly anxious to get out of the apartment. "I'll be by to collect my things tomorrow."

Without another word, she ended the call. She typed a harried text message into her phone, grabbed her purse, and headed for the door.

She had the start of a magnificent plan. But she needed a business partner, and she knew just who she wanted it to be.

• • •

Kip paced the carpet and glanced at his phone for the hundredth time in about a minute.

Meet me in our room ASAP. ♥

There were so many things about this text from Victoria that he could get caught up on, but what he chose to focus on was that little heart.

Because he'd seemed to hang his own on it.

She'd never sent him anything like that before. So, while he could be pissed that she'd sent him what could just be a booty call, that heart gave him hope.

*That heart, and, ya know, the fact that she put me above herself at great sacrifice.*

There was a clicking on the other side of the door, and like Pavlov's dog, his body recognized the telltale sounds of Victoria using a key card to get into their room.

He spun to face her, catching her just as she was opening the door. The moment their gazes locked, they both froze. Kip was holding his phone out, in the process of checking the damn message again; Victoria was gripping both the doorframe and her bag so tightly her knuckles were white.

He wanted to run to her. To sweep her up in his arms. He hadn't seen her in days, and it suddenly felt like he'd battled his way through purgatory to catch just a mere glimpse of her. But he had to make sure. Had to know why she had called him here. Why she had done what she did with Mr. Davis.

"Why did you keep my secret?" he asked.

At the same time, she asked, "Why did Mr. Davis call and offer me the contract?"

They both smiled, and everything tight in Kip's chest loosened.

Victoria stepped into the room and shut the door behind her, but she still didn't come to him. Kip fisted his hands at his sides to make sure they behaved.

"I'll answer first," she whispered. "Promise not to freak out?"

Kip raised an eyebrow. *Well, that's a promising start.* Nevertheless, he nodded.

She closed her eyes. "I … think I love you."

Kip actually gasped. Victoria's eyes fluttered open. That blush he loved spread across her cheeks.

He was across the carpet in the next second. "My turn." His voice was a barely audible rumble. "Promise not to freak out?"

The hint of a smile edged her lips.

He reached for her hands and wove his fingers through hers. "I think I love you, too."

Her eyes widened. "Really?"

He dropped one of her hands so he could trace his fingers up her arm. "Really, really."

"But we've only known each other for—"

"I don't care."

"Your mother hates me—"

"I really don't care."

"I'm …" She licked her lips, and Kip wanted to kiss her so badly, he thought he would die of it. "I'm unemployed."

That got his attention. *Just what the fuck had happened today?* He wanted to know, but she was what he wanted even more. "Hmm, actually, I am, too."

He saw the full import of his words hit her, but just as quickly, however, her smile faded. "I said"—her eyes filled with tears, and Kip felt the first stirrings of alarm—"horrible things to you." She squeezed his hand. "Kip, I'm so, so sorry."

"Oh, honey." Dropping all restraint, he finally allowed himself to gather her into his arms. With a hand to the back of her head, he pressed her to his chest, kissing her golden hair. "Thank you for saying that." He pulled back a little so he could look at her. Her eyes still swam with tears. He gently cupped her face and brushed them away with his thumbs. "You know what? I think standing up for me when it counts makes up for that."

She sniffed. "I like standing up for you."

God, his chest was going to explode. "And I like standing up for you."

She grew serious. "There's one more thing I have to say."

*Oh, God.* Kip's chest tightened again.

"Will you go into business with me?" she asked.

He blinked several times.

"I mean," she said quickly, "you don't have to. I want to be with you no matter what. Unless, you don't want to be with me now because I just asked you to go into advertising with me, and

I have a feeling you're conflicted about advertising given who your mother is, and—"

"Wait." He tilted his head. "You did ask me if I want to go into business with you?"

She blinked. "Well, yeah. You're kind of brilliant."

"I thought I was hearing things," he muttered. "This is real, right?" He looked around the room for any obvious sign that he was dreaming, like a horse standing beside the bed or someone in the closet with an ax.

She laughed, drawing his gaze back to her since he could never look at anything else when Victoria laughed. "Yes, this is real. I have several clients to get us started, but there probably won't be a lot of money in it for a while yet, and—"

"Yes."

She paused. "Yes?"

"You can stop trying to talk me out of it. My answer is so much fucking yes." God, he needed to kiss her. He stepped even closer. Now, her breasts pressed against his ribs.

She licked her lips. He'd be doing the same in a moment. "Want to get out of here?" she whispered.

"Out of here?"

"I want to … make love, I guess?" She blushed. "At one of our places. Yours or mine. Just not—"

Here. Because their relationship had taken a very different path. Kip bit back a grin. "How about mine then yours?"

Her eyes twinkled. "I'm pretty sure I'm supposed to come first."

Kip shrugged with one shoulder as he slowly rotated his hips, pressing his growing erection into her belly. "That's true. Yours, it is."

When their lips finally connected, they were both smiling.

# Epilogue

*One year later*

"Oh, God."

*That's right, baby.*

"Oh, *God!*"

Kip arched his back beneath her, the blunt ends of his fingers digging into her hips. His breath started bursting out of him in quick catches: Victoria's favorite sound, and a sure sign that he was about to tip over the edge.

She started riding him hard, the telltale fluttering of her own orgasm beginning.

He opened his eyes and grinned up at her, knowing exactly what those muscles against his cock meant.

She swallowed down the small moan that rose in her throat as she coasted over the edge with him.

"Fuck, I love you," he groaned.

Though her eyes wanted to close, she forced them to stay open, her gaze locked with his. "I love you, too."

The came down together, and Victoria collapsed on Kip's chest. He wrapped his arms around her, and she snuggled into his warm skin with her cheek, the still-rapid thud of his heartbeat resounding in her ear.

A moment later, their alarm went off. With a groan, he stretched over to slap it off, and she made a small noise of disappointment that their afterglow was coming to an end.

Then again, they'd managed some morning delight before having to get up and started on this very busy, very important day, so she couldn't be too disappointed.

Kip's large, warm hand skated up and down her spine. "You ready for today?"

She bit her lip to keep from smiling too broadly, because if he saw the size of her smile, he'd start asking questions.

Today, they would meet with the former Mrs. Davis to sign a campaign contract. She'd gotten The Ricchezza in the coup of all divorce settlements—their prenup having an adultery clause that favored Mrs. Davis greatly. Though Kip had never told Mrs. Davis what he knew, Vegas was, for all its grandeur, a small town at heart. In the end, Victoria was getting her "dream" after all. Only now, it was even better, because she was getting it with Kip, and she'd come to realize that what they had together was a dream in and of itself.

No, the reason Victoria's grin was so big was not because of Mrs. Davis. Every day for the past three months, Kip had asked her to marry him. Every day, she'd responded with *maybe someday*.

Today when he asked? She'd already reserved a chapel for tonight. In about—she squinted at the clock—fourteen hours, she and Kip would be best friends, business partners, lovers, and man and wife.

Life couldn't get better.

She crossed her arms over Kip's chest and propped her chin on top of them. Meeting Kip's gaze, she said, "Today is going to be perfect."

He leaned up and pressed a soft kiss to the tip of her nose.

And then they got out of bed and started to get ready for the best day of their lives.

# About the Author

Micah Persell lives in Southern California with her husband, 1.9 children, and menagerie of pets. She writes romance with strong women, smart minds, and scorching love. She loves connecting with readers. You can find her at *www.micahpersell.com*, on Facebook at *www.facebook.com/MicahPersell*, and on Twitter @ MicahPersell.

# Praise for Micah Persell

Don't miss these Micah Persell titles:

*Uncharted Waters*

"Science: love or maybe both? See for yourself. You won't be disappointed. Plus, come on…the cover? Dang…" —Harlie's Books

**Operation: Middle of the Garden series**

*Of Eternal Life*

Winner of the 2013 Virginia HOLT Award of Merit in the paranormal category.

Second place in Lyrical Press's first annual "How Lyrical Is Your Romance" contest.

*Of the Knowledge of Good and Evil*

*Of Consuming Fire*

*Of Alliance and Rebellion*

"If you enjoy military suspense and a strong romance try this book. *Of Eternal Life* is a good page turner to the end." —Night Owl Reviews

"I give this action-packed, sexually-charged story a definite thumbs up … the author has a good series going, and I was left gasping for breath and searching for more pages … I can't wait to hear more." —4 stars, The Romance Reviews

“I fell in hopelessly in love with the lead male character, Jayden. Wow! He is absolutely divine in every sense of the word.” —5 stars, Romancing the Book

**Wild and Wanton series**

*Emma: The Wild and Wanton Edition*

*Persuasion: The Wild and Wanton Edition*

“Micah Persell has near perfectly captured Austen's voice and explored some of the subtle nuances of Persuasion that Austen hinted at but never ventured to pursue . . . As . . . a fan of Austen retellings, I appreciated how seamlessly the additional text was worked into the classic storyline.” —The Romance Reviews

“Micah Persell exceeded my modest expectations, however, by deftly and for the most part seamlessly working in backstory, dreams, and interior monologue in very Austenesque language . . . it’s just ideal for a reader such as me—one who loves Persuasion but also can take pleasure in a talented wordsmith’s having a bit of fun with it.” —Romantic Historical Lovers

Printed in the United States
By Bookmasters